CROSSFIRE

AXEL BLAZE THRILLER
(BOOK ELEVEN)

BILL RUNNER

RUNNER HOUSE BOOKS, LONDON
www.bill-runner.com

First eBook edition July 2025

978-1-917652-04-9

www.bill-runner.com

From Soldier to Vigilante: Blaze's Path

Dear Readers,

First off, thank you for joining Axel Blaze on his journey. Whether you've been with him since *Blaze Returns* or are just diving in now, I'm thrilled to have you along for the ride.

When I first created Axel Blaze, I envisioned a man who couldn't stand by when innocent lives were at stake—a man who acts decisively, even when it means crossing dangerous lines. In his first adventure in *Blaze Returns*, he was still tethered to a semi-official role, stepping in to help his old boss at the U.S. Marshals track down a missing Deputy.

But as the series unfolded, Blaze began carving his own path, driven by his unwavering sense of justice and a deep disdain for the wrongs he saw around him. In the first seven books—*Blaze Returns*, *Lethal Force*, *Hard Target*, *Mean Streets*, *Unchained Fury*, *No Escape*, and *Fear City*—all set across different American cities, Blaze operates as a lone ranger. He steps into situations where innocent lives hang in the balance, doing what others can't—or won't.

Starting with *Dead Calm* (Book 8), the series takes a deeper dive into Blaze's past. In *Dead Calm*, we see him as a Captain in the U.S. Army Rangers, followed by his Delta Force missions in *No Mercy*, *Warpath* and *Crossfire*. These stories explore the intense operations and personal losses that forged Blaze into the man he is today.

The upcoming Book 12, *Nemesis* (November 2025), will be the final book exploring Blaze's military career. It's a deeply personal story where Blaze seeks justice for his brother Ryan—a U.S. Marine. This pivotal story will mark the turning point in Blaze's life, as he ultimately decides to leave the army. Disillusioned by the failures of the system, he becomes a man willing to cross lines to ensure justice prevails. Beginning in 2026, Blaze will be stepping fully into a world where the lines between right and wrong blur, and he's left to rely on his own moral compass to guide him.

In his words: You have to pay your dues. Period.

Your feedback and support have been instrumental in shaping this series. Blaze's journey has been as much yours as it has been mine, and I can't thank you enough for coming along for the ride.

Thank you for being part of Blaze's story.

Sincerely,

Bill Runner

CHAPTER 1

It wasn't like breaking into a prison was on my bucket list. But then again, neither was helping terrorists stage a jailbreak. And yet, here I was.

I have hopped borders under sandstorms, crossed minefields under purple skies, and fought my way through compounds full of men who would love nothing more than to hang me from the nearest rooftop. But a midnight break-in to a Yemeni prison with my Delta boys on my six? That was a new one even for my crew of seasoned operators.

Turns out, when the threat's big enough and time's running out, even the suits in D.C. don't blink before sending in the unlisted crew—the kind of people they will swear they have never met if shit hits the fan.

The plan was textbook—slip in, extract two targets, and vanish before the locals figured out we weren't their regular Tuesday night visitors.

Textbook plans are my least favorite kind. The textbooks never include what happens when the alarms go off early.

"Someone remind me why we're playin' jailhouse Santa for a coupla rats who probably don't even like us?"

The voice crackled through comms—dry, sarcastic, and unmistakably Ninja Man. Call sign of Staff Sergeant Buck Conway. Fast with a blade, faster with a wisecrack—he lived for close quarters and bad jokes in the worst of places.

I gave a slow head shake as I peered through my night vision. "Because those rats are going to get us intel that might keep the U.S. embassy from getting turned into a barbecue pit. You sleep through the briefing again, Ninja?"

"Nah, boss. I was wide awake—just wondering when the Pentagon decided our pure, innocent, patriotic souls were fair game."

"You telling me you once had a pure soul," another voice rumbled low over comms.

Staff Sergeant Jackson Cole, call sign Raptor. Six-four, two-twenty of walking destruction in close-quarters battle (CQB). He didn't say much, but when he did, it carried weight—usually just before something broke.

"You've got no idea, big man. Used to be white as snow. Remember the good old days when we just shot bad guys and went home. Now it's coke runs in Mexico, jailbreaks for terrorists... what's next? Babysitting cartel kids on Christmas?"

Ninja was taking a dig at our last operation in Mexico, when we ended up stealing a truck filled with a cartel's cocaine stash.

Raptor chuckled softly. "I still can't believe we hauled three tons of nose candy through Mexico."

"Yeah, man, building quite the résumé. From Delta Force to Delta Freight," Ninja retorted.

"Relax," I cut in. "That coke job was government approved. Chain of command stamped it, blessed it. No blemish on your pure soul."

"Well, there you go, Cowboy. Always know how to soothe a man's injured spirit."

Cowboy was my handle. Captain Axel Blaze, 1st Special Forces Operational Detachment–Delta, Sabre Squadron. My job was to lead the team, keep them alive, and finish the kind of missions the government doesn't talk about.

And this was one mission Uncle Sam surely wasn't planning on ever talking about.

It was September 2014—a real shitshow of a time in Yemen. The Houthis were making a hard push toward Sana'a, the capital, and the Saudis were lighting up the skies with airstrikes, trying to clip their wings. We weren't exactly waving pom-poms on the sidelines either. Officially, the U.S. wasn't involved. Unofficially, our fingerprints were all over it.

Now, the Houthi dudes never had much love for Uncle Sam. But thanks to the Saudis flying U.S.-made jets and dropping U.S.-guided bombs, they had bumped that hate up to the deluxe package.

Add Al-Qaeda in the Arabian Peninsula into the mix—AQAP for short—and the stew really got spicy. The AQAP bunch wasn't just radical—they were overachievers. Their dream was turning Yemen into a nice little Islamic Emirate, one car bomb at a time. If the Houthis hated Americans, AQAP wanted us crucified on live stream with subtitles.

They had already turned the U.S. trade office in Sana'a into a smoking crater. Suicide bomber. Embassy was probably next. Or some tourist bus filled with morons who thought Yemen sounded "adventurous". Chatter on the dark web was getting louder by the day, but the intel stream had gone bone-dry. The CIA was blind, and D.C. was freaking out behind closed doors.

That's when our phone rang. Turned out, they needed deniable assets with no business cards.

security cell block. That's where our two "extraction targets" were being kept. Access was through a secondary hatch that opened onto the catwalk. Tight fit, but doable.

Up on the ridge behind the prison, Hawkeye was in overwatch. Custom-built suppressed M110 on bipod, 10x scope dialed in, wind call already calculated.

The second he dropped the guards, Ninja and I were to launch grappling hooks fitted with anchored lines up onto the tower's parapet. The hooks were carbon steel, spring-loaded to latch deep into the ledge. We would climb fast, breach the hatch, and move along the rooftop walkway to the cell block. Quick cuts with the bolt cutters, grab the targets, and get moving.

Raptor was our extraction man. He was waiting in a Black Hawk tucked in a dead zone behind Hawkeye's hill, bird powered up, rotors ready to shred the night as soon as we signaled. Once we had the targets, we would move them across the roof, signal Raptor and the helo pilot, and they would come in low. Raptor would lay down suppressive fire with the door guns while we hustled the targets aboard.

Nothing fancy. Just brutal efficiency.

We had worked tighter exfils with worse odds. The plan was good. As good as it could be with the little intel we had. If things stayed on course, we would be wheels up before the Houthis figured out they had been played.

But missions like this don't like to stay on rails. And I had been in this game long enough to know that smooth sailing was often the prelude to getting sucker-punched by fate.

Hawkeye's voice broke in again, crisp and calm. "Targets marked. Confirming clean shot. Cowboy, we're green."

"Stand by," I said over comms, and then keyed up for the team. "Alright boys. Show time. We do this clean and fast. Move on my call."

"Copy," came Ninja's voice, all business now. All the sarcasm had bled out.

"Standing by," Raptor reported. "Let me know when you need me to knock."

Just like that, the game was on. No more jokes. No more banter. The switch had flipped. We weren't clowns on comms anymore—we were the scalpel headed straight into the artery.

The kind of silence that came before a breach wasn't just quiet. It was thick. Like the air itself was holding its breath. We were about to knock on the enemy's doors—layers of unknowns, shifting loyalties, and the kind of men who would light you on fire just to make a point.

But that's where we lived. Right at the edge of the map, where reason stopped and violence took over.

And now it was time to step across.

CHAPTER 2

Everything was in place. The recon was done, the angles studied, and the timing synced tight. Each of us knew the mission plan down to the last second.

I keyed my comms. "Hawkeye, take the tower."

No hesitation. Two soft pops came through the earpiece like distant knuckle cracks. The M110 rounds traveled at nearly 2,600 feet per second—high-velocity death. The first caught the guard in the upper chest, turned his insides into vapor. The second hit his partner center mass, folding him like laundry. Lights out. No alarms. Just silence.

A second later, Hawkeye's voice, calm as hell: "Tower's cold. Both down."

Ninja and I were crouched in the shadows behind a ridge of busted concrete, just out of sight from the lone guard at the front gate. That guy didn't have a line of sight to the tower.

I gave Ninja the nod. We launched our grappling hooks. Heavy-duty titanium claws on paracord line—good gear, the kind that wouldn't slip if the world fell apart beneath you. The hooks clanged once as they latched onto the parapet's lip. We gave a sharp tug to test them. Solid.

We climbed. Fast and quiet.

The tower wall was old-school concrete and limestone, rough enough to grip. Our boots scraped as we ascended, but the wind was enough cover. Less than a minute later, we rolled over the parapet and hit the rooftop in a low crouch, rifles ready.

The compound sprawled below us, a patchwork of stone and metal lit by flickering yellow bulbs near the barracks and admin buildings. But the pathways between the towers were cloaked in darkness.

The other tower, on the western end, maybe seventy-five yards off, stood quiet. That one had two guards in it, but they were too far to see or hear anything unless we turned this place into a Fourth of July barbecue.

From up top, the prison looked like it was cobbled together by angry drunk men with a grudge against architecture. Built into the slope of the hills, stone walls met sheet metal, patched with concrete blocks and makeshift wiring.

The place had changed hands just two days ago—Houthis had rolled in and overrun the joint, busted out their pals, let Al Qaeda stew in cages, dumped new "enemies" into cells, and declared themselves the new wardens.

The result was a prison run by goat herders with AK-47s. Not trained guards. They had no SOP, no chain of command—just rebel fighters who knew how to pull a trigger. But there were a hell of a lot of them.

If all those AKs get generally pointed in your direction and the triggers squeezed, the probability of you catching a few goes up dramatically. Quantity over quality could still get you killed if you weren't smart.

We didn't stick around. No sightseeing. We dropped low and jogged along the narrow rooftop catwalk toward the cell block. Concrete lip on one side, a sheer drop on the other.

Ninja took point, sweeping ahead with his suppressed HK416 shouldered tight. I followed close, scanning arcs. One good thing was that there were no cameras. Back in 2014, most of Yemen's prison tech was stuck in the 1980s, and security systems hadn't caught up. One less thing to worry about.

Halfway to the hatch, a rooftop guard stepped out of a side access door, scratching his gut and lighting a cigarette near a vent.

We froze, dropped low behind an HVAC unit. I leaned around the duct, lined up my suppressed Glock 19, and put a 9mm through his skull. The man dropped like a marionette with its strings cut, his cigarette still glowing between two fingers. I retrieved the body, dragging him into the shadow beside the vent.

We reached a roof access hatch, just like our intel said. Rusted, dented, and padlocked, but not reinforced. I pulled a compact Halligan from my rig, wedged the fork into the latch, and gave it a slow twist. A few seconds of gentle persuasion, and the lock popped. We eased it open.

Inside was a maintenance ladder with bolted rungs. We descended into the guts of the building. The place stank of wet rock, mold, and piss. Narrow beams overhead, rusted pipes dripping in places, a thin layer of dust on the floor that muffled our boots. I stayed crouched, gun low and tight.

Halfway through, we passed over a grated mezzanine that overlooked the cell block below. At the far end, we reached a narrow stairwell down to the cell level. As we approached, music wafted through—a scratchy Arabic pop song playing from a busted plastic speaker plugged into a dangling socket.

I stopped three steps short and fished out my angled inspection mirror on a telescopic wand. Eased it around the corner.

Two guards slouched in folding chairs near the corridor entrance, rifles leaning against the wall. One was nodding off, the other was chewing something, eyes glazed.

I signaled Ninja. He dropped them both with two suppressed shots—center mass, then a second round to the head for insurance. The dull thuds were barely louder than the music.

We moved in and I grabbed the keyring off one of the bodies—cheap metal, a dozen padlock keys jingling against each other. I pocketed them, then we pushed forward into the corridor, weapons up.

The cell block was a single strip—twelve cells total, six per side, separated by a narrow corridor of cracked tiles. No doors—just thick iron bars and padlocks straight out of the Cold War. Two ceiling bulbs flickered overhead, casting sickly light and leaving plenty of corners in shadow.

The place reeked of sweat, blood, and fear. Each cage was jam-packed—ten, maybe twelve men each. Some slept, some stared blankly, others just huddled in corners, eyes hollow, faces drawn.

I scanned the cell numbers. They were painted in Arabic, old and chipped. But I had memorized them from the intel packet. Cell 7. The number kind of looked like a slightly crooked letter "v".

"Far end," I whispered to Ninja. "That's our pen."

I sighed. “Oh man, this mission just became a game of beard roulette.”

Ninja adjusted his grip on his rifle. “I vote we grab the two who look fastest.”

“Sure. Any other bright ideas?”

We had minutes—maybe less—before this place woke up. And if I picked the wrong two, we would be dragging out dead weight and leaving the real targets behind.

Ninja grinned, barely. “Nope. But look at the bright side—at least it wasn’t twenty.”

He had a point. But picking two out of five was still a gamble.

And this wasn’t Vegas.

CHAPTER 3

It hit me the moment those five bearded jackasses stood up like they had won the lottery—Ibrahim and Hassan weren't exactly rare names in this part of the world. Hell, half the prison block probably had a cousin named one or the other. The briefing had only given us first names, which, in hindsight, was like showing up to a rodeo and asking for "Bob".

I racked my brain for the detail I had filed but hadn't needed till now—their father's name. Khalid Al-Mansour. Yeah, that was it. Had to hope the guys remembered their own damn bloodline.

I took a breath and called out, low but clear, "Ibrahim Al-Mansour. Hassan Al-Mansour."

A slight shift in the air.

Two of the men who had stood sat back down without a word. Three still remained on their feet. What the hell?

I narrowed my eyes and went name by name. "Ibrahim Al-Mansour?"

The man in the middle raised his hand. No hesitation. Eyes locked on mine.

"Hassan Al-Mansour?"

The other two exchanged a glance—then both raised their hands.

I shook my head "Well, I'll be damned."

Behind me, Ninja muttered, "Maybe they're triplets."

I stepped forward and signaled the three to move closer. No arguments from them—they came up to the bars like they had been waiting for this moment their whole damn lives.

Time to check them for identifying marks intel had told us about. Ibrahim had a raised scar on his upper arm, shaped like a hook or a sickle. Supposed to have gotten it in a welding accident when he was a teenager. Hassan had a dark birthmark high on his left shoulder blade, shaped roughly like a thumbprint.

We flicked on our tactical flashlights, cones of light slicing across faces drawn tight from weeks of hell.

I rolled up the sleeve of the guy who answered to Ibrahim. Sure enough, there it was: a keloid scar, maybe four inches long, curling like a hook just above the bicep.

"That's Ibrahim," I said, more to myself than anyone else.

Ninja spun the second man by the shoulder and yanked the loose shirt back. Under the collar, just beneath the skin, sat a coffee-colored birthmark, the size of a silver dollar.

"That's Hassan," he said, tapping once for confirmation.

We both looked at the third guy. He looked back like he knew his ticket just got canceled. He stepped forward like he was about to say something, but Hassan beat him to it.

"He is our brother," Hassan said, voice low and rough. "He come with us."

The English was broken, but the meaning came through loud and clear.

"No," I said flatly. "Two assets. Ibrahim and Hassan Al-Mansour. That's it."

Hassan's face hardened. "We not leave him."

I had heard that line too many times. Hostage rescues, extractions, evac jobs—they all go sideways the second emotions get a vote. You give them an inch, they dig in. Start pleading, bargaining, delaying. Then the next minute someone's bleeding out, or worse.

I took one step closer, enough for him to feel the weight behind my words.

"You *will* leave him," I said, low and cold. "Because this is a one-time offer. You walk out with me now, or you stay behind and rot with him. Either way, we're leaving."

I didn't wait for a reply. I grabbed Ibrahim's arm—he didn't resist, but he looked back and forth like he couldn't believe it was going down like this. Ninja picked up on the signal and fell in beside me.

Behind us, Hassan let out a sharp curse in Arabic, then turned to the third guy and said something quick and clipped—sounded like an order or maybe just goodbye. Then he followed.

As he passed, he muttered, just loud enough for me to catch it—"fucking Americans".

I stopped. Reached out and slammed him into the wall so fast the breath shot out of his lungs. My forearm pinned his throat, eyes level with his.

"Let me make this real clear," I said, voice quiet, even. "The last thing I want is to give you a shot at dodging a bullet from the Houthis. Only reason you're breathing is because pulling your sorry ass out helps save lives."

Hassan tried to pull air in through his nose. His eyes darted sideways—right into Ninja's.

Ninja didn't say a word. Just stared. Cold. Smiling. The kind of smile that said: *you bleed easy, and I enjoy messes.*

I leaned closer. "You so much as breathe wrong, I'll break a couple of bones just to feel better and tell my boss we couldn't find you. You get me?"

He blinked, coughed once, and nodded. "Yes."

I let go and shoved him forward. "Good. Walk."

I turned back, ready to pull the cell door shut, when three other men got up and lunged, grabbing the bars. They weren't after us—they just wanted out. But that didn't mean they wouldn't rip us apart if we got in their way.

"Back!" I snarled, forcefully pushing the first one back. Ninja used the butt of his rifle to crack another one across the chest.

We slammed the door shut and jammed the padlock back in place, metal scraping on rusted iron.

The block exploded in Arabic fury. Men slamming the bars, fists pounding steel, a rising wave of hate echoing off the cement walls.

I couldn't make out most of what they were yelling, but one phrase rang out above the rest: *Kalb al-Amrikiya!*

American dogs.

Lovely.

It didn't take a linguist to know that meant we had overstayed our welcome. The word *American* alone could get a crowd foaming at the mouth in this shithole.

I tapped my comm. "Cowboy to Raptor, get hot. Package in hand. We're exfil bound—fast."

"Raptor to Cowboy. Solid copy," he replied, voice calm and crackling over the comms. "Skies are clear for now."

I glanced at Ninja. "Let's go before this turns into a bonfire."

We moved fast through the block, keeping dead center between the rows of cages. The echoes of Arabic curses chased us like a swarm of wasps.

The inmates were in a frenzy now, every last one of them screaming, howling, spitting, arms clawing through the bars, reaching for anything they could grab—an arm, a shirt, a miracle. But we kept moving, keeping to the center, rifle ready, boots pounding stone. Ninja was on point, silent and surgical. The two assets followed close, doing exactly what they were told.

"Don't get sentimental," I muttered, as one pair of hands grabbed for Ninja's vest and he shoved them off with a hard jab.

"Not my type," Ninja grunted, eyes forward, rifle up.

We hit the stairwell like a storm. Just as I put a boot on the first step, I heard it—footsteps rushing up from below, boots hammering stone, voices shouting in Arabic. We dropped to one knee and opened fire before the first head cleared the flight.

Three Houthi fighters hit the top landing and died right there—two dropped by my bursts to the chest, the third caught a round from Ninja's suppressed pistol right between the eyes. He folded like wet laundry.

But the fourth man—he was smart. Dove back down the stairs, barking into a handheld radio. I didn't need a translation. I knew the whole damn hornet's nest was coming now.

"Shit," I hissed. "They're calling in the cavalry."

I looked at the two brothers. Their faces were pale and tight with fear, but they were not stupid. They knew what would happen if those guards got to them first—execution on the spot, no questions, no trial. The Houthis didn't waste prison space on Al Qaeda men they hated.

"Up," I growled, jerking my chin toward the next level. "Move!"

They didn't hesitate. Fear makes for obedient cargo.

We pounded up the next flight, hitting the mezzanine above the block, boots thudding across the grated catwalk. The cell block echoed below us—yells, curses, pounding fists. The whole place was boiling over.

"Ladder's ahead," Ninja pointed out.

"I'm right behind you," I replied, eyes sweeping the catwalk, weapon ready.

We reached the maintenance ladder. Rungs bolted to the wall, the same one we had used on entry. Ninja went up first. The two assets followed, climbing like their lives depended on it—which they did. I brought up the rear, rifle slung, one hand on steel, the other gripping the hatch handle.

Ninja crested the hatch first—and that's when I heard him.

"Contact!" he barked. A gunshot cracked, and then chaos erupted.

I shoved the hatch open and burst out, pushing past the brothers with a shoulder check. "Stay the fuck down!" I snapped.

I cleared the hatch just in time to see Ninja slam his elbow into a man's temple, sending him sprawling into the gravel. Another came at him swinging an AK like a club. Ninja ducked, drove a punch into his gut, then spun and snapped the guy's neck like he was wringing out a rag.

Two down for him.

I charged into the fray.

First one came at me with a bayonet, low and fast. I deflected with my forearm, stepped inside his swing, and hammered a knife into his ribs. He screamed. I pulled it out, reversed the grip, and buried it straight into his eye socket. Lights out.

Second one came in behind me. I felt him, turned fast, grabbed his wrist mid-swing and broke his elbow with a downward crunch. He howled—until I slammed his own knife into his throat. He fell gurgling, hands clutching his neck.

Across the roof, Ninja was dancing with two more. One came in high with a clubbing strike, the other low with a blade. Ninja dodged right, parried the blade, and kicked the high one in the knee so hard I heard it snap. The guy went down howling—Ninja stabbed him twice in the chest and moved on. The low attacker slashed, caught Ninja's arm—a shallow cut—but it earned him a brutal reward. Ninja kicked his feet out, straddled him, and shoved a combat knife up under his jaw.

That made four for him.

Back to me.

A thick bastard came in hard, swinging a folding-stock AK like a baseball bat. I ducked, surged forward, and tackled him to the gravel. He went for my throat—I flicked his hand aside and headbutted him twice until he went slack. Then I finished it with a blade under the chin, straight into the brain stem.

One left.

He tried to run. I chased him down, tackled him from behind, and slammed his face into the concrete rooftop until it split like a melon. Blood smeared the stone, warm and dark.

Silence. The rooftop went still.

Eight men, dead or dying. Rooftop reeking of blood and cordite.

I stood, chest heaving, blade dripping. Ninja wiped sweat from his brow with the back of his gloved hand.

"You good?" I asked.

He nodded. "Four and four."

"Damn right," I muttered. "We should do this more often."

He looked down at one of the bodies. "Sure. Next time let's charge extra for rooftop entertainment."

I snorted and turned toward the hatch.

"Let's get the brothers moving. Before the next wave shows up."

Raptor's voice crackled in my earpiece, low and tight with rotor wash in the background.

"Raptor to Cowboy. We're wheels up. One mike to LZ."

"Copy. Moving to rally point," I replied, eyes already on the target.

The eastern watchtower. The same route we used to breach the roof. One minute to get there. We moved.

Ninja and I ducked low, herding the two assets across the gravel rooftop, rifles up, eyes scanning. Gravel crunched under boots as we made a beeline for the tower, hugging the rooftop cover, avoiding open lanes.

Thirty yards out.

Then the night lit up as all hell broke loose.

CHAPTER 4

A heavy machine gun tore into the night from the western tower—green tracers zipping past like glowing hornets. The rounds slapped into the rooftop behind us, kicked up dust, shattered brick, and made a hell of a racket. Sounded like God was dumping a bag of steel bolts in a blender.

"Incoming! Two o'clock, elevated! Get low!" I barked, grabbing Hassan and dragging him down behind a rusted exhaust duct. Ninja yanked Ibrahim by the collar like a sack of rice and shoved him behind a water tank.

Debris rained down. Somewhere below, alarms were blaring, and the whole compound was waking up hungry.

But I knew the men firing didn't have eyes on us. They didn't even have a clue who they were firing on. They weren't aiming—they were just dumping fire to deny the route. Blind, suppressive, panic-spawned. Didn't matter. That shit still kills.

I keyed comms. "Cowboy to Hawkeye. You got eyes on that gun nest?"

Hawkeye came back after half a beat. "Negative. No visual on the tower from this angle."

I switched channels. "Cowboy to Raptor. We're pinned by MG fire from the western tower."

Static, then Raptor's voice, cool and sharp: "Copy that. Bird inbound. Night vision on. Stand by for sweep."

The Black Hawk came in low and dirty, dark as sin, no lights, blades chopping air like a reaper's scythe. Pilot was good—nap-of-the-earth approach with his goggles locked in.

I caught a glimpse of Raptor in the open door, harnessed in, leaned out, hands on the M134 six-barreled rotary machine gun.

Then the gun spun up.

The gun screamed and it was like the full wrath of God followed. Fire poured into the western tower, as the six barrels spun a thousand rounds per minute, rounds chewing through concrete, sandbags, steel, men. Bodies flailed and folded. Chunks of tower sprayed into the air like clay pigeons. It was a goddamn meat grinder.

"Western perch is soup," Raptor's voice came through, calm as ever. "You're clear."

"Appreciate it," I muttered, hauling the two assets up. "Move!"

We bolted low and fast across the last stretch of roof to the top of the eastern tower, feet pounding metal, ducking low as fresh rifle fire erupted from below. The prison yard was awake now—gunmen yelling in Arabic, firing upward blindly. Muzzles flared behind chain-link fencing and from the gaps in the walls. Poorly aimed, but luck's still a killer.

We reached the tower. Rotor wash hit us like a truck. The Hawk was hovering just above, twenty feet out, blades churning the night air into chaos. Raptor waved us to the hoist rig but Ninja froze, scanning the far perimeter wall.

"RPG!" he roared, pivoting on his heel. "Perimeter wall—ten o'clock!"

I spun and caught sight of the man lining up the tube. Ninja was faster—two shots from his HK416 cracked through the night. The gunman dropped, the rocket launcher clattering away harmlessly.

But that wasn't the end. More shadows, more RPGs. One runner on the parapet opposite. Two runners, maybe three, darting behind vehicles below, loading up RPG tubes.

Then a single suppressed shot cracked through the air, distant but sharp.

"Runner on the parapet's down," Hawkeye's voice said over comms. "That one I had. Clean shot. No eyes on the ground rats though—they're under my line."

I grunted. "Roger. Good kill. Stay sharp."

I had to make a call. Could have asked the pilot to light up the whole damn compound—guns, Hellfire, the works. Would have turned this place into a crater. But that would have blown the whole op sky-high. We needed deniability. What we had done so far could pass as a rogue Al Qaeda bust-out. But a Black Hawk leveling a Yemeni prison? That's a whole new ballgame.

Couldn't risk the helo getting hit either. Or a rocket taking us all mid-hoist.

I keyed comms. "Cowboy to Raptor. Abort rooftop. Going to ground. Hawkeye, spin up Plan Bravo."

Raptor's voice came back. "Roger. Bird moving off. Bravo in play. Good luck."

I watched the Black Hawk peel off hard, rising into the dark like a ghost bird, banking left and vanishing into the dark like it was never there. Time to move to our fallback plan.

Plan Bravo... yeah, that was our just-in-case. The one we hoped we wouldn't need. Original plan, Plan Alpha, had Hawkeye posted on overwatch to the east, with a local asset called Ali as his spotter. They were set up in a sniper hide overlooking the prison. From there, they would support our rooftop exfil. Once we were airborne and clear, they were supposed to pull out, make their way down the back slope to a waiting truck driven by Youssef, our local wheelman. Then we would all regroup a couple of ridgelines out, at an LZ where Raptor in the bird would scoop us up.

But that went sideways the second the RPGs showed up. So now we were flipping to Plan Bravo. In this version, Youssef was coming in hot to pick us up, straight from the valley road near the outer perimeter. Hawkeye and Ali would hold their overwatch until we were rolling, then peel off and rendezvous on the far side of the ridge. From there, all of us would push to the secondary exfil point—a dry flat beyond the next couple of hills—where the Black Hawk and Raptor would be waiting with the engines hot. Not as clean. But still doable.

We just had to get off that damn tower first—fast and vertical.

I turned to the two assets—wide-eyed, sweating, barely standing.

"Alright, gentlemen. Time to ride the snake."

I pulled a pouch from my ruck and snapped it open. Inside were two quick-deploy rescue slings—the kind used when you have got to drag some poor bastard out of a hole fast. No padding, no dignity—just a nylon strap and a carabiner between you and gravity.

Ninja rigged a rappel line to a brace. I clipped Ibrahim in first—looped the sling across his chest under the armpits, cinched it tight, and snapped him into a descender I rigged to the rope.

"This might hurt," I told him. "But don't let go, don't flail, and don't scream."

"Will it break anything?" he stammered.

"Only if you land wrong," I said, pushing him.

He slid down the line in a half-controlled freefall, boots bouncing once off the side of the wall, and hit hard on the ground below. Rolled over, groaned.

Ninja already had Hassan hooked up. "He pukes on me, I'm sending him back up," Ninja growled.

Hassan went down head back, eyes shut, feet flailing like a kicked frog. He landed a second later and dropped to all fours, vomiting onto the gravel.

"Better than shitting yourself," Ninja muttered, then looked at me. "You next or me?"

"You go," I said, tightening my gloves. "I'll cover till you're down."

We took the rope in pairs, fast and dirty. I clipped in, went last, boots sliding and gloved hands burning on descent. My knees jarred when I hit, and I had to swallow the urge to grunt.

We were down, and we were moving.

Ibrahim limped, said something about a broken ankle, but he could still run. Hassan was wiping puke off his face with his sleeve, eyes wild, but he was upright.

We crouched low behind the ridge of busted concrete where we had hidden earlier, and scanned the horizon.

From the massive steel gates at the prison's front, chaos unfolded.

Headlights flared as reinforcements rolled in from the access road beyond, vehicles kicking dust, shouting in Arabic, gunfire popping off like popcorn. They didn't know where to shoot yet—but they would soon.

And we were running out of shadows.

CHAPTER 5

Hawkeye's next message brought some sense of relief.

"Hawkeye to Cowboy," his voice came low and calm over comms. "Package Mule is two mikes out. Stand by."

Package Mule. That was our ride—the backup ride. Not our usual ride, but a beat-to-hell Toyota Hilux pickup, the kind that blended in with every other rusted-out farm truck in the damn country. Meant for low-vis exfil. Originally it was for Hawkeye and Ali to ghost out quiet after we were up in the bird. But things went sideways, and Plan Bravo got punched in.

Less than two minutes later, the truck came barreling up the ridge, fishtailing gravel, headlights off, engine snarling. At the wheel was the guy called Youssef. Local fixer. Beard braided, ballcap sweat-stained and faded, grin like he was heading to a party instead of a hot zone, eyes hidden behind scratched aviators.

Seriously? Who the hell wears shades in a warzone at night? Apparently, our driver did.

But apart from his fashion sense, I had heard good things about him. Old-school Yemeni warrior with enough grit to chew through gravel. Carried an AK folded across his chest and a bandolier of mags like a damn fashion accessory. Sleeves rolled high to show off old scars and older tattoos.

As for the Hilux, it wasn't much to look at. Rust in every seam. No rear gate. Jerry cans lashed to the bed with sun-bleached straps, panels held together with hope and baling wire. But the engine still purred like a diesel-fed devil and never died. It rode like a wheelbarrow full of bricks, but it could climb a rock wall blindfolded with a toothpick for traction. Not exactly the extraction I had in mind. But here we were.

Youssef barely braked as we piled in.

"Up, up, let's move!" he shouted, slapping the side of the truck with one hand and spinning the wheel with the other.

We piled into the truck—Ninja first, then me, hauling Hassan and Ibrahim by their collars. No time for grace. Just deadweight and urgency.

At the same time, two cargo trucks full of fighters rolled to a stop at the prison entrance, lights bouncing, boots hitting the gravel. One of the guards barked something in Arabic and pointed right at us. Showtime.

Youssef reversed in a spray of gravel, turned around, and then floored it, kicking up a storm of dust and heading back the way he came.

"Hawkeye, we got pursuit," I barked into my mic.

"Copy," came Hawkeye's dry reply.

Hawkeye's M110 cracked from its perch up the hill, the suppressed rounds moving at nearly 800 meters per second. Two quiet cracks. No flash, no thunder—just soft punches of fate. First vehicle veered left, then smoke poured from its hood like it was crying. Second truck's windshield caved in as the driver's head vanished into a red mist. It skidded sideways and crumpled into the first one. And just like that, pursuit was canceled.

Youssef grunted approval. “Good shooting. That’s our ghost sniper, yes?”

We hit the backside of the ridge, shocks groaning like a dying animal. The truck bounced over the rocks, dipped into a dry creek bed, and roared up the other side.

Ninja blurted out: “You sure those shades ain’t killing your night vision, dude?”

“Not a problem,” Youssef yelled back over the noise. “I know these roads so well, I can drive with eyes closed. Want to see that?”

“No, bro, I’m cool. Let’s make what we can of those lovely eyes of yours. Counting on divine intervention while driving really ain’t my thing.”

Youssef chuckled before he skidded into a clearing, killed the lights, and idled down. Out of the trees came Hawkeye and Ali—both grinning like devils.

Hawkeye had his ghillie half-rolled down, M110 slung tight. Dust on his boots, blood on his knuckles, face streaked with grime and sweat. “Took your damn time, boss.”

“Traffic was a bitch,” I replied. “You blow up both trucks?”

“Nah,” he shrugged. “Gave the second one a gentle nudge. Might still be usable.”

Ali wore a chest rig like he was born in it, short-barreled AK slung tight. And yeah—shades at night, just like Youssef. Apparently tactical blindness was trending in Yemen.

Ninja couldn’t hold back. “You gotta be kidding me. What is this, midnight fashion week? Ali rocking shades too?”

Hawkeye shot back: “That’s how he scopes targets. With style. Doesn’t like being temporarily blinded by any muzzle flash.”

“Long as he hits what he shoots at, he can wear a damn disco ball,” I chipped in. “Climb in—we’re burning moonlight.”

The Hilux growled forward, suspension howling like it hated life, bouncing through the dark. Prison behind us, exfil ahead.

I keyed my comms. “Cowboy to Raptor. We’re en route to secondary LZ. Four mikes out.”

“Copy that, Cowboy,” came the reply. “Bird is dark and tight.”

Youssef wrangled the Hilux through the hills like he was herding a drunken mule—suspension screaming, engine snarling, tires crunching over loose shale and cracked earth. The road—if you could call it that—was a busted goat trail wrapped around loose rock and blind turns.

We crept up over a rise and the ground leveled out just enough for a flat clearing cut into the slope—bare rock, dried grass, wide enough for one quiet demon bird. And there she was.

Black Hawk silhouetted against the half-moon, crouched low and dark, rotors whispering as she idled in full blackout mode. Dark as sin. No running lights, no IR beacons, blacked out instrument panel, just ghost tech and steel nerves. NVG-mode cockpit glowing faintly green from inside. Those pilots of 160th SOAR trained for this—flying blind except through green phosphor and God-given guts. They were Night Stalkers for a reason.

“Eyes on,” I called out. “LZ looks clear.”

Raptor's voice came through again, more amused this time. "You should've let me light up that yard, Cowboy. We would've cooked the whole damn hornet nest."

"And left crater-sized headlines for Langley and State to explain? Suits back in D.C. would've shitted flaming bricks for a week." I shook my head. "This was a ghost run. Plan Bravo was the only call. Quiet, dirty, and forgettable. Just how we like it."

Ninja chimed in. "Forgettable? I nearly got murdered by a guy with flip-flops and a machete. That's gonna stick."

"Builds character," I shot back.

Youssef slid us to a stop. We dismounted fast—Hawkeye and Ali flanked wide, rifles up. Raptor was already waving us in, flight helmet on, visor down, gloved hand making tight signals. Ninja helped the assets onboard while I did a quick visual. Minor scrapes. Nothing bleeding bad. We were lucky. Damn lucky.

"Everyone green?" I asked.

"Green as it gets," Hawkeye replied, tossing his ruck aboard.

Ninja wiped a cut from his forehead. "Just a little character development. I'll live."

I checked my own side—rib felt bruised, probably from the fall or the brawl on the rooftop. "Good. We're still pretty. Let's lift."

We climbed aboard. The rear ramp hissed shut, rotors spooled higher, and the bird lifted like a phantom into the night. Just a shudder and then the ground fell away beneath us.

From up there, the prison looked like a toy fort left behind in the sand. But the fire down there was real. So was the blood.

That was hurdle one. A warm-up. The real storm hadn't hit yet.

Sana'a was still standing—barely. The Houthis were tightening the noose by the hour. Their forces were circling like wolves and the city was coughing smoke from every wound. Meanwhile, the suits at the embassy were still busy holding meetings about whether to stay or bail while the whole place burned.

Until someone made a decision, we would be running point. No backup. No fanfare. Just us, mopping up hell one corner at a time and trying not to get buried under it.

This mission wasn't over.

Hell, it had barely started.

CHAPTER 6

Until the day before, I had no clue we would be knee-deep in Yemen, working our way through Al Qaeda backdoors and Houthi checkpoints like it was just another Tuesday.

That's how it went in our line of work. One day you're scrubbing blood and sand out of your boots, the next you're boarding a bird to another hellhole with your gear, your team, and zero margin for error.

We were parked at Camp Lemonnier, Djibouti—a slab of heat-blasted real estate squatting in the Horn of Africa. Population just north of a million, not counting the goats. The place smelled like diesel, sweat, and geopolitics. It was the U.S. military's crown jewel for counterterror ops in the region, sharing the neighborhood with Somalia, Ethiopia, and enough bad actors to fill a watchlist. The place sat just across the Gulf of Aden from Yemen, separated by about a hundred-plus miles of choppy water and pirate ghosts. Felt closer when you knew what waited on the other side.

Camp Lemonnier wasn't pretty, but it ran like a war machine. Blazing sun overhead, gravel crunching under boots, and cargo planes cycling through the airfield like clockwork. The compound itself was a maze of sandbagged Hesco barriers, blast-proofed barracks, comms shacks, chow halls, and rows of tents that cooked like ovens by noon. Generators hummed, helos thumped the air, JSOC operators in multicam moved like ghosts between briefings and workouts, and somewhere in the background, some poor bastard was always doing pushups for doing something stupid.

My boys and I had just come back from Somalia—quick in and out on an Al-Shabaab compound. Eliminated a high-value Al-Shabaab courier, scrubbed a safehouse, and torched a few ratlines on the way out. Textbook hit, fast and brutal.

We had been rearming and debriefing since wheels down, soaking up what little downtime we could. But in our world, peace was just the gap between missions. And it never lasted long. I had barely stowed my gear, popped the cap on a warm Gatorade, and was thinking about grabbing rack time when the call came through.

"Colonel Flynn wants you in his office."

That was Flynn—my CO.

So much for downtime.

I had no clue what Flynn wanted. I had already debriefed him about Somalia—how we dropped a building on that Al-Shabaab asshole and punched out before sunrise. Nothing was on the board after that. So I figured maybe it was something administrative. A pat on the back, maybe a slap on the wrist—same difference in this game.

But when your CO calls, you don't ask questions. I dumped the drink, holstered my sidearm, and headed across the compound. Sun beat down like a punishment as I moved through the grid of metal and concrete. Marines marched in formation to my left, a Black Hawk kicked dust into a cyclone on the pad to my right, and a pair of agency spooks in polos and Oakleys skulked past like they had just invented espionage.

Flynn's office was tucked in a block of modified conex containers stacked and reinforced like a fortress built from old war stories. I knocked once and opened the door.

Inside, I was in for a bit of a surprise. I wasn't expecting two civilians waiting for me in his office.

Well, not civilians exactly. Not with that posture.

The woman looked like she belonged on the cover of a fashion magazine—if the theme was "lethal elegance". She sat straight-backed, legs crossed, hands folded neatly in her lap. Ponytail pulled tight, like the kind of woman who didn't like things loose—discipline in every line of her posture. She wore a light field blouse and khakis, but there was nothing soft about her. The way her eyes moved, clocking me before I even fully stepped in, said she had been places most diplomats wouldn't survive five minutes.

The guy next to her was built like a blunt instrument. Square shoulders, salt-and-pepper hair, that hardline look that screamed D.C. suit, but the kind that did his time downrange. He leaned back slightly in the chair, relaxed in the way that said he wasn't. The kind of guy who watched the exits, timed reactions, and measured every heartbeat in the room. He was about forty, give or take, but his eyes were older.

Flynn was flipping through a folder thick with red tabs and what I could only imagine wasn't good news. His desk looked like it had been dragged through three deployments and a bar fight.

Flynn looked up and nodded at me. "Blaze, come in."

No smile. That wasn't his thing.

I stepped inside and shut the door. "Sir."

"This is Captain Axel Blaze," Flynn introduced me to the two. "Fresh off a mop-up in Somalia. Clean op. His team just came in yesterday."

He didn't say more, and I didn't expect him to. Somalia wasn't for public consumption.

"Take a seat, Captain," he said. "We've got something that needs your kind of touch."

I dropped into the chair across from the pair, leaned back slightly. Didn't slouch. Just enough to show them I wasn't there to be impressed. I gave the two a once-over again, up close this time. Yeah—field people. The real kind. I remembered the pair of spooks I saw skulking past earlier near the air pad, decked out in polos and Oakleys. I wondered if they came in with these two.

Flynn nodded at the woman first. "This is Caroline Maddox. National Clandestine Service—Case Officer. Based in Sana'a."

Her deep blue eyes met mine with zero hesitation. Steel behind that pretty face.

I knew that NCS—the CIA's National Clandestine Service—didn't hand out that title unless you had run real ops in the dirt. The kind with blood, bribes, and broken cellphones. Running human intel networks—tribal contacts, NGO fixers, ex-military sources. Often embedded under diplomatic cover, especially in conflict zones like Yemen. Which meant half the guys in Sana'a probably thought she was a cultural attaché or something equally useless. And they would be dead wrong.

"Captain," she said, voice smooth but firm. No flirting, no fake smile.

I nodded. "Ma'am."

She looked like she was about to say something, but changed her mind when Flynn began speaking again. My guess was she didn't like being called "Ma'am".

"And this," Flynn continued, "is Reed Atwood. Deputy Chief of Station, Amman. He's here because the intel Caroline received wasn't the kind you sleep on. Reed brings operational weight."

No kidding. Amman, Jordan was CIA's regional hub. The guy was like Langley's forward hammer in the region, running ops from Amman and flying in only when things got twitchy. Caroline called, and he got on a jet. These two surely hadn't flown in for sightseeing. Whatever this was, it was real.

Flynn turned toward them. "Why don't you lay it out for the Captain before we talk specifics."

Atwood nodded once, then turned to Caroline. "Go ahead."

She clicked open a small folder and pulled out a tablet, but didn't look at it yet. Her voice was even, clipped—pure field cadence.

"Situation in Yemen's deteriorating faster than expected," she began. "Houthi rebels have entered Sana'a's outskirts. Saudi airstrikes are pounding Houthi positions across the north—with some quiet help from us."

I caught the emphasis. Quiet help always meant some boots, a lot of drones, and more headaches.

"The Houthis blame the U.S. for backing the Saudis. That's not a stretch. They're gunning for us. Meanwhile, AQAP—Al-Qaeda in the Arabian Peninsula—has been stepping up its own campaign to form their Islamic Emirate of Yemen."

She took a pause before continuing. "They hate us more than the Houthis do."

"Nice," I observed. "Real neighborly."

She suppressed a smile before continuing. "Last week, AQAP hit the U.S. trade office in Sana'a. Suicide bomber. Ten civilians dead, most of them locals. The message was clear—if you're American or helping Americans, you're a target."

I nodded. That was all over the news. Hell of a blast. Hell of a mess. No glory in that kind of war.

"The U.S. has advised all personnel to evacuate. Most have. But a number of soft targets remain at risk. Contractors. NGO staff. Embassy support. You name it."

I didn't say anything, but I was thinking it. If Yemen's circling the drain, why the hell are we still there? Just pack up and let the place implode. Would save guys like me a lot of trouble dragging diplomats and desk jockeys out of burning buildings when the curtain falls. But suits don't do simple. They can't. Too much pride. Too many half-finished policies. I kept my mouth shut.

Caroline continued. "That blast wasn't random. It was a probe. A test."

I leaned forward. "What are they warming up for?"

"That's what we didn't know. Until two days ago."

Caroline tapped her tablet, brought up a photo—grainy, zoomed in from a distance. Arab male, around fifty, wiry frame, glasses, thinning hair, dressed like a nobody. Soft features, not your typical battlefield type.

"Know this guy?" she asked.

"No."

"This is Khalid Al-Mansour," she said. "He's AQAP's banker. Ghost operator. Built their funding networks, moved millions through front companies. Moves their money through fronts across the Gulf. No operational ties on paper, but if AQAP has explosives, food, vehicles, or comms—it comes through him."

That got my attention.

Caroline continued. "Two days ago, I got a ping through a cut-out in Marib. This source told me Al-Mansour wanted to meet. I didn't know if it was legit. Could've been bait. I took it anyway."

"Where did you meet?"

"Backroom of a hardware shop in Marib. Place run by his nephew. I didn't know that until after."

"Brave," I said. "Or reckless."

She gave me a look. "I had backup. A local asset. Ali. Ex-Yemeni army. Capable man."

Good enough for me.

"I made visual ID," Caroline continued. "It was him. And he said something I didn't expect. He wants out. Disappear. Dead to the world. Wants us to fake his death and vanish him."

Well, I didn't see that coming. I used to think nothing could surprise me anymore. After Baghdad, Helmand, Aleppo—after watching men burn for a cause they barely understood—I thought I had seen it all. Turns out I was wrong. Sitting across from two CIA officers discussing how to fake a terrorist financier's death so he could vanish into the wind? That was a new one.

Just proved one thing: no matter how deep you go in this line of work, there's always another level beneath. And this one smelled like rot. I didn't like it. But I was already in.

And something told me this op wasn't going to end where they thought it would. Not even close.

CHAPTER 7

I raised a brow. "You mean the terrorist suddenly grew a conscience?"

"Not really. He had four sons. Two are dead. He claimed Al Qaeda had pulled them into the fight. Two other sons are rotting in prison. He knows he's next."

"And he can't just run away," I completed her thought.

"Not a chance. Al Qaeda will kill his entire family—extended relatives included—if they think he turned. And they'll hunt him down wherever he goes."

"Sounds about right," I muttered.

Truth was, scum like Al-Mansour didn't deserve second chances. He had a hand in financing pain, suffering, death. Men like that didn't need to pull triggers—just shuffle funds, grease the right palms, and bodies dropped like dominos.

Still, this wasn't my call. No one at Langley was asking for my opinion. I wasn't the one making deals—I was the tool they used to execute them. In this machine, my job wasn't to question orders. It was to carry them out, clean and quiet. I kept my mouth shut.

Caroline continued. "He knows we're the only ones who could make it happen. Said we were the only ones with the skill to fake a death and disappear someone in this part of the world."

"What's he offering in return?" I asked.

“All intel he has on AQAP. Time-sensitive stuff. He said the bombing at the trade office was just a test run. That Al Qaeda’s planning a string of attacks. Not next month. Not next week. In the next few days.”

Caroline tapped again. A satellite shot came up. Building, squat, industrial. Tin roof. High walls. No signage. Out in the mountains, north of Sana’a.

“To prove he wasn’t just screwing us around, he gave me the location of a hidden bomb factory. Al Qaeda’s been producing car bombs and suicide vests there. Quiet, low signature. Off-grid power. No drone footprint. And they’ve been testing devices on livestock to keep their blast radius tight.”

“Charming,” I muttered. “And you think it’s legit?”

She looked at Atwood.

He finally spoke. Calm voice, but there was iron under it.

“It was legit enough for me to fly in.”

That spoke volumes.

Atwood continued. “We looped in our Ground Branch guys—local surveillance assets. They deployed micro-drones. Snuck them in through a busted window vent. Captured thermal footage of bodies moving inside. Machinery. Racks of devices.”

Ground Branch was the CIA’s paramilitary arm. The door-kickers. If they were involved, this was already past the talking stage.

“They’re keeping eyes on the building,” Atwood went on. “Haven’t moved yet. Orders were to observe only.”

“Why wait?” I asked.

"Because we don't just want the building," Atwood explained. "We want Al-Mansour. He's sitting on target intel—locations, names, dates. The works. The kind of stuff that doesn't just stop one attack. It disables their entire attack infrastructure."

Caroline continued. "There are multiple attacks in motion. Days, maybe hours out. We bring him in, we shut them down. We don't—we lose people. A lot of them."

Silence settled for half a second.

I leaned back in the chair, arms crossed. "Does this Al-Mansour know you're planning to pull him out?"

Caroline gave a sharp nod. "I sent a message through the same cut-out in Marib. Told him it's in motion. To be ready. He knows it'll happen in the next day or two."

Atwood added, "I pulled every string I had to get the green light. Black op status. No names, no paperwork, no deniability issues because there's nothing to deny. Once the clearance came through, we caught a flight and landed in Camp Lemonnier."

I gave a slow nod. Yeah. This smelled like a black op all right. Something no D.C. pencil-pusher would want showing up in a Senate committee hearing. Covert, no cavalry, and if it went sideways, we were just ghosts in the dirt.

Flynn cut in, eyes steady on me. "This is where you come in, Blaze."

I glanced his way. "Figured, sir."

"I know your team hasn't had proper downtime since Somalia," he said. "But this is top tier. High priority."

"No complaints, sir," I said. "My boys will be ready once we've got a plan."

Atwood leaned forward slightly. "I was... strongly advised to approach Colonel Flynn. And to specifically request for you, if you were anywhere in this part of the world."

I looked at him. "Huh? How come?"

Flynn gave a small nod. "He's talking about Director James Davis."

The name hit like a call sign in the dark. James Davis—Deputy Director of Operations, CIA. Man liked clean ops, quiet footprints, and operators who didn't flinch when the mission got dirty. My team had pulled a few rabbits out of hats for him in places we weren't supposed to be—Afghanistan, Lebanon, Syria. Ghost countries. We had also dragged his daughter, Madison, out of a hot zone, earning a lifetime of goodwill with him.

I cracked a grin. "Well, hell. The big man's still watching from up in D.C."

"Apparently so," Flynn said.

"Well, I'm already in," I replied. "But good to know Davis is still thinking fondly of me."

I shifted in my seat, posture changing. Mind flipping into the mission zone.

"All right. What's the timeline you're working with?"

Caroline's answer came fast. "That depends on how fast your team can be in Yemen. We're under severe time pressure."

Atwood added, "If Al-Mansour's intel holds up—and we've vetted it through every filter we have—then coordinated attacks are already being staged. Every hour we wait increases the risk of one detonating."

I turned to Flynn. “Understood. Once we finalize the operational plan, infil and exfil routes, platform assignments, and I have command authorization, I’ll need six hours to prep my team— intel brief, weapons check, gear loadout, final recon, comms sync. We can be wheels up by 1800 hours.”

Flynn gave a sharp nod. “Six hours is tight, but manageable. Let’s start locking things in.”

I looked at the map Caroline had projected on the screen. “If we want a clean extraction with plausible deniability, we use the bomb factory as the target site. It’s isolated, out of town, no civilian clutter, no adjacent infrastructure. If we hit it at night, we can neutralize the facility, make it look like a catastrophic munitions failure, like one of their bomb monkeys slipped up. The whole place goes up in a fireball, nothing left but twisted metal and carbonized bone fragments. Zero bodies left to ID.”

Flynn summed it up. “There won’t be enough left to identify any remains. Al-Mansour disappears in the chaos, and AQAP is left thinking they lost their financier in a tragic accident.”

I nodded. “Exactly. It’s not like AQ will send a forensic team digging for Al-Mansour’s DNA. And we’ll have zero collateral. As we’re literally sitting on a timer, we can’t afford to lose any time and risk attacks happening. We can aim to do it tonight.”

Atwood sat up straight, practically sparkling with excitement. “That’s exactly what I was hoping for. If it were just about neutralizing the site, we could’ve dropped a Hellfire and toasted it days ago. But for an extraction—your plan gives us deniability and misdirection. It's the cleanest option on the table."

Caroline looked less convinced. "I agree the site makes sense tactically. But it may not be possible for Al-Mansour to be out there during the night, let alone being there tonight."

I shook my head. "If we're staging an accident, the op has to happen at night. You increase your risk profile during daylight—foot traffic, loiterers, chance of local security patrols. You want it clean and quiet? It's got to happen under the cover of darkness. In daylight, it'll be a gamble with witnesses."

She still hesitated. "I get that. Only problem is, it might be difficult for Al-Mansour to make a night appearance at the factory. He's not your average foot soldier. He's the group's financial brain. Guys like him don't stroll into bomb shops after dark."

"Maybe," I said. "But the man's not stupid. He knows his clock's running out. And he won't get a second chance. He'll figure it out. It's about self-preservation. His life, not someone else's."

I paused, then added, "I also think he gave us the factory location on purpose. He's thought this through. He knows blowing that place sky high is his best shot at disappearing off the grid."

Atwood pulled weight and took the call. "I'm with you on this. The only reason we're doing this is to prevent any attacks in the pipeline. We can't take the risk of something blowing up tomorrow morning. Let's get it moving."

Caroline still didn't look happy. I wasn't sure if that was because she was still unconvinced, or because her boss had just sided with an outsider.

Atwood looked over at Caroline. "Send the message. Confirm extraction tonight. No delays."

Caroline gave a curt nod. "I'll relay it now."

Flynn stood up. "You've got the green light, Blaze. It's your op."

"Roger that," I said, rising to my feet.

I stepped out of the briefing room and into the hallway, already pulling up my comms tablet.

Time to round up the boys.

CHAPTER 8

I held the briefing in the corner hangar, laying out the mission on the whiteboard—full schematic, target details, and contingencies.

As expected, they weren't thrilled.

"We're rescuing terrorists now?" Ninja muttered, arms folded, his tone dry as sand.

"Langley says he's an 'asset'," I replied. "I guess that sounds better on congressional memos than 'terror financier'."

"They also use phrases like 'minimal resistance' and 'low probability of compromise'," Hawkeye added from the back, adjusting his ball cap. "And we all know what that means."

"Yeah," Ninja said, "it means we'll be crawling through goat shit with suppressed weapons while some desk jockey in Virginia runs PowerPoint."

Raptor snorted. "Last time someone said 'minimal resistance', I got peppered with shrapnel from a twelve-year-old with an RPG."

I let them get it out. They earned the right to bitch. But they also knew the job.

"Alright," I said, voice firm. "I know this stinks. I get that. But if this intel's right—and I believe it is—we're cutting off multiple attacks. That's civilian lives. Women, kids. It's real."

They fell quiet. Heads nodded. No more wisecracks.

Time to go to work.

At 1800 hours sharp, we were wheels up out of Camp Lemonnier in a Black Hawk packed with gear, firepower, and exactly zero enthusiasm for what lay ahead. The bird lifted off the tarmac with a gut-deep rumble, rotors chopping air like a meat grinder, and we banked east out of Djibouti, headed over the Gulf of Aden.

The Gulf stretched out under us like a sheet of hammered steel, calm and cold, catching the last glint of sunlight in broken shards. We flew low and fast, skimming thirty feet above the water. Too high and radar picks you up. Too low and you're shark bait if something goes wrong. But the pilots—both 160th SOAR—had hands like surgeons and nerves like steel. Best damn pilots in the world—guys who could land on a postage stamp in a hurricane if you asked politely.

The team sat strapped in with the kind of stillness you only see in people who have done this too many times. Raptor sat across from me, arms crossed, eyes shut—resting, not sleeping. Hawkeye stared out the porthole like he was already ranging targets in Sana'a. Ninja seemed focused whittling a piece of wood into a shape that I couldn't quite figure out.

We crossed open water for about eighty miles. Then land reared up beneath us, rugged and raw, the kind of terrain where every rock had a sharp edge and every village had someone watching with binoculars and a Kalashnikov. The Black Hawk threaded through mountain passes and low valleys, hugging terrain like a shadow. The Gulf behind us, Sana'a ahead, we dropped into the real world. High-value territory, high-risk airspace.

From there it was another hundred-seventy-odd miles inland, terrain rising fast. The ridgelines to the north caught the last blood-orange sliver of sunlight as we curved west toward Sana'a. Sunset hit around 1830 hours. That golden half-light turned the mountains into jagged black teeth, and then it was gone—just us, the rotors, and the hum of a bird full of bad intentions flying blind through a land where every fire on the ground could be a checkpoint or a cook fire for militants.

Total flight time was a hair under two hours. We ghosted in low to the western outskirts of the city and set down on a hard-packed strip behind a walled property that looked like it hadn't been used in a decade. Broken gate, dead trees, rusted water tank on the roof. But the perimeter tripwires and infrared sensors told the real story. This wasn't some forgotten homestead—it was a covert site, either Agency or JSOC-run. Hard to say and didn't matter. We were there, and it was secure.

As the rotors wound down and the dust cloud settled, I gave the signal to dismount. The team filed out with practiced rhythm—packs slung, rifles low, heads on a swivel. No nerves. Just the usual sense of purpose, coated in a thin film of professional distaste.

None of us liked the idea of pulling a known AQ financier out of the fire while pretending he died in it. That went against every muscle memory we had. But taking out a whole Al Qaeda bomb factory while doing it? That was something we could get behind. Even the worst jobs came with silver linings. This one just happened to be wrapped in Semtex. But it made the whole thing palatable. Almost.

We were locked in and ready. Targets, timeline, terrain—everything had been drilled and red-teamed on the flight in. Now we just had to wait for the word. And when it came, we would burn that factory down to the last bolt and disappear with the ghost no one wanted to admit existed.

The safehouse was quiet, humming with diesel power and encrypted comms. No flags, no insignias—just hard men moving with purpose. Mission clock was ticking. We would rest when it was done. Maybe.

I didn't get time for a breather as I was immediately led to a briefing room.

The room was the kind of place where secrets went to breathe—cinderblock walls, no windows, one heavy-duty door, and walls painted in that usual no-nonsense government gray. Caroline and Atwood were already seated at the table when I walked in—Caroline focused, tapping her pen against a folder, Atwood sitting back with a look like he had seen everything twice and was bored both times.

When Caroline looked up at me, there was something in her expression—focused, keyed up, maybe even a little excited, the corners of her mouth just barely lifted like the mission hitting green lights had done something for her.

"He's confirmed," she almost burst out. "Al-Mansour will be at the extraction site at midnight."

Her voice was calm, but there was a charge under it. Not nerves—something sharper. Determination, maybe. Excitement, for sure. I had seen it in field operatives before—when the plan starts moving and your blood knows it before your brain does. And I had to admit, she looked even better when she was keyed up like that—sharp eyes, sleeves rolled to the elbows, hair pulled back but already a strand escaping.

Whatever heat she had carried earlier at Lemonnier when I had overruled her on timing—it was gone. Replaced by that subtle shift in posture you only see when someone realizes they were wrong, and they are glad for it. The mission mattered more than being right. I respected that.

"He gave in faster than I expected," Caroline went on. "I thought I'd have to strong-arm him—'take it or leave it.' But he didn't even push back. Just agreed. I was a little surprised."

I was halfway to saying "*I'm not surprised at all*", but caught myself. No point acting like a smartass and rubbing it in. She didn't need a smug "*told you so*" right then.

So I just nodded. "Good. That locks it in."

Caroline leaned back slightly, eyes narrowing in thought. "But the time he picked—midnight—that's odd. It's late. Too late for him to be 'inspecting the grounds' or whatever excuse he usually feeds them. No obvious excuse for him to be there unless someone's covering for him hard."

Atwood chimed in, his voice low. "It's a risk, yeah. But maybe he figures the late hour gives him fewer eyes on the ground."

I nodded, but something itched at the back of my neck. Midnight made sense for us— low visibility, fewer locals around, tighter op window—but not for a guy like Al-Mansour. A financier like him usually sent runners to do his dirty work. Showing up in person was bold. Maybe desperate. It smelled off. I just couldn't put a name to the stink yet.

Caroline moved on, opening the folder and flipping to a photo of a black device shaped like a pocket vape. "We passed this tracker to him. A

Talon-5 tracker. GPS-based beacon, low-profile. Passive until activated. Magnetic slide switch on the bottom. It'll give us a clean signal the moment he turns it on."

"He asked specifically for it to stay cold," Atwood added. "Said he won't turn it on until he's at the site. AQ's been sweeping aggressively. He's paranoid they'll catch any live signals if he's carrying one hot. So he's playing it safe. Once he's at the site, he says he'll be isolated enough."

"Fair point," I said. "And he knows that beacon's his life jacket once things go loud."

"Exactly," Caroline said. "Once it's hot, you'll get a ping and real-time location data."

I nodded. "We'll be in position a couple hours ahead. My team will have eyes on from multiple angles. Once we see that ping, we move."

"I'll have the drone overhead as soon as we're wheels down in the AO," Atwood said. "Thermal and real-time ISR ready to feed directly to your taclink."

Just then, there was a knock on the door. Caroline stood and opened it.

A man stepped in. Mid-forties, medium height, lean, built like someone who didn't just lift weights but had carried real loads across mountains. Close-cropped hair, clean beard, dark eyes that scanned the room like he was calculating angles. He wore a dusty brown field jacket over tactical slacks, a battered watch on his wrist, and boots that had seen more than one war.

"Captain Blaze," Caroline said, voice formal. "This is Ali. He's the one who accompanied me to my first meeting with Al-Mansour. Ex-military—

Republican Guard. Knows Sana'a like the back of his hand. He's our best local field asset."

I stood and offered my hand. "Good to meet you."

Ali shook it with a firm grip. "Delta Force," he said, smiling slightly. "I've worked with some of your teams before, Captain. You boys move like ghosts. I'm looking forward to another midnight job. Feels like old times."

I liked him instantly. There was no try-hard bravado in his tone. No pretense. Just the kind of man who kept his head down and got the job done.

"Glad to have you on board," I said. "You'll meet the rest of the team in five. We've got final brief in the gear room."

Ali gave a nod and stepped aside.

I looked at Caroline and Atwood. "We better drop the formalities now that the op's live. Callsigns only. Mine's Cowboy."

Atwood raised an eyebrow. "Cowboy, huh? I get the feeling there's a story behind that."

Caroline gave me a sideways look, that same spark back in her eyes. "Oh, there's definitely a story."

I gave them both a shrug. "Not much to tell. Grew up on a ranch in Colorado. Horses, fences, the whole thing."

Caroline tilted her head, not buying the simplicity. "I've got a feeling there's more to it than that."

I gave her the hint of a grin. "I'll let you figure it out."

For a moment, something hung in the air—quiet, not spoken aloud, but unmistakable. The kind of look you don't throw around in an ops room unless you mean it. She held my gaze half a beat too long, and I didn't mind one damn bit.

Atwood stood and stretched. "Alright, we're green. Let's keep it that way."

We broke up after that and filed out. I motioned for Ali to follow. The hall was quiet, footsteps soft on tile. Behind us, the door clicked shut.

The op was on. Midnight extraction, one slippery terrorist, and about a hundred things that could go wrong.

Business as usual.

CHAPTER 9

"Eyes on movement," Hawkeye's voice crackled over comms. "Backside of the target compound. Pickup truck. Two men loading some stuff. Hard to tell what exactly."

"Copy," I replied, scanning through green-lit NVGs from my prone position atop a wind-scoured ridge.

I adjusted my angle to get a better view of the squat, ugly building below. Tin roof, high walls, no signage—just an unremarkable structure in the middle of nowhere. One road in, same one out. This was a bomb factory, plain and simple. CIA's latest intel said they had stockpiled several hundred kilos of precursor compounds and finished explosives in there. Enough to turn Sana'a into smoke.

We were parked on a low ridge to the north about 500 yards out—me, Ninja, Hawkeye, Raptor, Ali, and Youssef, the wheelman-slash-backup trigger if things got noisy. The terrain around us was harsh, dry, the kind of place where the wind scoured everything clean. Quiet, except for the occasional rustle of boots in the dust or the static in my earpiece.

"Unless these guys are prepping a midnight food drive, that's not rice they're packing. They're handling the stuff with too much care," Ninja murmured, his voice flat.

He did have a point. The men weren't just flinging the stuff in the back.

Youssef, our local wheelman, leaned forward, chewing a sprig of something green I didn't ask about. "They're moving the good stuff. That's not routine loading."

No kidding. CIA's intel had said this facility was sitting on a pile of HME—homemade explosives, military-grade accelerants, the works. If they were boxing it up now, it wasn't for spring cleaning. It meant operations. Big ones. Suicide vests, IED convoys, coordinated strikes. The clock was ticking.

The time was 2235 hours. No tracker ping yet from Al-Mansour. Which was weird—because I already knew he was in there.

The moment I had left the briefing room with Ali, I had hit up Echo.

Corporal Kevin King—callsign Echo. Our digital wizard with a buzzcut and zero patience for protocol. Guy could hack a comms net, track a SIM card through six proxy hops, and bring down a drone feed with one hand while eating a protein bar with the other. Officially, he was with Delta's CNO Squadron—the Digital Devils. Unofficially, he was the all-seeing eye. If it emitted even a whisper of signal, Echo could find it.

I had called him from the hallway as soon as I exited the meeting room.

"You really don't sleep, Cowboy, do you?" Echo commented, voice crackling over the secure line.

"Sleep's for civilians, Echo," I replied. "I need some info. An asset we're chasing has a tracker on him—Talon-5 model. He's not turning it on until he's at the site, but I want eyes sooner. You know if those things push out anything before activation?"

Echo chuckled. “That depends. You want the truth or the classified answer?”

“Whichever’s faster.”

“Right. Talon-5s have dormant backscatter. Low-power passive GPS. It doesn’t chirp, but it hums. You just need the right ears. Lucky for you, I’m the bat.”

“So, you can track him?”

“Ballpark him. You won’t get movement vectors in real-time, but I can triangulate based on drone sweeps and ambient signal noise. Your guy might think he’s dark, but I can sniff his shadow.”

“That’s all I needed to know.”

That conversation happened at 1900 hours. But just a few minutes ago, I got a second call from Echo.

“Cowboy, you up?”

“Take a guess, Echo.”

He laughed. “Well, I’ve got news for you. Got your guy. He’s there. Southern side of the structure. No movement in the last fifteen minutes. Tracker’s still dark, but the passive signature’s clean.”

“You sure?”

“I’ve got three satellite passes saying the same thing. He’s in. He’s early.”

That didn’t sit right with me. Al-Mansour was supposed to arrive at midnight, flip the tracker, and wait for our exfil. That was the deal. But here he was—already inside, quiet, and not lighting the beacon. And what the hell were his guys loading?”

“Something’s off,” I said, almost talking to myself.

“Think he’s not as straight as our intel experts hope he is?”

"No doubt about it. That's one crooked SOB. Anyway, keep sniffing. Let me know the second that tracker lights up."

"Roger that," came Echo's voice. "Just promise me if this guy screws you over, you let me write the eulogy."

I gave a half-smile. "Only if you make it funny."

I shifted in the dirt, eyes still fixed on the building. Something down there wasn't adding up. The early arrival, the loading, the silence on the tracker. Could be nerves. Could be coincidence. Or it could be something worse.

"Let's get eyes inside," I said over comms. "Hawkeye, time to let the bird stretch its wings."

"Copy that," he replied. "Launching the Hornet."

Hawkeye reached into his pack and pulled out a matte-black case. Inside sat a Black Hornet Nano drone—roughly the size of a hummingbird but meaner and a hell of a lot more useful. Built for recon, stealthy as sin. He powered it up, and its rotors gave a faint whine before stabilizing into a whisper.

The Hornet zipped off the launch pad like a ghost in the wind—silent, fast, almost invisible to the naked eye unless you were staring right at it. Which nobody down there was.

While it made its way across the open ground, Hawkeye unfolded the control module—a ruggedized tablet tethered to a compact joystick rig. The screen lit up green with live-feed telemetry. We crouched in tighter, our NVGs lifted, eyes locked on the display.

"Fifteen seconds to ingress," Hawkeye muttered.

The Hornet skimmed over the outer wall and threaded through a narrow opening—some kind of louvered window with no glass. Inside, the feed sharpened.

The interior was a single, large industrial hall. Dimly lit with yellow fluorescents that flickered now and then. Sheet-metal walls, cracked concrete floors, old machinery pushed to the sides. A few prefab panels had been set up to form makeshift rooms along one wall—plywood and tarps, just enough to break line of sight.

“There’s our workspace,” I whispered.

There were three men inside. One was hunched over a vest on a steel table, stitching something into the lining—looked like wiring or detonator loops. The other two were sorting through bins stacked with components. I saw racks with nails, bolts, wiring looms, soldering stations. It was a damn hardware store for suicide bombers.

“Outside, two tangos,” Ninja reported. “One at the main door, armed with an AK. One by the truck—just smoked a cigarette down to the filter. No discipline.”

No sign of Al-Mansour, though.

He was supposed to be there. Echo wasn’t the kind of guy who got fuzzy with intel. The man was inside. But I didn’t see him.

“Move the drone right,” I said. “Check those partitioned rooms.”

Hawkeye guided the Hornet along the edge of the wall. First room—empty. Second room—closed door. Third—door open.

And there it was—a narrow flight of stairs leading down.

“Bingo,” I muttered. “They’ve got a basement.”

Hawkeye angled the drone down the stairs, keeping it slow and tight to the walls. The signal got a little jittery, but the feed held. The stairwell ended in a reinforced concrete room—bare floor, no windows, high-density rebar in the walls. The kind of place built to hold more than just junk.

We panned the drone inside.

Three steel storage cabinets lined the far wall. Industrial-grade—thick hinges, triple-bar latches, and built-in locking wheels. Not something you would buy at an office supply store.

Center of the room was a metal field table—cold steel legs, scarred top.

And standing over it—Khalid Al-Mansour.

"Well, there's our snake," I said.

He was bent over a stack of papers. Not in a hurry. Focused. Methodical. A man doing business, not making a run for his life. Two other men stood nearby, not doing much, more like hanging around, AKs slung across their backs, waiting for orders.

"Looks like a ledger," Raptor noted. "Maybe financials?"

A minute later, Al-Mansour stacked the papers, then placed them into an open strongbox—metal construction, with reinforced corners and an integrated locking system. Looked like a mil grade cash safe, the kind you would transport in high-risk environments.

He added two small burlap sacks—probably cash, maybe coin, maybe something nastier. Then he shut the lid, locked it with a key, and gave a short nod to his men.

One of them lifted the safe—real heavy, judging by his stance—and they started moving up the stairs.

"That's not bomb-making material," I said.

Ali gave a low grunt. "Operational funds."

I nodded. Made sense. The place wasn't just a factory. It was a goddamn war chest. They weren't just building weapons—they were stockpiling resources. Money, documents, maybe even IDs or safehouse intel.

And Al-Mansour... he wasn't acting like a man defecting from a terror network. He was acting like a logistics officer prepping an asset drop.

"Why's he moving their cash?" I said out loud. "He's supposed to be cutting ties. Midnight rendezvous, tracker lights up, we extract, he gives us the intel. That's the deal."

"Doesn't look like a man cutting ties," Ninja replied.

No, it didn't. But why?

He wasn't going to see a dime of that money. Those two gun-toting guys carrying it weren't dumb porters. They would carry the stuff to another Al Qaeda stronghold.

So why move the war chest? Why not let it all burn along with the rest of the shit that we were there to blow up sky high? What the hell was Al-Mansour playing at?

I stared down at the building, jaw clenched. Whatever this was—it smelled like a backup plan. And I hate backup plans I don't know about.

CHAPTER 10

No way in hell I was letting that money land in Al Qaeda's bloody hands.

That cash wasn't just pocket change. It was operational lifeblood—funds meant for safe houses, guns, bomb parts, and payoffs. In the wrong hands, that kind of war chest could bankroll a dozen attacks across continents. And from the looks of it, Al-Mansour had just signed off on a withdrawal.

It was time to act. I keyed my mic. "Raptor, Ali, Youssef—heads up. If that truck rolls, you three are tailing it. We're not letting that cash fall into Al Qaeda's hands."

"Roger that," Raptor's gravelly voice came through instantly.

I paused a second, thinking it through, laying it out clear.

"Youssef, run black. No headlights unless you need them. Use the terrain, tuck behind ridgelines and structures. That Hilux of yours has night-assist tech—use it in pulses, don't drain the battery. Keep visual contact but don't crowd them. We need to know where the hell it's going."

"Copy that," Youssef replied.

"Rules of engagement?" Raptor asked.

"Soft follow, full stealth. You keep eyes on it, find out where they're taking it. You see anything hinky—weird stops, route changes, external vehicles joining—you call it out. Try not to engage. But if this goes sideways and you need to engage, don't hesitate. You light them up and take that damn truck."

"Copy that, Cowboy," Raptor confirmed. "We'll keep it clean unless it gets dirty."

"Echo, you watching this circus?" I asked, switching channels.

"Always, Cowboy. Bird's in the sky. High-alt drone feed. Got full thermal and visual overlay. Nothing but darkness and bad intentions out there."

"Good. Let me know if anything smells off."

We didn't have to wait long.

"Truck's about to move," Hawkeye said quietly over comms, watching through his spotter scope.

I shifted my eyes back to the pickup. Three men climbed into the truck—driver and two trigger-happy passengers with AKs slung lazily across their chests, one riding shotgun and the second riding bed security. Al-Mansour stood by, arms folded, watching like a proud father at a send-off.

The truck's taillights flashed faintly before it dipped behind a low berm and turned onto the dirt trail heading north—away from the city and into goddamn nowhere. That confirmed it. They weren't heading to Sana'a to redistribute that cash through the usual Al Qaeda logistics pipeline. They were heading into the empty wild. Which meant they were either burying the money, or it was going to a remote stronghold we didn't know about.

Back on team comms, I gave the go.

"Alright, move. Keep shadow distance and check in every five mikes or on change of contact. And Echo's watching, so if you get cut off, he'll keep us in the loop."

I watched through my binos as Raptor's vehicle peeled off from the low defilade we had parked in, rumbling quietly across the dark slope. Solid SUV, local plates, nondescript. Fit in just enough to not raise eyebrows from a distance. Night-assist headlights kicked in as a flicker, then went dark as Youssef shifted into passive mode, navigating like a mountain cat through the tracks.

"Keep feeding us updates," I told Echo. "They pull any fancy moves, I want to know before their brains even catch up."

"Roger that. Road's empty for now. This is ghost country. Nothing but hills and shadows."

Ten minutes later, Echo's voice returned.

"Cowboy, vehicle's approaching a checkpoint. Looks like... temporary structure. Small shack, overhead lamp, two tangos out front with a makeshift barrier."

"Copy," I replied. "They stopping?"

"Affirmative. Barrier's down. Truck's halted. Hold—wait one—"

A few seconds of silence.

Then, Echo's voice jumped. "Shots fired! Multiple rounds. No idea who lit up who. Looks like—hold on—yeah, yeah, the checkpoint crew opened up. Truck team's down."

"Say again, Echo. The checkpoint's hitting the truck?"

"Confirmed. Truck team's down. Two bodies dumped in the truck bed. They're pulling more bodies from the shadows—damn, they just staged a swap. Cowboy, this isn't a checkpoint—it's a planned hit."

I clenched my jaw. "Raptor, I need a sitrep."

"We saw the same," Raptor confirmed. "We're two hundred yards out, holding behind a low wall. Three new tangos took out truck crew. No shots from the truck, no resistance. This was an ambush. Clean and fast. Now loading the bed with something else. Bodies stashed. Truck's still running."

"Copy."

Then Echo's voice cut in again, sharper now.

"Tracker just went live. Our favorite finance guy just turned it on. Signal just went live in that bomb factory. I'm getting a clean ping."

I stared hard at the map on my tablet. The tracker pinged—a blue pulse radiating on the screen.

I narrowed my eyes, the puzzle pieces snapping into place. Then it hit me like a boot to the teeth.

Son of a bitch. That slick bastard was playing us.

Al-Mansour hadn't come there tonight to defect with clean hands. He came to empty the war chest. He wasn't delivering anything. He was stealing it.

Those guys in the truck were Al Qaeda loyalists. The checkpoint was his people. He set the AQ guys up. Sent them out with the war chest, then tipped his own crew off. They ambushed the shipment, eliminated the witnesses, and now the money was under Al-Mansour's control.

Once his boys secured the goods, he flipped the tracker, just like a good little asset. Called in Uncle Sam to come scoop him up and disappear him into a five-star safehouse somewhere in Europe.

A hell of a retirement plan. And if we hadn't been watching, we would have never known a damn thing. No wonder he had answered Caroline's message about a night exfil without hesitation and opted for midnight rather than earlier in the night. He wasn't making a snap decision—his whole damn scheme was already in play.

"Well, I'll be damned," I muttered, shaking my head.

Ninja glanced over. "Something funny?"

"Yeah. Al-Mansour's retirement plan."

I pointed at the tablet screen. "The bastard wasn't defecting. He was cashing out. Stealing Al Qaeda's money, handing over a fake defection, and planning to ride into the sunset with a suitcase full of jihad cash and a big American exit. This whole tracker routine was a green light to move once he knew the money was secure. That truck was never meant to reach AQ. His men intercepted it, and now he's sitting pretty thinking he just bought himself an escape plan."

Hawkeye let out a short laugh. "Ambitious little weasel."

Ninja snorted. "A jihad pension fund, huh? That's a new one. Wonder if it comes with dental."

"Too bad for him," I said flatly. "This is where the fairytale ends."

I keyed my mic again. "Raptor, change of plans. Take that truck. Neutralize the ambush team, secure the cargo. Make the truck and bodies disappear. Bury it if you have to. I want that truck to vanish off the face of the earth for a couple days. Keep it clean and covert."

"Copy all," Raptor said, tone sharp and clipped. "Going in quiet. Moving to engage."

The comms went quiet, broken only by the soft breeze over the hills and the occasional click of NVG adjustments.

I glanced at the tablet, watched the blue tracker pulse steadily from Al-Mansour's location in the basement of that bomb facility. The signal was strong now, perfectly timed.

I waited, eyes scanning the horizon where Raptor's team had gone dark.

Two minutes.

Three.

Then Raptor came back, voice steady.

"Target eliminated. Truck secured. Cargo intact. Bodies buried off-trail. Vehicle's covered with tarp and stone. No visual from air."

"Good work," I replied. "Make your way back."

"Copy, Cowboy. Out."

I leaned back on my haunches and looked out over the dark horizon. Cool mountain wind whispered across the rocks. Quiet out there—one of those nights where you could almost forget the world was burning, if not for the blood and betrayal riding on every decision.

Al-Mansour thought he had played it smooth—one move ahead of the Americans, two moves ahead of Al Qaeda. Selling them out while keeping his hands just clean enough for a CIA retirement plan. Not bad. Real slick.

But luck didn't lean his way tonight.

He didn't know we had eyes in the sky, boots in the dirt, and a tracker on his playbook. Didn't know we had seen through the curtain before he even pulled the string.

I would keep stringing him along, let him believe his con had landed. Let him think he had fooled us all.

Smart, Al-Mansour. Real smart. Just not smart enough.

CHAPTER 11

Ten minutes later, I heard tires crunching softly over gravel. They parked the Hilux in a shallow defilade, tucked in beside our second vehicle—out of sight, nose angled for a quick rollout. Doors cracked open and boots hit dirt. Raptor joined us on the ridge, Ali covering rear, Youssef staying behind the wheel with engine warm and eyes scanning the darkness.

At 2350 hours, we moved.

Me, Ninja, Raptor, and Ali slipped down from the ridge in a low, silent descent. Moonlight barely kissed the ground, and that was just fine—we didn't need much to work with. The landscape was all scrub brush and shale, with jagged hills cutting silhouettes against a starless sky. The building below sat squat and ugly in a small saddle between two rises, like it didn't want to be noticed. A single dim bulb was glowing yellow over the entry door like it was trying to convince the world it was just a mechanic's shop and not a ticking death trap.

Intel from the drone recon had painted the layout clear. One guy outside on the door, three inside in the workshop. Al-Mansour was somewhere in there too, and I could bet my last mag he wasn't standing too close to the fireworks. A man like him didn't get to the end of this kind of game without knowing how to survive the splash zone.

Ninja peeled off left to sweep the perimeter. Two minutes later he came back, and gave me a short nod.

"No other doors. No patrols. It's a one-door party."

"Good," I said. "Let's crash it."

I took point, moved on the guard first. The terrain gave me cover—small rocks, low brush, the kind of landscape that eats sound and keeps secrets. He stood under a bulb barely holding on to its last watt, more worried about his cigarette than anything tactical.

Double tap to the head. He dropped like a sack of onions.

We flowed in fast and quiet. The interior was lit just enough to see the targets and not much else. Three of them—bent over a workbench, tinkering with something they shouldn't have been.

They didn't even have time to turn.

Suppressors hissed like snakes. Three bodies hit the floor. Clean, surgical.

And then—

There he was.

Al-Mansour stood near the far corner like he had been posing for a painting. Just far enough from the action, hands raised, holding up a white placard like a damn greeter at the airport. "KHALID AL-MANSOUR" scrawled across it in blocky, awkward English.

Jesus.

I blinked. He had used a marker thick enough to read from across the room. Even underlined his name. Twice.

Well, at least he was thorough.

But talk about a welcoming committee. All he needed was a fruit basket and a customer satisfaction form. I had seen warlords fake surrender with a smile, watched narcos piss themselves mid-capture—but this guy? I half expected him to start humming the Star-Spangled Banner.

I felt a bit daft doing it, but I had to ask—it was protocol. "Khalid Al-Mansour?"

He nodded like a man confirming a dinner reservation.

Then he pointed to the closed metal door on the far side. His hand signals were military-clear—three men inside. No hesitation. Like he was helping us with the sweep. Trying to earn that ride out.

I didn't blink.

"Raptor, Ninja—stack up."

They moved like clockwork. Raptor took lead, Ninja right behind. They breached clean—no flashbang, no noise—just swift, suppressed fire. Three more bad guys down before they even knew they were being evicted from this life.

I turned back to Al-Mansour.

"What's in that other room?" I asked, pointing casually at the door that led to the basement.

He shrugged, eyes wide with false innocence. "Just storage. Empty. Nothing of interest."

Yeah. Sure.

I gave him a nod and pretended to buy it. Just a grunt with a gun, right? Couldn't read a blueprint if it bit me.

"Ali, Raptor—escort our guest to the trucks. Keep him comfy."

Raptor grabbed Al-Mansour by the arm. "Move."

Al-Mansour tried to object. "Wait—I am cooperating."

"Then cooperate faster," Raptor said flatly.

No more arguments. Out they went.

Once they were out, I turned to Ninja. "Time to blow up the place. Make it look like a test run gone bad."

Ninja was already pulling C4 from his kit. While he rigged the plastic explosive on structural beams, I headed downstairs, just to satisfy my curiosity.

The basement was a cement-walled bunker—empty strongboxes scattered like an abandoned vault. Whatever had been stored there was long gone. I checked every crate, every corner. All empty. The money had moved. That part of the plan had worked.

But Al-Mansour wouldn't know we knew that.

I came back up. Ninja had the explosives in place, all timed, tight, and tucked behind load-bearing joints. One spark and the whole place would pancake.

We moved out, smooth and silent. The mountain air was cooler now, the kind that made you feel like the night was holding its breath.

I climbed into the lead vehicle and signaled to Raptor. He nodded, pulled a black hood from his gear, and slipped it over Al-Mansour's head.

"This is unnecessary—" he started.

"No, it's standard," Raptor replied, his tone like a coffin lid slamming shut.

That shut him up.

Nobody else said a word. Silence was part of the plan. No chatter, no comfort, no friendly glances.

Let him think he was cargo, not company. And even wonder if this was a pickup or a hit.

I switched channels on comms. "Breaker-One, this is Cowboy. Package is secure. En route to designated drop."

Caroline came back quick. "Copy. Proceed."

No names. No locations. Protocols tight as ever.

We rolled out. The road twisted hard up into the hills—tight switchbacks and drop-offs where a wrong turn could make you part of the canyon wall. Youssef drove like he was born on those roads. He killed the headlights for a stretch, flipped over to night driving assist. Screens lit up the path in grayscale. The Hilux glided like a ghost.

I gave Ninja a nod. He pulled out the detonator, flipped the guard, and hit the button.

A second later, the world behind us erupted.

The main charge gutted the building from within, a deep concussive *thump* that echoed across the slopes like thunder rolling off steel. Secondary blasts popped off in chain—fuel tanks, acetylene, maybe a box of leftover detonators.

Fire spewed from the roof, then sucked in as the structure collapsed. One final boom sent a shockwave up the hills, rattling stones and setting off a chorus of barking dogs down in the valley.

Then it was gone.

Nothing left but smoke and a heat shimmer.

No bodies. No evidence. No fingerprints.

Al-Mansour sat silent in the back, hooded, breathing hard. Still thinking he had pulled it off.

That was fine.

Let him enjoy that, for now.

The truth would come later—slow, cold, and permanent.

CHAPTER 12

I was back in yet another debrief room—bare walls, humming fluorescents, a table that had probably hosted as much bad coffee as intel, and chairs designed by someone with a grudge against the human spine.

But the vibe that night was different.

Caroline was pacing like a caged bobcat, her boots tapping out a sharp rhythm across the tile. Her hair was pulled back in a no-nonsense knot, and her sharp eyes were flicking between the floor and the far wall like she was mentally eviscerating someone. Anger rolled off her in waves—but even in full-blown frustration, she looked good. Not the fragile kind of pretty, but sharp, precise, dangerous. The kind of woman who could walk into a war zone in heels and come out with actionable intel and a body count.

Meanwhile, Atwood leaned against the wall with his arms folded, jaw grinding slowly like he was chewing on a bad thought.

Caroline was the one to snap first. She stopped and turned on a dime, arms crossed tightly over her chest.

"I still can't believe he was playing us. All this time. Every call, every coded message—we were just feeding his plan."

Atwood still stood with his arms folded, expression unreadable except for the muscle ticking in his jaw. He let out a low chuckle that sounded like it was dragged through gravel.

"I've got half a mind to dump his ass in the streets, let Al Qaeda pick him up. See how fast he prays for CIA protection."

Then, a beat later, he exhaled hard and shook his head.

"Just venting. We all know I can't do that. Much as I'd love to watch him sweat on some jihadi livestream."

I leaned forward, forearms on the table, voice calm.

"Yeah, the guy's a snake. But a useful one. He's got intel we need—real stuff. Targets, financing networks, logistics. And more importantly, he's scared. He was scared to begin with, but now with the stunt he's pulled stealing AQ money, he must be terrified. That makes him a goldmine."

Atwood raised an eyebrow. Caroline stopped pacing, before shooting me a sharp glance. "You trust him?"

I snorted. "Hell no. But I trust his survival instinct. He pointed out the three gunmen in the back room. Didn't have to, but he did. Gave the signal, clean and clear, like he knew we'd smoke them and keep his ass safe. Didn't hesitate. Saved us time and maybe a bullet or two. That's not loyalty—that's desperation."

Atwood nodded slowly. "He's burned every bridge he had."

"Exactly. He's banking everything on the CIA being his ticket out. Right now, the only thing keeping him breathing is staying useful. And he knows it."

Caroline crossed her arms. "So you're saying he's cooperative now?"

I shrugged. "He's cooperative like a drowning man is helpful to the guy with the rope. But yeah—he'll give us what we want. And he'll keep doing it, because he thinks there's a soft couch and a bag of millions waiting at the end of the ride."

Caroline looked thoughtful, then sighed, dragging her fingers through the end of her ponytail like she needed something to do with her hands.

"So what—you think we just keep letting him believe he's on track for that safe house in the Alps and a fresh passport?"

"Damn right," I said. "Let him keep dreaming. He still thinks his millions are waiting for him somewhere sunny. That's our upper hand. He thinks we're dumb enough to fall for his act. So let him."

Atwood cracked a smile. "So we play the fool and bleed him dry."

"Exactly. He wants to believe he's the smartest guy in the room. Fine by me. Makes it easier to run circles around him."

There was a pause. Then Caroline tilted her head, eyes narrowing in mock suspicion.

"Did he really hold up a placard with his name on it? Or were you pulling our leg?"

I couldn't help the grin.

"Dead serious. Block letters. Khalid Al-freaking-Mansour. Like he was waiting for TSA to call him forward at gate B12. Was probably two seconds away from waving a little American flag and singing the Star-Spangled Banner."

She let out a laugh—short, surprised, and almost unwilling. But when she smiled, it lit up her face, softened the hard lines that anger had carved into her.

"That's insane," she said, shaking her head.

"Not insane," I replied. "Calculated. You don't survive this long in his world without knowing how to read a room. He read ours loud and clear: walk out slow, hold up your name, and don't get shot."

Caroline leaned back against the wall, arms loose at her sides. The fight in her had cooled, but her eyes were still locked on mine. Then she looked at Atwood for a second... then back to me, holding the gaze this time.

"You... and your team... you're sticking around, right? Until the threat's dealt with?"

The way she said *'you'* first, then tacked on *'your team'* after a breath... It was subtle, but I caught it. Could've been nothing. But I had a hunch it wasn't. A little slip. Just enough to make the room feel warmer for half a second. And yeah... I would be lying if I said I didn't like that.

Atwood turned to me. "Well, Cowboy?"

I gave a small shrug and leaned back in my chair.

"Mission's still hot. My boss hasn't called me home yet. So yeah... we're here."

She seemed satisfied with that. Not surprised—just reassured.

Then she turned to Atwood. "Shall we bring him in? It's time we had a little chat with our moneyman."

Atwood cracked his knuckles. "Yeah, let's see what he's got left in the tank."

He looked at me. "You want to observe? We've got a spot set up. Room with a one-way. We call it the fishbowl."

I smirked. "Wouldn't miss it for anything."

Atwood led me down a quiet corridor to a soundproofed room, dark glass stretching across one wall. Beyond it, the interrogation room—sterile as a morgue. Gray walls, steel table bolted to the floor, three metal chairs, and a surveillance camera in the top corner. It didn't scream hospitality.

A minute later, two security types brought in Al-Mansour. No cuffs or shackles. Just two well-built six-foot reminders not to try anything stupid.

Al-Mansour took a seat without a word.

He wasn't what most people picture when they hear "Al Qaeda financier". No scars, no unruly beard, no warlord swagger. Just a wiry, soft-looking guy in his early fifties, thinning hair, rimless glasses, button-down shirt a size too big. Looked more like a middle school math teacher than the man who funneled millions into suicide vests and IED factories.

But he was trying to play it cool—shoulders back, hands folded in front of him. The man had played his hand well—slipped out of AQAP's inner circle just before the floor gave way, defected with enough secrets to make himself useful. Now he sat there, trying to look calm. But I saw the nerves under the surface—the way he tapped his fingers against the table, the dart of his eyes to the corners of the room.

And I knew what he was thinking. He still believed he had a payday waiting on the other side of this. That once this was all over, he would step into some new life, maybe Switzerland or Uruguay, pop open a safe deposit box, and live off blood money in peace.

Caroline and Atwood made him wait. Let the silence stretch. Old-school psyops—let a man sit with the weight of his own future pressing down on him like a steel ceiling.

Then they walked in together—her with that calm, razor-sharp focus, and Atwood with his quiet menace. Al-Mansour sat at the far end of the metal table. He watched them take their seats opposite him, eyes calculating, but I could already tell—he didn't have much gas left in the tank.

Caroline didn't bother with pleasantries.

"You've got what you asked for, Khalid," she said, voice cool and direct. "Now it's your turn. We need everything—targets, names, comms hubs, safehouses. We know something big's coming. You're going to tell us what and where."

Al-Mansour didn't blink. He adjusted his glasses, leaned back a little like he thought he still had a seat at the table.

"I'll tell you everything," he said carefully, "but first, I need to know—what do I get in return?"

Caroline leaned forward just an inch. No expression. No emotion. Just cold precision.

"You're breathing. That's what you get. And for now, so is your family."

Al-Mansour's jaw tightened.

"You think your Al Qaeda buddies would let them live if they knew you were here, talking to us?" she continued. "You're only safe because they believe you died in the explosion at the bomb-making site. As far as they know, you're a martyr. Your sons, your wife, your entire bloodline—untouched because of that lie."

She let that sink in. Al-Mansour blinked and looked down, like he was trying to do the math on how close his life was to being over.

"But let me be perfectly clear," she went on. "That illusion shatters the second we stop protecting you. And the second we think you're wasting our time, you'll be back on the street. Alone. Let's see how long you last out there once AQ realizes you sold out their secrets."

Atwood spoke for the first time, voice gravelly but calm.

"You're not walking into some new life in Paris with a new name and a pile of money. You'll be spending the next few years in black sites you won't find on any map. Off the books."

Al-Mansour's face tightened, his hands curling slightly on the table. "And after that?" he asked, low voice almost a whisper. "Is there a future after… the sites?"

"That depends," Atwood said flatly. "On the quality of your intel. You help us neutralize the threat and dismantle this network, and we can eventually give you a shot at something close to a life. New face. New name. Far from here."

He hesitated, then gave a final try. "And my family?"

Atwood leaned in just enough to make it uncomfortable. "If they're smart and stay out of this, they live their usual lives. You drag them into your mess, that's on you."

Caroline cut in again, sharper this time. "But let me be clear. If even one attack goes off while you sit here trying to haggle like it's a damn bazaar, we'll leave you out there to explain to AQ what the hell happened at that facility."

Al-Mansour's mouth opened. Closed. He swallowed hard. The air in the room changed. His posture sagged just slightly, like the fight went out of his spine.

Then he nodded. "All right. I'll talk."

And just like that, the vault opened.

He started slow—head down, voice tight, testing the water. A safehouse here, a bombmaker there. Caroline and Atwood were good. Kept nudging him on. Once he warmed up, he started rattling off locations, names, cell structures, codes. And damn if he didn't have the goods.

By the time he was done, the war room looked like someone dropped a hornet's nest on a map of Sana'a. We had multiple credible threats and enough actionable intel to send us scrambling across the city.

Caroline and Atwood were on the line with Langley, and I had Hawkeye and Echo cross-referencing the threat matrix. We weren't walking into a battlefield—we were about to live in one for the next 24 hours.

CHAPTER 13

Next day, we barely had time to breathe. My team didn't stop moving all day, chasing down threats like a fire brigade in a city made of matches.

But we had to play it smart.

The thing was, if Al Qaeda got wind there was a mole in the ranks, they would pull the plug on every op and start again from scratch. And if that happened, Al-Mansour's intel would turn into toilet paper overnight. So we had to make it look like we were reacting to random noise, not reading from their playbook.

The CIA spun up a little theater to sell the illusion. First act? Chatter planted on dark web jihadi forums claiming that Khalid Al-Mansour—praise be to the martyr, peace upon his devoted soul, all that usual bullshit—had perished in the righteous explosion at the bomb-making facility. Pictures of some charred corpse with a blurred-out face got passed around. Al Qaeda ate it up. No suspicion. No whispers. No heads turning.

The second part of the plan? Let a few attacks look like wins. Not the big ones—just enough to feed the beast and keep them cocky.

The first "success" was a fuel depot used by U.S. convoys. AQAP had a cell set up in the hills, ready to pop RPGs at the tanks at dawn. Thanks to Al-Mansour, we were ahead of the curve. The depot had already been cleared out hours before—what was left behind were rusted-out shells and dummy fuel tanks. When the RPGs hit, the explosion looked real enough for cable news. Big ball of fire, cameras rolling, jihadis cheering. But in reality? Nothing lost but scrap metal and a few gallons of diesel for show.

Second staged win was an IED on a diplomatic convoy route. They had wired a decent-sized charge under the pavement, set for remote detonation. We rerouted the actual convoy the night before and rolled out a decoy—two armored trucks loaded with nothing but rubber dummies, sandbags, and remote driving tech. The bomb went off and flipped the lead vehicle on its side. Good show. Al Qaeda's boys thought they had bagged a few diplomats. Little did they know, they just blew up an empty ride and gave us a reason to tail their signal crew.

While the smoke cleared from that sideshow, we got to work on the real threats.

First hit was at a western café downtown, popular with embassy staff and expats. Intel said it was going down mid-morning. Joint sourced chatter pointed us to the café near Haddah Street—modern, glassy, espresso-sipping crowd, full of expats and diplomatic staff who didn't know how close they came to eating hot lead for brunch.

Me, Ninja, and Ali rolled up in an old Hiace van, blacked out, no plates. Echo had hacked traffic cams, gave us real-time visuals of three men in security guard uniforms posted out front—too clean, too stiff, and no company ID tags. They weren't guarding jack. They were casing the joint. We breached from the alley entrance, just minutes before go-time. We went in quiet—SIGs suppressed, fast and surgical. Quick and clean—

double taps, no collateral. Nobody heard a shot. The patrons inside kept sipping their lattes, not knowing how close they came to becoming a headline.

Second threat came in fast, just an hour later. Echo flagged unusual movement near the International Hotel—a soft-target high-rise known to house western journalists and contractors. Three men dressed as kitchen staff had come in from the loading dock. Caroline confirmed the place wasn't expecting any deliveries.

We were there in time to stop them. I came in through the stairwell while Ninja and Ali approached from the rear maintenance corridor. The men had weapons taped under the sink units—MAC-10s and homemade grenades. They didn't get to unwrap the party favors. We went in hard. Close quarters, brutal. One tried to pull the pin on a frag. Didn't work out for him. When we were done, the hotel's real staff were still clueless. We pulled out silently, left the cleanup to the local liaison.

Third op took us east. A tip from Al-Mansour mentioned "a delivery to the British", which turned out to be AQ-speak for a car bomb headed to the British diplomatic offices. We passed the tip to MI6's local boys. They beefed up their perimeter, set up overwatch, and flagged a beat-up Toyota Crown, loaded to the axles with ammonium nitrate, wrapped under plastic fruit crates.

We coordinated with their field lead. No cowboy moves. Brits don't like drama. Their team pulled a textbook intercept using a roadside trap—two SUVs boxed the vehicle. Driver reached for the trigger—sniper took out his brainstem before he could sneeze.

Three ops, seven kills—clean, fast, no exposure. But none of us were smiling. Because while we were putting out fires, something bigger was brewing.

At 1640 hours, Echo came over the comms. His voice was flat, but with that low edge I had learned to listen for—the kind of tone that meant something wasn't just suspicious, it was about to go kinetic.

"Cowboy, we've got a situation. Repeating chatter across multiple encrypted networks. They're all circling one codename."

I sat up straighter. "Talk to me."

"Codename appears in at least seven jihadi nodes on the dark web. Same phrase over and over. *Midnight Scimitar*."

My jaw tightened. That wasn't a code you used for some lone-wolf shit. That was war talk.

"That a new op?" I asked.

"Unknown. All signs say yes. It's been spiking in the last six hours—mentions in channel traffic, buried keywords in forum headers. Always tagged with timestamps around 0000 hours."

"Midnight on the dot?"

"Yeah. And get this—tonight's the last quarter of the moon. It'll rise at midnight local. Like clockwork. That can't be coincidence."

I felt the tension coil behind my ribs.

"Al-Mansour mention any of this?" Echo asked.

"Not directly. He gave us the fuel depot, the café, the hotel. But nothing about this. Closest he came was something cryptic: 'The true blade doesn't swing at noon.'"

"Hell does that even mean?"

"No clue. We thought it was poetic nonsense. Now I'm not so sure. But if AQAP's saving their biggest play for midnight, it tracks. Letting the day's attacks distract us—maybe wear us down—while they line up a real kill shot when visibility's low and defenses are stretched."

I had seen this playbook before. Throw out chaos all day long—force us to burn manpower and resources chasing every firecracker they light—then hit us when we were blind, tired, and thinking the worst is over.

Echo pulled up traffic spikes, signal dumps, route monitoring—everything suggested coordinated movements across multiple sectors of Sana'a. But what we couldn't pinpoint was what exactly was supposed to happen.

Theories started flying.

Could be a multi-front hit—assassinations, embassy attacks, a plane hijack, maybe even a chemical or biological strike. One thing was certain—this wasn't just a headline grab. This was meant to be a generational message from Al Qaeda: "We're still here. We're still lethal. And we still choose the hour."

I glanced at the time: 1800 hours. Six hours to go.

That was enough time to stop the nightmare. Or walk straight into it.

I told Echo to keep scraping every byte he could. Then I called Caroline.

"Echo's picking up heat. Something called *Midnight Scimitar*. Some kind of coordinated hit, most probably happening at midnight. I'm heading back to the safe house now. Start squeezing Al-

Mansour. See if he knows what the hell that means."

By the time I rolled up to the safe house, adrenaline was already sharpening my edges. My boots hit the concrete floor at a run. One of our local guys led me down the tight hall toward the glass-walled op center called the fishbowl—the soundproofed room with the one-way glass overlooking the interrogation room.

Inside the fishbowl, the air was heavier than a sniper's breath before the trigger pull. Caroline was pacing. Atwood looked like he had chewed through three cigars and was working on the fourth—without lighting any of them.

I stepped in. "What's the word?"

Caroline turned, looking pissed as hell. "You're not gonna like it."

She pointed through the glass at Al-Mansour sitting alone in the interrogation suite on the other side of the glass. Calm. Collected. Like he was waiting for tea service.

"He confirmed it. Midnight Scimitar is a major op. Multiple targets. Coordinated. Goes live at midnight."

"Alright," I said. "So what's the holdup?"

Atwood snorted. "He says he won't give us the targets unless we meet another demand."

I looked between them. "Let me guess. He wants to get his hands on the money?"

Caroline shook her head. "It's not about money. Not anymore."

"Then what?"

She looked at me. "He wants us to get his two sons out of a prison on the other side of the city. A fortified hellhole called Al-Mizan."

I blinked. "Wait—prison? You're telling me the price for stopping a mass-casualty op is a jailbreak?"

Caroline ran a hand down her face. "Yeah. That's what I'm telling you."

"You've got to be kidding me."

"Nope," Atwood said. "He says that was the real reason he reached out to us in the first place. Not to save his own ass—but theirs. Wife's dead. Two other sons already gone. These two are all he's got left. Says if he'd asked for their release up front, the Agency would've shut the door in his face."

"He's not wrong," Caroline added quietly.

"So he played the long game," I muttered, staring at the glass. "Got us to pull him out, gave us just enough intel to prove his value... save a few lives... little victories... then dropped the real price tag once he got leverage."

"Exactly," Atwood agreed. "And now he's got us by the balls. The next phase of his intel could prevent a catastrophe tonight."

Caroline added, "He waited until now—until we need the rest of what he knows. He says without him, we won't be able to stop what's coming at midnight. And when that hits, it won't just be the body count—it'll be a political bloodbath."

Atwood exhaled. "He's got leverage. He knows it. And he's not bluffing."

I looked at Al-Mansour through the glass again. Calm. But behind the calm was steel. I had seen that look before—men who had already accepted their death if it meant a shot at saving someone else. He wasn't bluffing. No amount of threats was going to move him.

"He knows we can't torture the targets out of him," I said. "He's made his peace."

"He said it himself," Caroline added. "These two sons are all he has left. If they die in there, he dies with them. But if there's a chance..."

"He'll take the risk," I finished. "We threaten to drop him back on the streets, hand him to Al Qaeda, he'll flinch. But he still won't break."

Caroline nodded.

I turned to Atwood. "What about pulling strings? Can the Agency get him a favor?"

Atwood's lips twisted into a grimace. "Can't pull what's already snapped. Al-Mizan isn't under government control anymore. Houthis took it two days ago. Government has no say."

"So it's a militia-run black site now?"

"Yeah. AQAP detainees won't last long inside. Especially not high-profile ones. Houthis treat them like dogs. He knows his sons are on borrowed time."

"You said Houthis took it two days ago. Isn't that when he made contact?" I asked Caroline.

She nodded. "He must've known this was his only shot."

So that was Al-Mansour's strategy from the start.

I sighed. "And I take it asking the Houthis nicely isn't on the table?"

That actually got a laugh out of Caroline. "Not unless you're bringing tea, qat, and a miracle."

"Jesus," I said. "Alright. These sons—are they active AQ fighters?"

"Affiliates," Atwood replied. "Members on paper, but Al-Mansour claims he's kept them out of the field. That they were being groomed as future assets, not current ones. They haven't seen combat. But we can't confirm it."

"So, not choirboys. But not full-blown martyrs either."

I let that sit for a beat. Then looked at both of them.

"OK. What do you want from me?"

Neither of them said a word. Just shared a look.

I gave them the look right back. "Don't pull that diplomatic shit with me. Say it."

Silence thickened.

So I said it for them. "You want me and my boys to go get them. Hit the prison run by hostile militia, yank those two scumbags out, and bring them here. Before midnight. That about right?"

Atwood looked at me. "That's an option we're... weighing."

"I don't think you're weighing anything. You're already tipping the scales. Clock's not just ticking—it's screaming. Let's be honest—there's no other move. We can try shutting off those cameras and letting me take a run at Al-Mansour, maybe I break him. But chances are, I don't. I've seen that look on his face. He's ready to bleed. I could put a knife in his ribs and he'd smile through the pain if it meant buying his sons a shot at life. We're out of time. We don't have the luxury of finding out if I'm wrong."

I pointed to the glass.

"He's made his decision. We don't have leverage anymore. What we've got is a ticking clock and a prison full of Houthis who don't know what's coming. If we're gonna get answers, it's not gonna be with threats—it's gonna be with action."

Caroline stared at the glass, then nodded slowly. "You're right."

“I know. The only option is we pull his kids out.”

Atwood crossed his arms and nodded. “We’re reaching out to ground sources now. Seeing who’s still breathing that can help us inside.”

“Good. You do that.” I stepped toward the door.

Caroline raised an eyebrow. “Where are you going?”

“I need a minute with him.”

“You planning to hit him?”

“No.” I paused, my hand on the doorframe. “But I’m going to make sure he understands something real clear. This is his last card.”

And with that, I stepped into the pressure cooker.

CHAPTER 14

The door hissed shut behind me with a metallic thud.

Al-Mansour sat at the steel table like he owned the room, fingers laced, posture straight. Like he hadn't just sold out everything to get his sons out from behind enemy lines.

He didn't flinch when I entered, but his composure stuttered for just a second. It was that tiny flicker of uncertainty you only catch if you have watched enough men struggling to appear braver than they really are.

I didn't say a word.

Just stood there. Stared at him like I was measuring a coffin. Letting the weight of silence settle in like a dead weight in the room.

He didn't like the silence. No terrorist ever does. They are prepared to resist pain, interrogation, isolation—but the weight of silence from a man who's done worse than ask questions? That's a different pressure altogether.

He shifted, tried to regain footing by folding his hands tighter, like he was holding himself together with prayer beads that weren't there. He locked his eyes on mine. Defiant. Hollow.

I walked around the table, slow, steady, putting my boots down like I was walking over landmines I already mapped. I stopped by his right side, planting myself between him and the wall. The overhead camera had my back. Wouldn't catch my lips or his expression. Good. This part wasn't for the archives.

I leaned in close. Not touching him. Just close enough for my breath to ride up his neck.

"I want you to listen real carefully," I said, voice low and even. "Every day, my men and I put our lives on the line to save people. Every op, every night, every firefight. We don't run our mouths about it. We just do it. Part of the job."

I let that sink in a second before I tilted my head.

"But there's a flip side," I went on. "We also kill people. Hurt them bad. Taking lives also comes just as natural to us. And we don't lose sleep over it. That's part of the job too."

His mouth tightened. Eyes didn't blink.

"You played your cards well. I'll give you that. You waited, measured your ask, saved the sons for when they'd cost the most. Congrats. But you're out of cards now."

Al-Mansour said nothing. But his breath slowed. Like he was trying to conserve oxygen.

"You want your sons back? Fine. I'll get them out. Prison's crawling with Houthis, but that's our problem now. We'll bleed for them, if that's what it takes."

I paused.

"But you'd better hear this next part like your life depends on it. Because it does."

His eyes tracked mine now. Focused. Calculating.

I leaned closer, just enough to make his jaw twitch.

"If—after I get your sons out—you don't immediately give up every single detail about Al-

Qaeda's attack... I'll shoot both of them in the knees. Leave them back there screaming in the dirt. And I'll hang around just long enough to watch the Houthis do what they do to escaped enemy convicts."

His face twitched. He tried to hold the defiant look. But his eyes knew I wasn't bluffing.

"Now, I'm not with the diplomats," I said. "This isn't a negotiation. You've already played every card. Now you deal with me, not the suits in the next room."

I nodded toward the door.

"They want your intel? Fine. I'll get your boys out. And when I do, I'll call you. Give you proof they're alive. But they don't come anywhere near here. Not until those two agents confirm you gave them every ounce of intel. Names, targets, comms, channels, plans. All of it."

Still no answer. But his eyes were doing all the talking. I saw the math running in his head. Cost versus consequence.

"You screw us," I said again, "and the next sound you hear will be their screams."

I stared at him dead on.

"Any doubts I'll do what I said?"

His jaw clicked once. Then his head moved, a slow shake. "No," he said, barely above a whisper.

"Tell me you understand."

"I understand."

I straightened up. "Good. I like it when things are clear."

I turned and walked out, shutting the door behind me without looking back.

Caroline stood just outside, arms crossed, leaning against the wall in that calm, CIA way that said she already knew too much. Her expression was cool, but her eyes tracked me like a sniper glassing a rooftop.

She gave me a sideways glance. "So... how'd the bonding session go?"

"He and I are practically family now," I said. "Just need matching tattoos."

She smirked. "You really threatened to kneecap his sons?"

I paused. "I thought this room wasn't bugged."

Her lips twitched. "We're the CIA."

I smirked. "Right. Forgot I was playing at home."

She waited. "Well?"

"Yeah," I said. "I gave him a nice bedtime story. Told him how his boys would scream if he lied to me."

Her brow arched slightly. "You're not bluffing, are you?"

I looked her square in the eye. "I don't bluff when lives are on the line. We're here to stop a massacre. That man in there needs to believe if he plays us and people die, I'll make damn sure he pays in blood."

After a pause, I added: "It won't come to that. He's smart. He understood me."

Caroline studied me for a second. Something flickered behind her cool exterior. Not fear. Not disapproval. Just... curiosity. Like she was seeing something she didn't expect and wasn't sure what to do with it.

"Most men who talk like that are either broken or full of shit," she said.

"Maybe I'm both," I replied. "But I get results."

There was a pause. The air between us got heavier.

"You always carry that kind of weight around?" she asked.

"Only when the stakes are real." I leaned in slightly, voice dropping. "And they're real now."

"You ever think of what happens after all this? When the mission's over?"

"Yeah," I said. "Usually while I'm cleaning a rifle."

That made her laugh. Low and dry, but real.

She looked at me longer than she needed to. Her jaw clenched, then softened.

"You're not what I expected," she said.

"I get that a lot."

Another pause. Her eyes didn't leave mine.

"Well," she murmured, straightening up, "just make sure you come back in one piece."

"I will," I said. "You planning to still be here when I do?"

She smiled. Small. Enough to mess with my pulse. "We'll see."

I looked at her for a second longer than I should have.

Then I said, "Let's get to work," and walked past her before I let the silence stretch.

For a second, I felt her eyes on my back like a live wire. She didn't say another word, but something told me she wasn't done with me yet.

And I wasn't sure if that was a good thing—or just the beginning of more trouble.

CHAPTER 15

The CIA's intel crew didn't waste time. Within the hour, they had me fully clued in, pulling up blueprints, satellite imagery, and internal schematics of the prison. High ground. Heavy walls. Reinforced gates. A goddamn fortress.

It was time to get my crew up to speed. As I walked down the hallway toward the briefing room, my boots echoed off the tiles like slow hammer taps. I wasn't looking forward to the next five minutes—breaking bad news to your team never got easier, no matter how many wars you had survived with them.

They were already waiting.

Ninja Man was sharpening his blade out back like we were headed into feudal Japan. Raptor sat hunched over the radio kit with a toothpick in his mouth and that bored expression he wore before a storm. Hawkeye stood near the window, arms folded, eyes locked on the shadows beyond the glass. And Ali—stoic, sharp, calm—stood near the map table, eyes tracking me like he already knew this was going to suck.

I stepped in, shut the door, stood facing them with my arms crossed, giving them a once-over before dropping the weight.

"Well, boys," I started, "hell of a day. We stomped out half a dozen brushfires in a single day without lighting ourselves up. And now..."

Ninja looked up, one brow raised. "Let me guess. We finally get to relax with beer?"

I shook my head. “Not quite. We’ve still got one more storm to ride before this night’s over. So enjoy the lull, because it’s about to get loud again.”

Raptor groaned. “Jesus, boss, we already tangoed with half the assholes in Yemen today. What now? Dinner with the Houthis?”

Hawkeye cracked his neck. “Please say it’s something quiet. Maybe a stakeout. Something with sitting.”

“Well, you do have some sitting to do on overwatch. As for the rest...”

Ninja groaned. “I don’t like the sound of that. We’re not sleeping tonight, are we?”

“Nope,” I said. “We’ve got a new op. High risk. No margin for error. CIA’s greenlit us to extract two individuals from a Yemeni prison.”

Silence. Then—

Ninja squinted. “Extract as in... escort duty? Prisoner transfer. US Marshals-style?”

I looked at him flatly. “No. Extract as in break in, breach, locate, and get the hell out. Like thieves in the night, but with more firepower.”

There was another beat of silence. Then Ninja snorted. “Well, damn. That’s gonna look nice on the ol’ resume. International prison break. Right between ‘black ops veteran’ and ‘reason for termination’. HR’s gonna love that.”

Hawkeye leaned back, arms crossed. “You serious, Cowboy. Next you’ll be telling us we’re rescuing Bin Laden’s gardener.”

I exhaled. “You’ve got no idea, Hawkeye, how close you hit that one.”

Ninja leaned forward. “That doesn’t sound promising. Who exactly are we busting out? Some poor sods caught in the wrong place?”

I hesitated just a second. “You’re not gonna like the answer.”

They waited.

“It’s Al-Mansour’s sons.”

The silence this time was deeper. More leaden.

Ninja dropped his whetstone. “You’ve got to be kidding me.”

Raptor sat forward. “You’re saying we just rescued daddy terrorist and now we’re going back to yank his spawn outta lockup?”

Ali just stared at me. Like he was trying to process a punch he didn’t see coming.

Hawkeye chuckled. “Hell of a family reunion we’re building out here.”

I gave them about ten seconds to vent—gripes, disbelief, colorful Arabic from Ali that probably involved someone’s mothers. Then I held up a hand.

“Look—I know how this sounds. I’ve been through this same pile of unhappy crap myself. But here’s the deal—this isn’t about Al-Mansour. It’s bigger. Intel confirms Al-Qaeda’s gearing up for a citywide assault. Codename: Midnight Scimitar. If it goes live, we’re looking at multiple coordinated strikes on U.S. assets, expats, embassies. Full-blown slaughter in the streets.”

That sobered them. The anger was still there, but it was quieter now. Focused.

“So what do Al-Mansour’s sons have to do with this?” Hawkeye asked.

“He’s the only one with the intel to help us shut it down. The sons are his price for it.”

“Son of a bitch. Saving his ass wasn’t good enough for him?” Raptor growled.

"Nope. That was his first play. All those fires we put out, he was just proving the value of his intel."

Then Ali spoke up, calm and cold: "Let me be alone in a room with him. Five minutes. He'll talk. That, I promise you."

I met his eyes. "I thought about that. Trust me, I did. But we're not after bits and pieces. We need full intel—timings, safehouses, chain of command. Torture won't get us all of that, especially not in time. This isn't about hurting him. It's about controlling him."

Ali nodded once, but his jaw was clenched. He wasn't thrilled, but he understood.

"And you sure he'll not come up with a new demand once we grab his pups?" Raptor asked.

"Yes. I had a heart-to-heart with him. Told him I'd skin those two alive if he even thought about stalling further. He won't."

"That I can believe," Ninja said. "Shoulda been there to see you putting the fear of death in him."

"I did enjoy that. Also, don't think this means Al-Mansour and his boys get a free ride. I've been promised that won't happen. Once we've got what we need, the gloves come off."

That sunk in. There were a few grim nods.

I stepped over to the map table and tapped the satellite image. "The prison's a hardened target in the mountains northeast of the city. Terrain's steep. Good for snipers but hell for vehicles. Front gate is a kill box—reinforced steel, two towers, overlapping fields of fire."

"Great," Raptor said. "So we're not using the front door."

"Right," I confirmed. "We breach through the eastern watchtower. It's got a narrow catwalk running across the outer wall—leads to the roof. From there, it's a clean drop into the high-security wing. We get in, grab them, and get out clean."

"And if it goes sideways?" Hawkeye asked.

"Then we paint the rocks red and fight our way to the helo."

They all nodded. Quiet now. Focused.

"Timeline?" Ninja asked.

"Wheels up by 2030. On site by 2100. Hawkeye takes overwatch from the east ridge, with Ali as his spotter. Raptor holds position with the Black Hawk, ready for my signal. Ninja and I breach the tower and lead the extraction."

I looked around the table. "You've all done the impossible today. But this right here? This is the price of playing in the deep end. Nobody's coming to back us up. It's just us. And if we screw it up, the whole city burns."

They nodded. One by one. Silent. Resolved.

Raptor snapped the pen in half and tossed it aside. "Let's go steal some terrorists, then."

By 2100 hours, we were ghosts in the mountains.

Hawkeye up on a shale ridge, rifle braced on a tripod, glassing every shadow. Ninja and I crouched below the eastern tower, charges set. Raptor's voice crackled once in the earpiece—"Wheels hot and waiting"—then went dark again.

We breached the tower, dropped bodies on the way in, and found our targets. Hassan and Ibrahim.

We extracted them, dealt with a shitload of angry Houthis firing on us with all they had, before the Black Hawk whisked us away from the madness.

CHAPTER 16

The Black Hawk's rotors churned hard through the thinning air, kicking up a cyclone of dirt and broken stone. I watched the prison shrink behind us—a box of concrete and misery stuffed into the mountain like someone was trying to hide it from the world.

I leaned toward the pilot. "Drop her into a hover. Ten seconds. Need a couple of snaps to send to HQ."

"Copy," the pilot replied, easing back on the collective. The bird steadied in midair, rotors churning above us like an angry god.

I turned back toward Ninja and Raptor. "Line them up. Make it pretty."

Ninja cracked a grin. "You want a family portrait, Cowboy? Or you want them lookin' like two guys who just shit themselves?"

"Something between mugshot and obituary," I said.

"Got it. Dead-eyed and disappointed. Classic terrorist sons pose."

He grabbed Hassan by the collar and nudged him toward the open door. Raptor took care of Ibrahim. By then, they had acquired the good sense to not resist.

Both men still wore faded gray prison fatigues—standard-issue stuff, cotton drawstring pants and tunic tops, sweat-streaked and threadbare. They stood in front of the open side door, wind whipping their clothes tight to their frames. Both looked like their guts were trying to crawl out through their throats.

Ninja and Raptor flanked them with their HK416s held loose and ready. Black balaclavas. No emotion. Just two angels of death in a steel coffin with rotor blades. Adding just the right kind of drama.

I stepped back and snapped two tight shots on my satphone.

Then I gave the pilot a thumbs-up. "Take us out of the hover," I spoke into the comms. "Let's move."

The rotor pitch changed, and the bird banked forward, pushing through the warm darkness again.

I keyed the secure comms and called Caroline.

Her voice crackled through a second later. "Go ahead, Cowboy."

"Package secured. We got both assets. Extraction clean. Minimal noise."

A pause. Then a smile in her voice. "That's really good work. You guys OK?"

"Affirmative. No holes in any of us. But we're still in the air, so let's hold off on the victory dance."

"Copy that," she replied.

I sent the photos through. "Sending you a couple of souvenirs."

"Visual confirmation?"

"Yep. Just sent them. Hassan and Ibrahim. With two very unfriendly escorts."

A pause, then her voice came back. "Got them."

"That's your proof of life. Now go to Al-Mansour. Show him the photos. Put him on speaker when he sees them."

She didn't reply immediately. I could picture her in that basement room—glancing at the image, jaw tightening, already walking.

"Done. What's the play?" she asked.

"I'll tell him he's got five minutes to spill everything about Midnight Scimitar. You'll confirm to me within five minutes that he gave you the full plan. If you don't confirm, we dust off and drop his sons back into Houthi arms."

"You planning to make that threat explicit?"

"Oh, I'll make it real enough to rattle his teeth. But you just sound outraged—try to talk me down, do the whole Langley rules-and-regs act. Make me look unpredictable as hell. Sell it."

She exhaled into the mic. "You ever stop to think how insane this whole plan is?"

"Every hour."

"You realize you're basically threatening to kill two prisoners mid-air while coordinating an international anti-terror operation?"

"I'm aware."

"And this is your calm plan?"

"Yep."

"Jesus," she said, not exactly sounding displeased. "Alright. I'll play my part. Outraged handler. Furious with your recklessness. Trying to stop you from going rogue."

"Good. Sell it hard. Call me back when he's in the chair," I said, and cut the line.

A minute later, my satphone buzzed. Caroline's voice came first, calm and clipped.

"Captain, we're live. I've got Al-Mansour in the room. He's seen the photos. You're on speaker."

"Good," I said, leaning forward so my voice carried. "Al-Mansour, you see those two fine young lads standing next to my men in ski masks?"

Silence. Then a grudging, "I see them."

"They're alive—for now," I said. "But I'm going to make this real simple. You've got five minutes to tell Caroline everything about Midnight Scimitar. Targets, timing, everything. No riddles, no 'maybe this, maybe that'."

Silence on the other end.

"You don't talk," I continued, "we take off, circle back, and throw them near the prison. And the Houthis will take it from there."

Caroline jumped in, voice tight. "Captain, wait. I'm going on record here—don't go rogue."

I cut her off. "We're the ones out here bleeding for this op. My team risked everything to pull these two out of that mountain hellhole. I'm not running a taxi service for terrorists. We did it to save lives—not to babysit a scumbag's kids."

I let that hang for a beat, then turned up the pressure.

"Al-Mansour. If I don't get confirmation within five minutes that you've spilled everything by the time that clock hits zero, I'm turning this bird around and throwing your sons out. The Houthis are still looking. Do you understand your deadline? Do you have any doubt that I'll follow through?"

His response was immediate: "No doubt. I understand."

"Good. Clock starts now."

I killed the transmission and leaned back. Now we would see how badly Daddy wanted to keep his little monsters breathing.

I looked up from the SAT handset and spotted Hassan and Ibrahim hunched shoulder to shoulder, whispering hard and fast. I didn't like it. No one swapped bedtime stories at 5,000 feet under rotor thunder.

Ali was sitting next to them, rifle across his lap, alert as ever. I caught his eye and gave him a silent signal—tilt of the head, two fingers tapping the ear. He nodded, turned slightly in his seat, and leaned just enough to eavesdrop.

It was soon time for us to change our rides. The Black Hawk dropped altitude fast, zeroing in on a landing zone that looked like the middle of nowhere—flat dust, broken rock. Two SUVs sat ahead—low-profile, blacked-out, waiting under faint headlight glow. Our wheels out.

We hit the dirt. I stepped off behind Ninja and Raptor, boots crunching under the rotor wash. My eyes swept the perimeter, scanning for any movement beyond the flood of grit and wind.

The pilot kept the bird at a hover for a beat, then peeled off hard—nose up and banking southwest. The bird was headed back across the Gulf, all the way to Camp Lemonnier in Djibouti.

CHAPTER 17

Ali jogged up beside me as we approached the vehicles.

"Got anything interesting?" I asked.

"You bet. Those two didn't know their father was alive. They thought he died in the explosion last night."

I stopped short. "You sure?"

He nodded. "Positive. But after hearing parts of your call just now, they're starting to suspect. They're not sure... and they're afraid to ask."

I let that sink in.

Echo's rumors had spread like wildfire. Word of Al-Mansour's "death" had made it past walls and guards, all the way into the prison. That meant our misinformation campaign was more effective than I gave it credit for.

"Ibrahim admitted to Hassan that he's scared. Hassan tried to act tough. Said he's not scared—just won't speak to Americans. Kept calling his father a traitor for working with the Americans."

That tracked. Hassan had tried to drag that third guy with him during the breakout. Wanted to bring a plus-one to his extraction. That wasn't panic—it was loyalty. Most probably to Al Qaeda. Daddy's pet project wasn't some misguided son after all—he was a true believer.

I snorted. "Brave little jihadist."

Ali smirked. "But Ibrahim... he looks like a boy trying not to break. He sounds like he was actually shaken up, like a normal son would be. But he didn't speak much—Hassan did all the talking. Loud, angry. Like he was in charge."

I glanced back at them. Ibrahim's shoulders were slumped, eyes bouncing from the bird to the SUVs like he was still trying to convince himself this wasn't some nightmare.

"Maybe that's one son who's actually trapped," I muttered. "And not just in the prison."

Ali gave a small nod.

"Keep your ears open," I told Ali. "They drop anything else, I want it fed straight into my comms."

He nodded and peeled off toward the vehicles.

That's when the satphone buzzed in my vest. Five minutes. Caroline, right on cue.

I brought it up to my ear. "Cowboy."

Caroline's voice came through, tight but clear. "He gave it up. It's real. We've got confirmation of multiple coordinated attacks. Everything kicks off at midnight."

"Targets?"

"Embassy, diplomats and their families, even the airport. It's the whole show."

I clenched my jaw. "You verify any of it yet?"

"I will," she said. "He gave up ops codenames, internal comms nodes, a server route in Mukalla. I've got our SIGINT boys scraping it now, and I'll cross-check what he gave me against deep-forum chatter. We flagged one of the keywords last week in TOR traffic. That'll tell me if he's bluffing."

"Send the whole damn thing to Echo," I said. "If anyone can validate, it's him."

"Already queued it."

"Good. I'll be at the safehouse in ten."

I cut the call and started toward the SUV. The rotor wash was starting to die down behind us.

Footsteps behind me. Light. Hesitant. Like someone walking across a minefield.

I turned. It was Ibrahim. Nervous. Like a scared stray—too spooked to come closer, too desperate to walk away. Hands twitching like he was about to get yelled at for something. He stopped a few feet from me, eyes down.

I turned and looked right at him. "You need something?"

He swallowed hard. "Sir..." he started, voice barely audible. "Is... is my father alive?"

I looked at him for a long second. There was no good reason to lie. And after everything, the kid deserved at least that much.

"Yeah," I said. "He's alive."

The relief on his face was damn near physical—like I had just pulled a steel beam off his chest. His whole posture loosened. Shoulders dropped. Breath came out in one slow exhale.

"Thank you," he said softly, and turned to head back.

I let him take two steps before I spoke again. Something didn't sit right.

"Hey," I called out. "Why'd you think he was dead?"

He turned back around. "Word spread in the prison," he said. "They said there was a big explosion at a facility. That he was there. That he died in it."

So the story we had spread reached them fast. Good. But there was something else I needed to confirm.

"You guys seemed almost ready to go when we landed in your prison cell. How'd you know someone was coming to get you?"

Ibrahim shifted his weight. "Our father sent word. Yesterday. Said he was... pulling strings. That someone would come. We were told to be ready."

Crafty son of a bitch, I thought. Al-Mansour had played it like a chess master. He had set the wheels in motion before he made his pitch. Knew exactly how the CIA would respond if he dangled the right bait.

Hell of a play. The kind of move only a guy who knew the game better than anyone else could pull.

"You still thought it was happening even after the explosion?"

Ibrahim shook his head. "No. We thought it was over. We assumed the plan had failed. That he was gone. So when you and your partner showed up in our cell—" he shook his head, "—it was a complete shock."

"Did you know it'd be Americans pulling you out?"

Ibrahim hesitated. Glanced back toward the SUV where his brother was waiting. Then back at me.

"No," he said. "We thought it would be... Yemenis. Or someone loyal to our father. Not Americans. Not in our wildest dreams."

Neither in mine, kid. That's the real punchline here.

I didn't say it. Just gave him a nod and motioned with my head. "Go on. Get in."

He shuffled back to the SUV and climbed in. Hassan didn't even look up, face a stone wall. No anger, no joy, no fear. That one was a brick wall—either stone cold or waiting to break.

I didn't trust that guy. I had seen eyes like that before—half-pride, half-poison.

Whole damn thing felt backwards. Us yanking Al Qaeda's golden boys out of prison while their father fed us playbook pages. But that was the op.

No one ever said saving lives meant playing by the rules.

We rolled out in convoy, two vehicles bouncing over hard-packed earth before hitting the road north. I sat shotgun in the lead vehicle, night air filtering through the cracked window. My eyes were on the road, but my head was a war zone of moving pieces.

We weren't even close to being out of the woods. Midnight Scimitar was real. And if even half of what Al-Mansour told us was true, we were about to face a full-blown coordinated hit on everything from barracks to towers to sleeping families.

Too many moving parts. Not enough men. No margin for error.

It was going to take a miracle if we stopped all those attacks. But miracles were above my pay grade.

I would settle for blood, sweat, and broken bad guys.

CHAPTER 18

We pulled into the safehouse compound ten minutes later. We got out and handed the two brothers to a pair of local contractors who whisked them away to a side room—no rough stuff, just gloves on, words minimal. Isolation. No comms, no windows.

I stepped into the ops room where Caroline and Atwood were already waiting. The air inside felt ten degrees colder than outside, and it had nothing to do with the AC unit in the corner.

Caroline looked up. Her face was a mask of control, but I could see the strain behind her eyes. Atwood stood next to her, hands on the table, glaring at the satellite photos like he could beat the attack out of them with pure focus.

"We've got a real problem," Caroline burst out.

"I figured," I said, peeling off my gloves and walking over. "How bad?"

She didn't flinch. "Four primary targets. Each one's a calculated strike—designed to cripple, not just shock."

Atwood tapped the screen, brought up a map of the city with four red markers burning like open wounds.

"Target one—obvious. The U.S. Embassy. It's still operational. Staff's limited, security's thinned out, but it's active. But it's the symbolic bullseye. We've got Marines inside, local Yemeni guards on the outer perimeter. If they get inside...," he left it unfinished.

He swiped to the next photo on the screen. "Target two—'The Quarter'. That's the secure compound where most of the diplomats and their families live. Guarded by a mix of local contract security and some active duty personnel. It's a soft target in comparison. Kids, spouses, unarmed. If they hit it, we'll have a bloodbath."

My jaw clenched. "But why are the families still here? After the deteriorating situation? Civil war right outside the gates?"

Atwood sighed. "About half the families have left. The rest—it's been a case-by-case thing. Ambassador doesn't want to raise alarm bells, not yet. He's trying to keep appearances, play it down."

"Jesus."

"He doesn't want to look weak in front of DC," Atwood added, shaking his head. "No one wants to be the guy who cried wolf and pulled out early."

I looked at the photo again. Guard posts, children's bikes, a basketball hoop behind one of the buildings.

"I've seen this play out before," I said. "Only difference is who gets buried after."

No one argued. Because they knew I was right.

Caroline moved to the next photo. "Target three— the Airfield Control Tower at Sana'a International. Hit that, and we're blind in the sky. No coordination for evac flights, no drone comms, no fixed-wing support."

I leaned over, scanning the overlays. "That's coordinated. Not just terror—it's strategic warfare."

"Exactly," Caroline said, then flipped to the final image. "Target four. The Marine barracks at the temporary Forward Ops Site.

I didn't need the photo. I already knew the layout.

Old Yemeni Army depot. Outskirts of the city. I had been there that morning—before we had started racing across Sana'a, snuffing out threats before they lit up.

The site was a quick-and-dirty fix—thrown together once the intel about terror threats spiked a few days ago. Half a solution to a full-scale problem. It was meant to cover evacuation routes, give the embassy some muscle, and stage quick reaction teams.

Ten Marines. Advance team. Setting up sandbags, wiring comms, keeping eyes on the perimeter. Holding ground like it was Fallujah '04, but with a fraction of the manpower and support.

Caroline laid it out. "As you saw this morning, they've got a decent perimeter, sandbags, concertina wire—but it wasn't built to take sustained attack. If they get hit with enough firepower—"

"They'll punch right through," I finished.

And they would. That depot might hold off a probe, maybe a mortar splash or some wild-eyed pickup truck crew. But not a real op. Not a coordinated, high-casualty assault.

And that's exactly what Al-Qaeda seemed to be lining up.

After the visit earlier that day, I had cornered Atwood and told him to get reinforcements. He hesitated—worried about how it would look... how the Yemeni government would take it. Optics. Politics. The usual D.C. theater.

I didn't care.

Eventually, he got the Ambassador to greenlight it. Extra Marines were in the pipe—ETA sometime after midnight.

The question was whether midnight would be too late.

I leaned forward, staring at the image. "How the hell did AQ even know we'd set that place up? We just opened it this week. It's not on any public maps. No chatter online."

Caroline's jaw tightened. "There's only one way they could've known."

I looked up at her. "Someone inside?"

She gave a sharp nod. "Inside the embassy. Someone who saw the movements. Got word out."

That meant this op was worse than we thought. It wasn't just coming from the outside. It was bleeding from within.

I didn't say anything right away. Just sat there, letting it all settle in.

This wasn't some ragtag jihadist hit squad tossing grenades and screaming for paradise. This was something else—tight, deliberate, surgical. It felt more like a military op than a terrorist spree. Coordinated. Synchronized. And built off solid intel.

I had seen this kind of planning before—but not from Al Qaeda. Not in this region. Not in Sana'a. Hell, half the city was still under government control. The rest was in Houthi hands. AQAP barely had a footprint there. Just whispers and sympathizers.

Now they were about to pull off a four-pronged blitz? All at once?

Where the hell were they getting the manpower? The gear? The intel?

Someone was helping them. And that meant we weren't just dealing with a terror cell. We were up against a goddamn shadow army.

I took a long breath, cracked my neck, and let out a slow breath. "Any timeline on the order of attack?"

Atwood shook his head. "That's the missing piece. Al-Mansour knew the targets and objectives but claims he wasn't told the sequence. The attacks are planned to start at midnight, that's all he knows for certain."

"Which means we don't know where the first punch lands."

"Exactly," Caroline agreed. "And if we guess wrong—"

"We lose people," I said flatly. "Maybe a lot of them."

I looked at the board again, eyes tracing routes, overlapping threat vectors. There was no clean way out of this mess. Every one of those targets could break us wide open. And we didn't have enough time or manpower to cover all four.

"We need sequence," I muttered. "Even a rough timeline. Something."

Caroline said, "I'm already running the raw intel he gave me through backchannels. I've flagged chatter nodes on dark web forums, trying to match phrasing or codenames. Cross-referencing geolocation pings from known AQ relay servers."

Atwood added, "We're feeding it all to Echo too. If anyone can corroborate it with signal intercepts, it's him."

Then something else occurred to me. "You believe him? Al-Mansour. You think he gave us everything?"

Caroline hesitated—not long, but enough to mean she had thought it through.

"Yeah," she said. "I think he's telling the truth. He's not holding back—not anymore. Your little chat with him earlier... That seems to have convinced him that keeping secrets wasn't worth the risk. You got to him."

"Well," I said dryly, "I do have a way with people."

She snorted, then grew serious again. "And he's given us more than just targets. He gave us a backdoor login to an encrypted AQ server. It's a comms relay node—he says most of their tactical chatter passes through it."

That got my attention. "You got anyone digging into it?"

"Yeah. My tech team's trying to mirror the content, scrape whatever's still live. All of it's been passed to Echo too. He's monitoring for signal spikes or redirects. If something moves, we'll see it."

If Al-Mansour gave us a server, it meant he was out of chips. That was good. But something still sat wrong in my gut.

"I talked to one of his sons," I told them. "Ibrahim. He told me Al-Mansour had already tipped them off yesterday—said a rescue was coming."

Caroline folded her arms. "So he'd planned it all."

"Apparently. Played a long game," I said. "Set it up before he even gave you the pitch. Hell, maybe because he gave you the pitch. It worked, didn't it?"

She didn't answer, but she didn't have to. Her eyes said it plain—*he played us.*

"I don't think he's done," I said. "He might still be holding something. And I think I can get it out of him."

Atwood crossed his arms. "You want to go in again?"

I nodded. "If that's alright with you two. I don't want to step on anyone's toes."

He didn't even blink. "Do it. If there's more in his head, let's get it on the table."

"Roger that," I said, getting up. "Better get word to your people inside the Yemeni government. Airport security beefed up—tight perimeter, eyes on the tarmac, checkpoints at every gate. And alert the security teams at all four targets. Especially the Quarter. Just a hunch, but I've got a bad feeling it'll kick off there first."

"Already on it," he confirmed, like he was reading my mind. "Teams are on alert. Working on pulling the schematics for the Quarter now. You think those ten Marines at the Forward Ops Site can hold off a full-on onslaught?"

I exhaled. "Wish I could say yes. They'll fight like hell. But that site isn't built for a siege. They've got a makeshift perimeter—sandbags, razor wire, some fallback points. But no blast walls. No reinforced bunkers. No layered defense. It's not a fortress. It's a speed bump. You throw enough firepower at that place, and it folds."

He nodded grimly.

"But they don't have a choice. Not unless we want to giftwrap the enemy a full weapons buffet. They were prepping it for the incoming platoon—getting the base in shape—and now they're sitting on a small armory. Enough gear to arm a battalion if it falls into the wrong hands. Abandon that site, and we might as well paint a welcome sign in Arabic."

Atwood nodded, slower this time.

"We're not leaving them to rot," I continued. "Thirty more Marines are en route. Birds should be wheels down in a few hours. If we hold the depot till then, it becomes an anchor point. Pull our ten guys now, and we're handing the incoming force a compromised LZ and a ghost base."

Atwood blew out a slow breath. "Alright. You've convinced me."

"Wasn't trying to," I said, walking for the exit. "I was just telling you how it is. Now let's see if I can get Al-Mansour to be a little more helpful."

The time was 2200 hours as I headed for the interrogation room.

As I passed by a window, I could see the lights of Sana'a in the distance. Somewhere out there, men were staging. Cleaning rifles. Loading magazines. Checking timers on vests.

The hits were coming. All four of them. And the worst part was I didn't know the order.

I could feel the tension building behind my ribs, tight and coiled. But panic wouldn't help. Rushing out there without intel would only get us killed—and still leave civilians in the crosshairs.

I had been there before. Too many times. Cities teetering on the edge of war, targets stacking up faster than you could process. You had to slow your pulse, shut out the noise, and think.

This wasn't about heroics. This was about strategy.

CHAPTER 19

I stepped into the interrogation room and shut the door behind me without a sound. Fluorescent light buzzed overhead like a dying insect. Al-Mansour was exactly where I left him a few hours ago, sitting on a steel chair on the other side of a metal table.

He looked up, trying to read my face.

I didn't give him anything. Just pulled out the metal chair across from him, sat down slowly, and let the silence settle like dust in a tomb. I kept my hands clasped, forearms on the table, leaned in slightly, and fixed him with the same cold, unblinking stare I had given him the last time I was in there—when I told him that if he played games, if he held anything back, I would leave his sons right there in that Houthi shithole and walk away without blinking.

He remembered that. I could see it in his eyes.

The silence stretched long. Ten seconds passed. Then twenty.

His expression didn't change, but the weight of that quiet started to press on him. The table between us felt smaller with every passing second. He waited... tried to read me. Couldn't.

Eventually, he broke.

"I've told your people everything," he said. His voice was calm, but there was an edge under it—a defensive twitch he couldn't quite suppress. "Everything I know about Midnight Scimitar."

I kept my eyes on him. Let it hang.

"I even gave them a backdoor login to an AQ comms server," he added. "It's encrypted, but I passed on the decryption sequence I had access to. Your people are trying to mirror the content now."

Still, I said nothing. I wanted to see how much he would keep giving just to fill the silence.

But he clammed up, waiting for my reaction.

Eventually, I gave it to him. Leaned forward a little, voice low. "You sure that's everything?"

He nodded. "Yes. That's everything."

I tilted my head slightly. "You're saying you have no idea about the sequence of these attacks?" I let the disbelief bleed into my voice. "No clue about timing, which target goes first, or how it's meant to unfold?"

He gave a small, sharp laugh. "Come on. If you were planning something of this scale... would you hand over the full blueprint to the unit's payroll officer?"

That almost got me. I felt the corner of my mouth twitch, but I killed the smile before it showed. I didn't want him thinking we were on friendly terms.

But hell, he wasn't wrong. The guys who moved the real pieces didn't talk to accounts. Not unless they had to.

I didn't nod. Didn't agree. Just let it hang, then said, "Maybe not. But you're not just a payroll officer, are you?"

He blinked.

"You've been Al Qaeda's financier for years," I carried on. "You sat at the table with the men who planned these attacks. Even if they didn't spell it out, you were in the orbit. You've seen enough operations to recognize patterns. Don't tell me you can't make an educated guess."

He looked down for a moment, fingers tapping lightly on the table, then back at me. "You're right," he said finally. "This operation—it's beyond anything I've seen. Ambition, scale, coordination. But yes, I can try."

He paused, studying my face. "Before I do, I need to know something."

I waited.

"My sons," he said. "Are they safe?"

I leaned back in the chair. Let the steel creak. Then I gave it to him straight. "That was the deal. You give me everything, I pull them out."

He nodded slowly, waiting.

"And I did," I continued. "CIA thinks you came clean. So I kept my end of the bargain. I dragged your boys out of that Houthi prison and got them here. They're upstairs. They're alive. They're safe—for now."

Al-Mansour's breath caught. Just barely. But I saw it. It was real. His mask slipped for a half second, and under it—just for a flicker—I saw something that looked like actual relief.

"But listen close," I added. "This place?" I motioned to the walls around us. "Might not last the night. Not with what's coming. So if you want them to stay safe, if you want to walk out of this with anything left—then you better dig deep and think, and give me something I can use."

He didn't answer right away. He looked off to the side, like he was watching a memory scroll across the wall.

"There's something," he said slowly. "Something I didn't say before. Not because I wanted to deceive you. Just... it's not intelligence. Not the kind your analysts want. It's just... a feeling."

I didn't interrupt.

"I've been wondering for a few days now," Al-Mansour continued, his voice low and deliberate. "Al Qaeda's never pulled off anything like this before. Not at this scale. Not with this level of synchronization. Someone's helping them."

That hit close. I had been chewing on the same thought minutes before I walked into the room.

The way everything lined up tonight—the targets, the timing, the boldness— it was too clean. Too deliberate. Didn't fit AQ's usual playbook. Hearing him say it just confirmed it wasn't my paranoia talking. It made me lean in. Maybe he wasn't just feeding me half-truths. Maybe he was starting to talk straight.

"I have a feeling," he said, "and it's just a feeling, that Al Qaeda has struck a quiet arrangement with a wing of the Houthis. Not an alliance—more like a handshake deal. A tactical understanding."

I narrowed my eyes. "You're saying AQ and the Houthis are working together?"

"Not all of them," he said quickly, shaking his head. "The Houthis are fractured. Tribal. Regional. But some factions are angry enough, hungry enough, and willing to cut a deal if it means hurting the enemy. Right now, America is the enemy they both need."

And he wasn't wrong. It sounded insane—AQ and Houthi fighters on the same side. But I had seen stranger bedfellows. In Kandahar. In Raqqa. In Syria. Groups that hated each other teaming up just long enough to bury a common threat. America had a way of making enemies find common ground. And my gut had been whispering the same thing since the first target popped up on the board. Whether I liked it or not, the man was making sense.

I caught a shift in his expression. The tight lines around his mouth relaxed just a notch. Like earning a shred of trust from me had taken a weight off his chest.

"You should understand," he added, "coming to you—coming to the Americans—wasn't my first move."

I gave a slow nod. Of course it wasn't. But the fact that he was telling me meant he was loosening up. That was good. Useful. Still, I reminded myself—he wasn't talking because he liked me. He was talking because I made it clear I would hold my end, but wouldn't flinch.

But I knew letting him ramble too much now would be a mistake. If I got too comfortable, I would lose control of the tempo. Still, if a man's willing to open up, you don't slam the door. Sometimes the best intel came when you let a man talk long enough to forget he was being interrogated. I let him talk, but I stayed ice-cold behind the eyes. It was all about control.

"When the Houthis took the prison," he said, "I asked AQAP leadership to intervene. Told them to use their contacts. Pull strings. Pay bribes. Do something. They just smiled and said to be patient. 'God will protect them,' they said." Al-Mansour scoffed. "I knew then—my sons would die in Houthi custody."

I didn't say anything. He didn't need sympathy. What he needed was someone who understood the stakes. And he could see it in my face.

“When I realized they wouldn’t lift a finger, that’s when I started planning this. Every piece. Every move.”

“Because you knew tonight would be the breaking point?” I asked.

Al-Mansour nodded. “If these attacks succeed, America will respond. Full force. It will be overwhelming. You’ll flood Sana’a with fire and steel. Every fighter—AQ, sympathizers, Houthi militias—will be wiped out. There won’t be anything left to protect. My sons, my name, my blood—it’ll all be ash. That’s why I had to stop this. Why I came to you.”

He leaned in slightly. “This was my only way out. My only chance to save my family. I took it. And I understand that it’s in my interest that the attacks fail.”

I leaned forward. “Then tell me more. What else can you give me about the sequence of attacks?”

Al-Mansour didn’t hesitate. “If I was planning it, I’d start with the easiest target. The Quarter. Where the diplomats’ families live. It’s exposed, lightly guarded, and high-value. Hit that first, take hostages, and claim victory before anyone knows what hit them.”

He was reading straight out of my own mental playbook. I had clocked The Quarter as the softest target—one good-sized assault force, and they could steamroll the contractors and private guards on duty. Chaos, panic, blood. Civilians taken alive. Maybe even used as shields. Human bargaining chips. Or worse—executed on livestream.

Once that was done, the next logical step would be the airport—cut the escape routes, ground any American airlift response. With that in their pocket, they could hammer the Marine site and the embassy till they cracked. Wear us out before reinforcements could get boots on the ground.

Al-Mansour mirrored my thoughts like he was reading them off a map. “Next, they’ll go for the airport,” he said. “Without it, your forces won’t be able to move. Without air control, you’re boxed in. Then they can siege the other two sites at their pace. No rush. No need to risk losses. They’ll have the momentum.”

He was laying it out like a military strategist. And I hated how much sense it made.

I gave him a hard look. A nod. “It makes sense. Tactically, you’d be an idiot not to follow that sequence.”

He gave a slow, almost imperceptible smile. Like he knew I finally understood the stakes on his level.

But there was something else in his eyes. Not relief. Not arrogance. Something deeper—buried, but twitching to surface.

CHAPTER 20

"What is it?" I asked. "What else is on your mind?"

Al-Mansour shifted in his seat, leaned forward, and looked me dead in the eye. "What's your impression of my sons?"

My first instinct was to shut that line down cold.

If we were passing around feelings, I had none. Neither did I have time for fatherly concerns about two wannabe jihadis. Didn't give a damn if they cried for their mama at night or whispered martyrdom verses in their sleep. They were assets—temporary ones. The only reason they were still breathing, and not zip-tied and dumped in a black site, was because their old man had information I needed to stop a massacre. Simple math. Save lives through their old man's information. That was the deal. Nothing more.

But I paused.

Because Al-Mansour wasn't the type to waste breath. There was a rhythm to his words—like everything he had said tonight had been a step toward something. He had been feeling me out the whole time, laying track with each sentence. This wasn't small talk—it was part of the structure. I could feel it in his posture, the way he had narrowed in. He was building toward something.

So I met him halfway.

"Ibrahim?" I said. "Doesn't strike me as someone who's going to die for the cause. Hell, I half expected to see a library stamp on his wrist.

That kid's built more for debating ideologies than planting bombs."

Al-Mansour let out a soft huff through his nose. Almost a laugh. A flash of something like fondness crossed his face, maybe regret.

"He was always quiet. Thoughtful. He likes books. Ideas."

"Yeah, well," I muttered, "he didn't exactly light the room on fire. More like... introverted scholar trying to impress the wrong crowd."

"And Hassan?" he asked, voice quieter now.

I didn't sugarcoat it. "That one? He should've stayed locked up. Looks like he's two steps from blowing himself up for a Facebook post. Hatred's baked into his bones. Called you a traitor without blinking. If Al Qaeda's looking for the next poster boy, they won't have to look far."

Al-Mansour didn't flinch, didn't try to defend him. Just nodded slowly, like he had already had the same conversation in his head a dozen times. He stared off for a beat, something hollow moving behind his eyes.

"I know," he said, voice distant. "He's not far from the edge. So close to the dark side it's a whisper away. But I believe God will speak to him. The way He spoke to me."

He went silent for a second, then leaned in slightly, voice tightening. "But I didn't bring them up just to talk."

There it was. The gear shift. He was done reflecting—now he was getting to the point. I stayed quiet, listening.

"I don't know the specifics of Midnight Scimitar. Not the whole playbook. But Hassan... he's been in that prison for two months. Surrounded by Al

Qaeda fighters. You know how it works—they talk. Plans circulate. Messages travel faster behind bars than they do in the open. The grapevine in a cell block like that? It's deeper than any radio chatter."

I didn't argue. Made perfect sense. Prison walls leaked secrets like cracked barrels. And fighters loved to run their mouths when they thought no one was listening.

"But if I ask him directly," Al-Mansour said, "he won't tell me. He'd rather bite his own tongue than tell me what he knows. Same with you. He'd rather die than cooperate with an American, no matter how... persuasive you get."

He wasn't wrong there either.

"But I know my son," he said. "I know how to provoke him. And if I speak to him—face to face—I can push the right buttons. I know what'll needle him enough to let something slip. I know how to get under his skin. He won't even realize he's doing it. He'll reveal more just trying to spite me than he would under threat of death."

I studied him, searching his face. Trying to see if this was just another long con. He had already played the room like a fiddle to get his sons out—what was one more trick?

He caught the look.

"I understand your hesitation," he said. "You're wondering if this is another ploy. But I've got no cards left to play. A meeting like this gains me nothing—except the hope of stopping something I never wanted to happen in the first place. And maybe saving a part of my family."

He looked tired now. Honest. Not in a performative way—just the kind of tired that sits in your bones after too many years of blood and loss.

He held my gaze, calm and steady.

"Ibrahim... and Hassan. Pulling him back from the edge. That's all that matters to me now. And I know—without a doubt—that none of that happens if Midnight Scimitar goes ahead."

He gave a humorless smile. "So here we are. You and I. On the same side, at least for tonight. Call it a... strategic alliance. Like Al Qaeda and the Houthis, only for a better purpose."

I let that sit for a second. He wasn't wrong. And despite everything in me that wanted to dismiss it, I couldn't.

He looked at me straight again. "Time's running out. If I can do something—anything—to help stop this, I will. Even if it means deceiving my own son."

That was it. The line. No performance. No pitch. Just the hard edge of truth.

I gave him a slow nod. "Alright. I'll arrange the meeting."

I stood up, turned and stepped out of the interrogation room, jaw tight from playing diplomat with a man who funded car bombings and called it faith.

Caroline and Atwood were waiting just outside. From the look on their faces, I knew they had heard every word. Probably didn't enjoy the part about Al-Qaeda and the Houthis swapping phone numbers.

Caroline met my eyes. "You handled him well," she said, voice steady but tight. "He's really going out of his way to cooperate."

"Yeah," I said. "Let's see if he can get that little shitbag of a son to spill something useful."

I didn't even need to finish the thought.

Atwood beat me to it. "Getting them in the same room sounds like a great idea."

"Damn right it does," I said. "Let's see if the family reunion rattles loose something useful before midnight rolls around and people start dying."

Two security guys collected Al-Mansour from the holding cell and walked him to the adjoining room where his sons were being held. The door opened with a buzz, and as soon as Al-Mansour stepped inside, Ibrahim rushed forward and threw his arms around his father like it was some kind of homecoming special.

Hassan didn't budge. He sat stiffly on the metal bench, jaw set, eyes full of judgment.

They started talking fast in Arabic. Too fast for me. But not for Caroline—she had the headset on and was translating on the fly while I stood next to her, arms folded, watching every twitch through the one-way mirror.

"Al-Mansour's telling them they're aligned with the Americans now. Says AQ left them to die and sold them out. He's putting pressure on Hassan. Trying to shake him."

"Good," I muttered, watching the body language through the one-way glass. "Rattle his cage."

I didn't need a translator to read the tension in the boy's clenched fists.

Caroline kept going. "Hassan's pushing back. Calls his father a traitor. Says Al Qaeda walks the righteous path. He says justice will be delivered tonight."

I glanced at the wall clock. 2230 hours.

Then Al-Mansour dropped the line he came in to deliver.

"Now Al-Mansour says he hopes the attacks fail," Caroline translated. "He's baiting him."

Worked like a charm.

Hassan leaned forward, smile spreading like oil across water, eyes lighting up with that glassy fanatic glow. "He says it's too late. That the fighters are already moving into position. That when the quarter moon rises—" Caroline glanced at the wall clock, "—at midnight, they'll kill the first hostages and announce it to the world."

That was it. Confirmation.

I didn't breathe, just watched. Hassan was on a roll now.

Caroline translated as he went on. "He's saying Midnight Scimitar can't be stopped. That no one will even realize when it begins. The Quarter's just the start. Says once they take the families, the rest of the targets will fold. They'll use them as human shields. Psychological leverage."

He was frenzied now—spewing holy war rhetoric, half-smiling like he already heard the gunshots in his head.

Then something shifted. Without warning, Hassan's expression changed. He caught his reflection in the mirror, and suspicion crept into his face. Eyes narrowed, like he suddenly realized the air had ears. Jaw locked. He clammed up like a switch flipped—one second preaching fire and brimstone, the next looking like he just remembered mirrors worked both ways.

CHAPTER 21

Caroline peeled off the headset. "He's done talking."

"Doesn't matter," I replied, already moving. "That's all I needed. We don't have a second to waste. They're already in motion."

I grabbed my tablet. "Caroline, shoot me the schematics for the Quarter on my tablet. Every house door, every blind spot, every fire exit. I want that place in my head before I hit the gate. And patch me through to security there."

She nodded, already working her touchscreen.

I turned to Atwood. "Better start planting the seed in the Ambassador's ear that a full embassy evac might not be a matter of 'if' anymore. Because if AQ and the Houthis are playing house, we're looking at a full collapse. We can't have Americans stuck here when that lid blows."

Atwood stiffened a little. "He's not going to love that. Worried about the optics... and pissing off the Yemeni government."

I gave him a deadpan look. "Yeah? When this city goes belly-up, the regime won't exist long enough to get upset. That government's gonna disappear faster than a bottle of Jack at a Delta barracks. If we're still here when the curtain drops, we'll be left standing around like a bunch of assholes wondering where the last helo went."

He didn't argue further.

I pushed back from the table and got up. It was time to move.

I had made it three steps toward the door when Atwood called out, “Blaze—wait. One more thing.”

I paused, turned.

“I got word to the Marines at the Forward Ops Site. Told them the situation’s heating up, and if things go sideways, they’ll need to hold the line until reinforcements arrive.”

“How’d they take it?”

Atwood gave a faint chuckle. “They sounded surprised I thought I had to tell them. Said they wouldn’t have it any other way. And there’s no damn way they’re letting terrorists lay hands on their gear.”

I smiled. That’s exactly what I expected them to say. No bitching, no hesitation—just steel.

“Whoever you talked to,” I said, “replied like a true Marine.”

Atwood nodded. “Staff Sergeant Logan Davis. He’s leading the unit there.”

Name didn’t ring a bell. “Don’t know him, but sounds like a fine Marine.”

“Well, he sure as hell knows you,” Atwood said. “When I told him Delta’s running an op to disrupt enemy movements and mentioned you by name—he lit up. Said if you had a minute, he’d appreciate a call.”

I nodded. “I’ll give him one.”

I stepped into the hall. Called Raptor on the satphone. “Tell the boys to saddle up. We’re rolling in ten.”

Next, I called the Marine. The line clicked after two rings.

“Staff Sergeant Logan Davis, FOS.”

“This is Captain Axel Blaze. Just touching base. Heard you wanted a word.”

A pause. Then his tone shifted—crisp, but respectful.

"Yes, sir. Appreciate the call. Heard you were running lead on containment. We're damn glad to have you."

"You and your Marines ready for a wild night?"

He gave a low, confident laugh. "Sir, we're Marines. We don't know how to do anything else. Ten of us here, fully loaded and dug in. No one's laying hands on our gear without bleeding for it. They come for our post, they better bring body bags."

"That's what I expected to hear. But tonight's gonna get loud. We've got reports of coordinated action. AQ and the Houthis, hitting multiple targets. They're aiming to overrun key positions across the city. Your post is a juicy one—ammo, comms, fuel. You're likely a high-priority objective."

"Copy that," Logan replied. "We've started hardening our perimeter. Got concertina out in two layers on the east and south. West has that busted wall, but we stacked up HESCOs and parked the MRAP in to plug the gap. Trying to cover our six."

"You got any elevated sightlines?"

"Only the ops shack roof. Got a private up there with an M110 and night glass. He's locked in."

"Good. Keep eyes up. You got Claymores?"

"You bet. Already spaced them around the chokepoints. Sandbag cover where we can, trying not to get silhouetted at nightfall."

"Sounds like you're dug in tight."

"We're not planning to let 'em breathe if they come near us."

"Copy that. My team's moving to hit the Quarter now. Once we mop up threats there, we'll try to draw heat off you with a flanking hit. If we split their force, you might catch a breather. All depends on how the opening salvos kick off around midnight. Stay sharp, and keep me posted."

"Copy that, sir. We'll hold."

"Call sign's Cowboy. Use that in all comms."

"Copy that, Cowboy."

"Any word about your reinforcements?" I asked.

"Thirty Marines wheels up at 0030 hours, ETA 0230 hours."

"That gives you two hours of hell before the cavalry shows up."

"That's two hours of free target practice."

I chuckled. "I like your style. By the way—how'd you know me?"

He paused, amused. "That's the interesting part, sir. The CO leading our reinforcement element... it's someone you might be familiar with."

I narrowed my eyes. "Hit me."

"Captain Ryan Blaze. My company commander. Told me once about his kid brother in Delta. When I heard your name, I put two and two together."

I blinked. Then laughed—couldn't help it. "Well I'll be damned."

"Yeah, figured you didn't know. Small world, huh? Captain Blaze talks straight, fights hard. You'd like him."

"I do. Been doing that since we were kids. I didn't even know he was going to be in-country."

"He didn't mention it either," Logan replied. "But when I heard your name, I figured I'd end up fighting alongside the Captain's brother. Gotta say—it's an honor, sir."

“Likewise, Staff Sergeant. You hold the line. We’ll raise hell on our end.”

“We will. Semper Fi, Cowboy.”

I ended the call, shaking my head. What were the odds? Two Blaze boys from Colorado converging on a hellhole like this. For a second, I just stood there, thinking about Ryan.

Then I turned and walked down the hall. No time to dwell. We had a Quarter to defend.

A few minutes later, we were done loading gear into two vehicles. The lead vehicle was a beat-up Land Cruiser that looked like it had survived three wars, hiding the fact that it was armored under the dusty exterior. The other was a blacked-out Ford Everest with a smooth ride and enough toys in the back to start our own insurgency.

Me, Ninja, Raptor, Hawkeye, Ali, and Youssef.

Loaded. Wired. Dead silent.

We rolled out. Full tactical kit.

Clock read 2250 hours.

Time to hunt.

CHAPTER 22

Ali took the wheel of the lead Land Cruiser. I rode shotgun, boots braced, rifle across my thighs, window cracked just enough to catch the scent of tension on the wind. Ninja and Raptor were stacked in the back, suited up and ready to roll. Behind us, Youssef handled the tail vehicle. Hawkeye rode passenger, long rifle case tucked by his feet, always ready to reach out and touch someone from distance.

The convoy rolled out with low lights and no chatter. The city outside had gone dark, not because of curfew—those had long stopped mattering—but because Sana'a knew something bad was coming. You could feel it.

The streetlights flickered like dying cigarettes. Smoke hung in the alleys. City smelled like burned wires and diesel—like it was coughing up its last breath. The kind of air that stuck to your teeth. The hum of power generators buzzed low like angry hornets in basements and rooftops.

The streets were tense. Not just empty—coiled. The kind of empty where you knew people were watching, waiting, guns ready just behind those drawn curtains and iron gates.

Every alley we passed had movement in it—shadows flitting back and forth, silhouettes slipping through doorways, rifles slung low, cigarettes glowing like sniper scopes in the dark. Some just stood there, bold as hell, Kalashnikovs over their shoulders, daring us to blink. No uniforms. No insignia. Just the loose swagger of men who had nothing to lose and were itching to shed blood.

Half the time I didn't know if they were militia, thieves, or just desperate men trying to guess who would be in charge tomorrow morning. And sometimes, you didn't have to guess—they made themselves known.

One guy stood dead center in a narrow intersection as we passed, legs apart, arms folded over a Heckler & Koch G3 slung across his chest. Yemeni irregular, maybe Houthi, maybe local muscle hired for the night. Not AQ—those assholes never posed. They hid and detonated.

He didn't move, just stared at us, like he knew what was coming.

Ninja leaned forward between the seats. "That guy's either high or ready to die."

"Probably both," I muttered, eyes on the side mirror. He didn't follow. Just kept standing there.

Off to the east, a burst of distant gunfire crackled across the rooftops—maybe a mile off, maybe more. Not a firefight. Not yet. Maybe just a warning shot from some checkpoint that didn't like who rolled up on them. Or an execution. A power shift being marked by muzzle flashes. I heard a vehicle rev high and fast in the distance, then cut off like it slammed into a wall. Probably did.

Raptor muttered from the back, "City's breathing heavy."

Ali agreed. "Yes, like it's been holding its breath all day and tonight it exhales fire."

They weren't wrong. Sana'a was sweating through its shirt. The kind of quiet that came before a thunderclap.

We passed through districts that looked like they hadn't seen plumbing or paint in decades—concrete skeletons stacked three stories high, sandbags in windows, kids with dirty faces and hard eyes watching from doorways. We rolled by remnants of checkpoints—burned-out tires still smoldering.

Then the landscape started shifting. Bit by bit. Less war-torn, more walled and guarded. Private compounds. Hedges started showing up. The walls got cleaner, straighter. Steel gates. Private generators humming like the heartbeat of privilege. Sprinklers running even though water was scarce.

The Quarter was less than ten minutes away.

It was set back from the main road, sitting on a slight rise overlooking the sprawl of the city—about thirty meters of elevation above the surrounding district. From a distance, in the dark, it looked like a fortress. A high-walled compound, topped with three strands of concertina wire that shimmered in the moonlight like silver barbed snakes. Angled lighting on the perimeter, discreet and directional.

One entry gate, guarded, with retractable bollards and blast-rated steel. The sign next to it just read: QUARTER RESIDENCE COMPOUND in three languages—English, Arabic, and French. Behind it, a reinforced guardhouse, tinted glass, and a double team in ballistic helmets.

Caroline had sent me the blueprints by the time we rolled out—files with site plans and interior layouts. I knew the specs by heart.

Inside the compound, the streets were narrow but paved, laid out in a U-shape around a central green. Hedges and low garden walls flanked the roads. You could almost pretend it was suburban America—if you ignored the sandbags, the security cameras, and the two guards with M4s posted behind the reinforced glass at the gatehouse.

Six two-story villas stood like fortresses wrapped in stucco and satellite dishes. Each within its own walled compound, palm trees and hedges screening the yards. Rooftop decks.

Off to the north side, one smaller building, three floors, held the temporary staff—apartment-style units for rotating aid workers, minor officials, or contractors waiting for reassignment. Six units—two on each floor. All the windows had reinforced shutters. One unit, 3B, was the designated residence for the embedded security team.

A narrow central green broke up the monotony—patchy grass, a few benches, and a swing set. At this hour, it was abandoned. No kids. No dogs. No sound but the hum of backup generators.

Near the green stood a repurposed operations shed, once a utility building or pool house. Caroline said it had been converted into a safe room—reinforced doors, backup power, hardline radio, basic sat uplink, and a panic switch that would ping the embassy—if it was still staffed by someone breathing.

What the blueprints also showed—but even most residents didn't know—was a secondary egress on the southwest wall. A small steel door leading into an alley behind a shuttered bakery. Permanently locked, camouflaged behind trash bins. It was meant for fire escape or last-ditch evacuation, if the main gate fell. I made a mental note: that door might just save lives.

The Quarter had eight or nine armed personnel on-site. Five or six static guards and perimeter walkers, all contracted through Sentinel Dynamics—an American private military company. Light loadouts. M4s, Glocks, radios. No drone feeds, no long-range comms. These guys were here to show a presence, not fight off an invasion.

The real muscle were the three ex-military embeds who lived on-site—quiet shadows posing as "consultants" or "relocation advisors". All three had Tier-2 or better backgrounds. Caroline trusted them. That meant something.

My point man for that night was one of them—a retired Army Ranger named Mark Ridley. Ex-2nd Battalion, 75th. Served in Iraq and Somalia. Word was he had done a stint training Kurdish Pesh in 2010 before falling off the grid and resurfacing as a private contractor.

The other two were: Abe Maddix, former Force Recon Marine, heavy on CQB and vehicle tactics, and Nick Calhoun, British Army—ex-Pathfinder Platoon, soft-spoken but surgical with a rifle.

All three lived in Unit 3B of the apartment block, two floors up, eyes on the courtyard, rotating shifts. Every family in the Quarter had one of them on speed dial.

I had called Ridley soon as we rolled out from the safehouse.

"Ridley, this is Cowboy. We're en route from the safehouse. ETA twenty mikes. How's the Quarter holding?"

Ridley's voice came through low and tense, with that clipped Ranger edge. "Copy that, Cowboy. Quarter's stable for now. Patrols doubled, rooftop overwatch in place. But the streets are off. No noise, no locals. Like someone hit pause on the whole city."

"They didn't hit pause. They're holding their breath. Threat level's high. Imminent. They're coming," I cautioned.

A pause. I could almost hear him glance at his watch.

"Understood. Are we looking at evac?"

"Could be our only real option. But do not move before we arrive. You take those families out without escort, you're walking into the unknown—crossfire, roadblocks, or worse. Stay put. Lock it down. Defensive positions. Head on a swivel."

"Copy that. Holding here. I've already got fallback prep going with Maddix and Calhoun."

"How many heads do you have inside the Quarter right now?"

There was a pause, paper rustling on his end.

"Three of the six villas are occupied. Only two have families—small kids, both under ten. The other villa's resident sent his family out last week—smart man. The other two families were planning to fly out tomorrow morning."

Tomorrow? I looked out at the streets, smelled the war in the wind.

Might be too damn late by then.

"And the apartment block?" I asked.

"Six units total. One's ours—3B. Only four for residential. All four are occupied: one married couple, two single women, one single guy."

"Everyone accounted for?"

Another pause. I could feel the hesitation before the bad news dropped.

"Negative. Single guy and one of the women—out together. Word is they're on a date."

I closed my eyes and sighed. "You're kidding me. They've been breathing the same air we have all day and can't smell what's cooking?"

Ridley's tone matched mine—exasperated, hard. "I've been asking myself if basic survival instincts are filtered out in Foggy Bottom HR. I called them as soon as the alert went up. They said they're heading back and I told them to keep low, keep quiet, and call me the second they're close so we can cover their approach."

I grunted. "Good. Keep hounding those lovebirds until some sense knocks through their romance-muddled heads."

"Copy that. I'll be in their ear until they're home or... let's not go there yet."

"Roger that. See you in twenty."

Ninja leaned forward as soon as I got off the call. "Trouble?"

"Two lovebirds from the Quarter out on the town," I muttered. "Decided tonight's a good time for romance."

Ninja smirked. "Guess nothing says 'hot date' like a collapsing city and incoming jihadis."

"Yeah. Let's make sure they get to tell their kids about the worst night of their love life."

Ali snorted. "In Yemen, even love has bad timing."

I looked out the windshield. A slow wind stirred the garbage lining the curbs, as if the city was quietly whispering secrets in Arabic no one wanted to translate. The night didn't feel random—it felt designed. Prepped.

The two lovebirds, whatever their names were, might have thought they were just grabbing some late-night kebab, chasing some sweet romance.

What they didn't get was that when you slipped the leash out here, you weren't just risking your own neck—you were pulling the pin on everyone else's grenade.

It was always the same. They wandered off script, we cleaned up the mess. That was the thing about operators—no matter who screwed up, we were the cleanup crew. And when things went sideways, it was always the operators who caught the shrapnel.

CHAPTER 23

I keyed my comms. "Echo, Cowboy. You got eyes on the Quarter?"

"Affirmative," Echo crackled back. "Thermals on rooftops show static heat—no movement. Nothing active. Perimeter's still quiet."

"Keep me posted. Anything changes, I want to know before the wind shifts."

"Roger."

We took a hard left onto an older street lined with crumbling stone facades and rusted roll-down shutters. The echoes of the Hilux's tires bounced off concrete like ghosts. We passed a shuttered corner kiosk where two men sat in the gloom sipping tea, rifles cradled across their laps. They stared at us. Expressionless faces.

About three blocks from the Quarter, Ali suddenly eased off the gas.

"Obstacle ahead," he said.

My eyes locked onto a makeshift barrier down the street—a low stack of tires, two broken plastic barricades, and a couple of rusted flatbeds parked nose-to-nose across the lane, angled just enough to force vehicles to squeeze through the center, slow and exposed. Their sides were painted with scrawled Arabic slogans and bullet holes, the kind left behind by warning shots—or executions.

Two men in faded police uniforms waved us down. No body armor. No badges. Just AKs slung low and too much attitude. Behind them were two more men—civilians with *keffiyehs* tied loose around their necks and cheap combat gloves. One held a shotgun with a sawed-off barrel, the other had a Czech VZ-58—no standard issue gear for any legit force.

I keyed the radio. "Youssef, Hawkeye. Maintain 50 meters behind us and hold. Watch for movement on your flanks and above. Any shadow twitches, call it out."

"Copy, Cowboy. I've got the rooftop scopes turning," came Hawkeye's measured response.

"Ali," I said quietly, "once you stop, keep her in reverse gear. Be ready."

"Always," he replied.

As we rolled to a halt, I clocked the uniforms—no sidearms, no patches, mismatched belts, and both men wearing beat-up sneakers instead of boots.

"Fake cops," I observed.

"Agreed," Ali replied, never taking his eyes off the one approaching his window.

The cop on the left came toward the driver's side. The other moved to my side, loose and cocky like he thought he had the high cards. He looked young. Maybe twenty. Maybe less. Dirt on his face, ragged beard. His hand rested lightly on the AK's grip.

I caught a faint glint of metal behind a pile of stacked bricks—one more rifle barrel poking out. Probably didn't even know how to zero the thing.

The cop by my window leaned in, tapping the glass with his knuckles.

"You... American?" he asked, with a half-smile and a glint in his eye that said he was more curious than afraid. Or maybe just high on qat.

"Doesn't matter what I am," I said flatly, scanning his hands, his posture, his too-casual smirk, making no attempt to slide down the window.

He was playing for time.

Ninja spoke low from the back. "Movement, two o'clock—rooftop, building with the rebar skeleton."

I didn't even shift my eyes. "Talk to me, Hawkeye."

Hawkeye chimed in on comms. "Cowboy, I've got two rooftop shooters. One northeast, second northwest. First guy's fully visible. Second's crouched, partial cover. I'm lased on the first."

"Copy," I said. "Ninja?"

"I've got a bead on the north-west guy," Ninja said. "Between AC units, crouching low. He's peeking with a Dragunov. Probably thinks he's subtle."

"Hold. Do not fire unless they line up." I asked Raptor. "You ready?"

He flexed his gloved hands and nodded. "Always."

The fake cop leaned in a little closer, tapping the window more insistently.

Meanwhile the cop at Ali's window started shouting. I didn't catch the Arabic, but I heard the tone—escalation. His voice rose like he was baiting Ali into some kind of panic.

I leaned into the radio. "Stay low. Keep weapons low-profile but hot. This smells like a hornets' nest."

Out the corner of my eye, I caught movement in the periphery. Five, maybe six figures creeping out from alleys and behind parked scooters. No uniforms, just rifles, patchy vests, and the kind of dead-eyed focus that came before drawing blood.

And then, in the sideview mirror—I saw it.

A sedan crept out of a side street behind us. Headlights off. Intent obvious.

Trap sprung.

"Trap," I snapped as I pushed the button to slide my window down. "Ali, reverse. Now. Ninja, clear threats on your side."

I grabbed a fistful of the fake cop's uniform through the open window and yanked him halfway through the open window, his legs flailing like a caught chicken. He hit the dash face-first with a grunt.

At the same time, Raptor's arm shot out of the rear window and snagged the other cop hard, pinning him between the Hilux's frame and his forearm like a vice. His AK dropped and clattered under the tire.

"Move!" I barked.

Ali floored it in reverse, tires chirping against broken asphalt, as the truck jolted backward. The two "cops" were now human shields—one shrieking half inside the cab, the other pancaked against the door by Raptor's iron grip.

The other gunmen were too stunned to react for a few seconds. Then they let out some wild shots, more out of frustration than anything else. None of the shots came close to hitting our vehicle, because they couldn't really aim that way with their boys plastered against the truck.

Then the dark sedan behind us lit up with muzzle flashes.

Ninja leaned out the rear window, braced his HK416, and stitched the front of the car with a three-round burst. The driver's window exploded, and the car swerved into a wall, dead weight. Passenger tried to bail and caught a round in the throat before he got his door open.

Hawkeye's voice rang clear on comms. "One rooftop down. Tango's out cold."

Ninja followed up. "Second guy's out of the picture. He ducked and lost angle."

Ali yanked the wheel and executed a reverse J-turn—tires screeched, and we pivoted 180 in a tight arc, dust cloud kicking up behind us. Textbook move. Call it what it is: a Bootlegger's Turn, the kind they don't teach in driver's ed.

Youssef mirrored the maneuver like a pro, tailing us as we roared back down the street we had come from.

"Youssef, follow us on the new route—go south two blocks, then cut east," I called. "Reroute toward the Quarter."

"Copy. Moving."

Behind us, the scene dissolved into chaos—shouts in Arabic, gunfire spraying uselessly into the air, and the fake cops screaming as we let go and they tumbled into the dust.

Ali gunned it as we tore down a side street, engine growling, the wind carrying the acrid scent of gunpowder and trash fires. Youssef trailed behind us in the second SUV, shadowing our every move like a seasoned wheelman.

We hit an open stretch just as my earpiece crackled.

"Cowboy, this is Echo. Be advised. I just saw movement near the Quarter. Not sure what to make of it yet."

I leaned forward, eyes scanning rooftops and balconies. "Go ahead."

"One car was moving down the straight road leading to the Quarter's entry gate. I can't make out the make—too dark, drone feed's too grainy. Looks like a mid-size sedan silhouette. But about five hundred yards from the gate, it got boxed in by two other vehicles. One came out a side alley to the left, the other from the right. They formed a T-block in front of it."

"Blockade?"

"Yeah. Fast and deliberate. Then... a bunch of foot mobiles spilled out of the buildings on either side. Multiple heat signatures. Could be a dozen. No visible weapons from this height, but formation's too clean for civilians."

I sat back in my seat, eyes narrowing. "The vehicle—stopped?"

"Yeah. Just sitting there. Nobody's getting out. Whole thing's frozen in place."

The knot in my gut twisted harder. I didn't say anything for a beat, just let Echo's feed play in my head. A car headed for the Quarter. Two vehicles suddenly appear and pin it. Armed men magically materialize from nearby buildings. Fast, coordinated.

Too fast.

The gears turned. It felt like déjà vu. We had just been through a version of that—same sudden roadblock, same armed mannequins popping out of the shadows like a street magic trick. Only difference was, that time, we had the wheel and the trigger.

I hadn't been sure earlier, but now it was screaming at me.

That roadblock we hit earlier... something about it had bugged me. The way it came together too fast. Not a checkpoint that had been sitting all day—more like someone had watched us coming, made a snap decision, and snapped the trap shut. Built on the fly, thrown up by locals who had seen us—reacted to us. Like they had instructions: white faces, gear bags, new cars—stop them, hold them, call for backup.

Which meant they had spotters. People watching intersections, watching buildings. The whole goddamn city was laced with AQ watchers—loyalists playing shopkeeper by day, warfighters by night. All of this... the roadblocks, the tailing cars, the sudden bursts of action—could be the opening act for something bigger.

Like Midnight Scimitar. Where invading the Quarter was the first episode.

CHAPTER 24

"Echo, keep eyes on that car. You see anything—windows down, doors open, anyone step out, you sing out immediately."

"Roger that—wait."

His tone shifted.

"We've got movement. Car's moving again. Slowly. But it's a convoy now. The two flanking vehicles pulled back just a hair. They're not surrounding anymore. Now they're trailing. Maintaining distance, like an escort."

"Could the car have made a break for it?"

"Doubt it. They're in formation, not trying to bolt. Now another vehicle just joined. Came from the north. Looks like a van, longer body, high roof. Can't see inside. Convoy's now at four vehicles total. The car is still in the lead. They're all headed straight to the Quarter's gate."

My jaw tightened.

Echo soon had another update. "Lead vehicle just stopped at the gate. The other three have pulled back slightly—like they're giving it space to approach. Maybe trying to remain invisible to the guards at the gate. Holding pattern."

I felt the hairs on my neck stand up. The lead car was the bait. AQ was using the two lovebirds as props to get the guards to open the gates and let them in.

I had seen this game before—and it always ended with an explosion or a bloodbath.

"Echo, stay on them. Don't blink."

"Copy."

I switched channels and called Ridley.

"Cowboy, just got a call from the gate. The two lovebirds are back. Claimed they were out for dinner. Said they're at the entrance now."

"That's not them," I yelled into the mic. "Don't let those vehicles in. I repeat, do not let them in. It's a setup. They're AQ. Lock that gate and arm up."

"Shit—Maddix! Calhoun! Get down there now! Lock it down—don't let anything in!"

I could hear him running as the line stayed hot.

"Step it up," I told Ali. "AQ's breaching the Quarter as we speak. Guys—lock and load. It's showdown time."

Less than a mile of straight road remained between us and the Quarter. As we crossed that halfway point, two pickups darted from a side alley and began falling into a blocking formation across the road.

The first was a plain Toyota Hilux with a few shooters in back—amateurs who hadn't gotten their heads down in time. The second was a different story. There was a heavy .50-cal mounted in its rear, a silhouette wrestling with the handles, trying to bring it to bear on us as the driver swerved to get the truck into position.

We weren't about to let anything get in our way. "Ali—ram the closest one. Take it on a diagonal. Push it up and over. Hawkeye—second truck's yours. .50 first. Take the gunner... then the driver, then whatever climbs up afterwards."

"Roger, Cowboy." Hawkeye's voice was icy calm.

The world seemed to slow just a bit—as it always did when shit got real. I felt the powerful diesel tremble under me as Ali pressed the accelerator. His knuckles were white on the wheel, the rear wheels hopped briefly over a pothole, and then we struck the first Toyota with a sickening crunch. Our bumper went in just forward of their rear quarter, a perfect pitting angle.

The momentum flipped their back end up and over. The Hilux tumbled side-on across the road, spinning in a cascade of sparks and tearing metal. Guys in the back flew into the air, a couple bouncing off the hood and into the ditch. The rest were stranded in the wreckage, taken out immediately by Ninja and Raptor.

At the same moment, Hawkeye pressed the trigger on his suppressed M110 sniper rifle from the follow-up vehicle. The 7.62x51 NATO round flew at over twice the speed of sound toward the rear of the pickup—a small shockwave visible in the air just above its path.

The gunner's silhouette folded nearly instantaneously, a perfect center-mass shot that opened him up like a bag of flour. His hands fell away from the .50-cal handles and the massive piece fell silent, unfired.

The second shot went through the windshield and turned the driver's face into a red mist. The driver slumped forward, dead before his nervous system could send a proper "Mayday", sending the pickup veering off into a stack of crates. The third and fourth shots followed a heartbeat later, cutting down two shooters who tried to rise in the back, dropping them over the side. The pickup careened forward a few more feet, then veered off into a pile of sandbags and fell silent.

"Target's eliminated. Road's clear." Hawkeye's voice was gravel-calm.

"Copy. Echo, what's the view from above?

"All four vehicles have crossed into the compound." There was a nervous tremor in his normally composed voice. "I'm keeping eyes. The gate's wide open. Another truck's rushing toward it. Gaining entry now. Cowboy... this isn't a small breach. It's a takeover."

"Copy." I switched channels. "Ridley, I need a sitrep."

No response. All I got back were the rips of automatic gunfire and occasional shouts—a messy chorus of soldiers trying to hold a collapsing perimeter. Whatever defenses were left were falling fast. And then the line went dead.

About two hundred yards from the gate, I pressed a hand against Ali's shoulder. "Slow. Stop here." Youssef fell into place alongside us, killing his headlights.

I got out, raised my binoculars and clicked the focus wheel a notch. The view jumped into crystal clarity under the green glow of the nightscope.

As I watched, the main gate—a massive, blast-rated monster of reinforced steel—was already closing up. A couple of seconds later, it shut up tight. The automatic bollards were raised back up, thick metal cylinders that could destroy a truck's undercarriage in a split second.

There were no vehicles visible—not a single set of headlights—which meant all their shooters were already inside.

If they had gone to the trouble of sealing the entrance, which also was the only way out, it was clear that they weren't planning on letting anyone get out of that place alive. But it also meant that they planned to stick around for a while, or else, they would have simply sprayed hundreds of rounds all over the place and made a quick exit. I could hear the echoes of sporadic gunfire, but they were a few short bursts here and there. Not heavy. That meant the civilians were still alive—for now.

Midnight Scimitar. A midnight deadline for them to commence their killing spree. That made perfect, sick sense.

I lowered the binoculars and leaned back against the cruiser's frame, letting the silence rush back into my ears. There had been no word from Ridley. I kept wondering if it meant he had gone black... or if a bullet had gotten him first. Guys like him were hard to kill. So I chose to believe it was the first. That meant we hadn't gone all the way into the worst case—yet.

Forcing our way through the gate was a non-starter. There were civilians in there—a lot of them—and friendlies we hadn't gotten to yet. If we went in hard and fast, we would be sending them straight into the blender alongside the bad guys. The shooters would execute everyone in their sights. That's what these guys lived for—a bloody showdown.

This was a delicate needle to thread—a messy breach could undermine everything.

But I looked at the positive side. It might seem hard to believe but there was a silver lining—they had closed up and sealed the compound. The hostages weren't going anywhere, and neither were their captors.

It would make hunting them easier.

CHAPTER 25

The only problem was getting in without announcing our arrival in large, capital letters.

Raptor hopped out of the rear door and fell in beside me. His silhouette was a blockier, more menacing mirror of my own—kit heavy, plate carrier bristling with magazines, HK416 slung across, backup sidearm on his thigh. "What's the play, boss?"

I pressed my shoulder against the quarter panel, letting a slow breath ease through me. "We've lost the advantage. AQ crossed the perimeter already. Once they gain control—which I think they already have—I doubt they're in a rush to execute everyone in there. They want civilians alive... for leverage... or a show trial. If we rush in now, we'll start a bloodbath we can't control."

"So a frontal assault is off the table." Hawkeye completed my thought.

"Bingo."

"That's a bummer. I was looking forward to our usual charge in and hope for the best routine," Ninja quipped.

"No, smartass. We need something more sophisticated."

"You don't say, boss. But you've got a backup plan, right?"

I nodded, trying to look more confident that I felt. "I think so."

"I knew it." There was a spark in his voice—the kind you hear when a soldier finds something to hang hope on. "Go on, we're all ears."

"There's a secondary egress—a small service gate near the abandoned bakery on the southwest side. Permanently locked, camouflaged behind trash bins. It was meant for fire escape or last-ditch evacuation. I think the time has come for us to use it."

"You said it, Cowboy. If there was a time for it, it's now," Raptor agreed.

"Well, we use it to breach quietly, move in without raising the alarm, find the hostages first... then we deal with the shooters on our terms."

"Sounds like a plan." Hawkeye paused. "How solid is that service gate?"

"That's the thing. It's a heavy-duty piece—not some rickety, rusted fence. It's meant to keep people in and danger out. We'll have to figure out how to breach it without making too much of a noise."

Ninja sighed. "So... breaching charges or a nice, clean shotgun blast to the hinges are a no-go."

I let a wry smile tug at the corner of my mouth. "You got it. We aren't doing the Fourth of July. It's a midnight break-in. We'll need something quieter. A Halligan, a hydraulic spreader... something we can pry without making a scene."

We got back into the SUVs and ghosted forward without headlights, grinding gravel under heavy-tread wheels, creeping into the side alley that paralleled the Quarter's outer wall. The abandoned bakery rose up on our left, its wooden sign dangling by a single rusted chain, a silhouette against a purple-black sky. We halted fifty yards short of it, hopped out quietly, and fell into a crouch, rifles at the low ready.

"Full-stealth from here forward." I kept my voice barely above a gravelly whisper, the kind that seemed to blend into the silence instead of breaking it. "Camo up. Black and green. Anything reflective gets covered. Tape it, spray it, whatever it takes."

The men fell into a well-practiced rhythm immediately—opening pouches, smearing face paint, clicking off infrared indicators, killing whatever glimmer might reflect a rooftop searchlight. The team tightened slings, pressed magazines home, threaded suppressors—making sure everything was dialed for close-quarter, clandestine killing.

I pressed myself against the rear corner of the abandoned bakery and listened. Anything—a rustling mattress, a shifting shadow—could be a danger we hadn't gotten a bead on yet. Then I turned and nodded toward Ninja. He fell in beside me without a word.

Behind the bakery, hidden by a stack of rusted oil drums and a pile of wooden crates, I pressed against a hidden steel service door—a heavy, fortified barrier meant to be an escape for those trying to flee the Quarter in a last-ditch scenario. But there was a problem—it was meant for people to get out... not in.

I pressed my gloved knuckles against it first, testing its resistance. There were no handles, just a flat plate with a deep-recessed deadlock.

I turned back toward Ninja, kept my voice a breath above a thought. "This isn't your average backdoor. It's a service gate... meant for exfil, not in."

He nodded. "Design's meant to keep people from forcing it."

I pressed an ear against it, closed my eyes, and listened. There were no movement vibrations on the other side, just a deep silence—a wall made for staying closed. In my mind, I walked through the options once again. A charge would be messy and noisy. Thermic would cut it, but we would light up the whole block.

Instead...

"There'll be a mechanical release on the inside—a drop-bolt."

Ninja nodded again. "Then we need someone to lift it. Mechanical breach without explosives would take too damn long."

He was right. There was a lot of metal we would need to cut through if we tried a mechanical breach. It would take at least ten minutes—time we didn't have—and make a shitload of noise we couldn't afford. Someone opening the door from inside was the only way of gaining entry quickly without waking the whole damn Quarter.

The clock showed 2320 hours. Time was bleeding away faster than I liked.

As if the universe decided it was a good time to cut me a break, my earpiece crackled to life.

"Cowboy... Ridley here."

I felt a rush of relief. I was feeling stuck when my key asset dropped off the net in the middle of a siege.

"Ridley. Good to hear your voice. What's going on inside?"

He exhaled quietly, then fell into a more deliberate, precise delivery. "It's FUBAR in here. Fifty AQ shooters crossed the gate. All heavy with AKs. Few RPGs in the mix. They're in the houses, walkways… rooftop positions. Taking hostages."

I pressed my knuckles against my forehead. Fifty. That meant we were going to be the ones surrounded, not the other way around.

"Fifty armed tangos? That complicates things."

"We managed to take out eight. So, about forty still active."

"Well, that sounds better. How many casualties on your end?"

"At least three of the six guards are dead. Main gate two are alive, or at least one of them. AQ needed them alive to operate the gate and bollards."

I nodded in the dark. That made sense—you need someone to spin the wheels when you want to move in and out. "Your team?"

"All alive. Calhoun's up on the apartments' rooftop with a suppressed HK417. He's silent for now, but ready to take out targets once we've got some kind of a plan in place."

"Tangos have no idea he's up there?"

"Not right now. But they are everywhere, and will eventually make their way up there."

"Copy that. And Maddix?"

"He got all four civilians into the safe room —all three occupants of the apartments and one guy from a villa. They're safely cooped up there for now. The room's reinforced, backup power, hardline radio. But we decided he'd stay off comms and not hit the panic alarm. We don't want to have a heavy-handed intervention and this turning into a full-blown hostage situation. We knew you Delta boys are around. Figured we'd be better off handling this ourselves with you."

That made sense. The last thing we needed were local cops involved and this descending into a messy showdown.

"Good call," I said. "How many hostages have they got?"

"Two families in two villas. And the two lovebirds—the ones who drew this shit-storm. You know what, I'd like to wring their necks myself."

I could feel his anger. I felt the same. "Save me a spot in the choke chain, pal."

He exhaled quietly, a frustrated rush of air. "Roger."

"Let's get this rolling. We're ready to move in. What do you suggest?"

"There's no way you're cutting through it without making a scene. I'll need to let you in from the inside."

"Where are you now?"

"About fifty yards west of the gate. Hidden in the hedgerows."

"Roger." I paused. "You or the others injured?"

"Got a few scratches from the CQB in the apartments. Nothing we can't handle. Otherwise we're green across the board."

"All right. We move in after five minutes. That enough time for you to reach the gate and lift it from the inside?"

"Affirmative. Five minutes. I'll be there."

The earpiece fell silent. I turned back toward my team and nodded. "Time to rock and roll."

I caught Ali's and Youssef's eyes in the dim glow from a nearby rooftop light. I had already briefed them. While we went in heavy, their job was to stay with the wheels, stay alive, and be ready to extract us the moment we called it. Side gate or main, whatever the situation demanded.

I pressed my hands against both men's shoulders. "Watch our backs. There's a strong chance reinforcements come in once we kick this hornet's nest."

They nodded quietly, one hand resting on the CAR-816s slung across their torsos—short-barrelled, piston-driven carbines built in the UAE. Easier to keep zeroed than old Soviet junk, and they fed clean.

The watch on my wrist glowed a dim green in the dark: **2325 hours**. **35 minutes to zero hour**.

CHAPTER 26

We fell into a stack formation at the side gate, all pressed against the wall, weapons up, muzzles trained forward.

The deadlock clicked and fell away. The gate opened a few inches and a silhouette filled it. Ridley. Tough, leathery face, piercing eyes that seemed a few decades older than his birth certificate. His close-cropped hair was matted with blood at the sideburns; a dark stain blossomed across his shirt just above his beltline. His walk was stiff—not dramatic, not weak—just a little off, a small wince with each stride. A Special Operations vet trying hard not to show it.

I nodded at him and we flowed in without a word. The gate closed quietly behind us with a deep metal *thunk*—no turning back now.

I fell back a step, letting the team move forward.

"How bad is it?" I whispered, falling in with Ridley.

He tried to straighten, winced. "Not bad."

I raised an eyebrow. "You sure?"

He pressed a gloved hand against his abdomen and whispered back, "Got a blade in the gut. Few stitches when we're clear."

"No shit. I did think it looked like more than a scratch."

He tried for a smirk. "Don't start crying over me just yet."

I nodded once—not much we could do for him now except keep him alive. "Stay close. Let me know if you fade. Lead us somewhere we can talk without prying eyes."

He nodded back, jaw tight against the pain, turned and led us inside the Quarter's labyrinth of courtyards and balconies. We fell in behind him—a silent stack melting into the shadows.

We crossed a gravel path, pressed against a retaining wall near the periphery. There, under a thick overhang of bougainvillea and in deep shadow, we halted.

I kept my voice to a gravelly hush. "All right. Tell me. Where are the families?"

He nodded toward the center of the compound. "Villas 2 and 4. About fifty tangos came in hard and fast—seemed to know the internal layout. Took out all the perimeter guards first, then fanned into the houses and apartments."

Ridley paused, drew a slow, painful breath, then pressed on. "Eight came into the apartments where Maddix, Calhoun, and I were waiting. We put all eight down... but we decided we'd gotten all the luck we were going to get. So we split. Maddix got the civilians into the safe room. I came back to find you."

I listened, filing it all away. "Status in the apartments now?"

He sighed quietly. "It's all quiet now. But if any of those guys go looking for their pals, they'll find them in a stack on the third floor. It's a bloody mess up there. We didn't have time to hide the bodies. But the good thing is that even if they try going to the rooftop, Calhoun's going to be fine for a while as there's a heavy steel-reinforced door between the stairs and the rooftop."

I nodded. "And the safe room?"

"Maddix and the civilians are tight. Few chances these guys just stumble across it. And if they do... it's a fortified box. They're not getting in."

"How about Maddix and Calhoun—their condition? Their 'scratches' as bad as yours?"

He slightly chuckled, then winced from the movement. "Calhoun is fine. But Maddix got cut. About the same as me. Guys got close... real close. When this whole thing suddenly started, we hadn't gotten suppressors on. But we needed to keep it quiet. So we went in hard, up close and dirty. Fists and knives. You know how it goes—close quarters, multiple opponents, you're going to get cut up."

I nodded quietly. Guys who hadn't fought with knives wouldn't understand. There's something raw about a knife-fight in a tight corner—a moment when the whole world drops away and it's just you and him, trying to stay a step faster, a bit more aggressive, a little more decisive. The blade's glimmer, the rush of movement, the shock when it finds a home. It's messy, intimate, and it leaves everyone marked, one way or another. There's no pure win in close-quarter killing; there's only survival.

"All right." I whispered. "Anything else I need to know before we kick this off, Ridley? Now's the time to spill it."

He gave me a nod. "Yeah... there's a jammer. Inside the safe room. RF-signal killer. Was the fallback plan. If we can't rescue the hostages, Maddix is supposed to trigger it."

I frowned. "When?"

"Five minutes to midnight. Atwood's orders. If we can't stop it, we sure as hell won't let AQ turn this into a goddamn snuff stream." He met my gaze, dead serious now. "No live broadcast of an execution. We don't let those bastards put on a show."

I nodded, tasting the bitterness in the back of my throat. Atwood was right. We had all seen enough of those barbaric videos—the orange jumpsuits, the blindfolds, hostages kneeling in the dirt, terrified eyes, blades glinting, masked cowards preaching hate while the world watched in horror. A life was erased on camera in the name of their ideology. I had seen the aftermath, too. Families broken. Recruits inspired by the spectacle. The kind of evil you can't undo.

It turned my stomach then, and it turned it now. I had fought this war long enough to know we couldn't let it happen. Whatever it took—a jammer, a bullet, a knife—we would do it. We would cut their broadcast. Choke their narrative. Deny them the show.

There was no way in hell I would let that happen here. Not on my watch.

I glanced at my watch: **2330 hours. Half an hour to zero hour.**

The kind of countdown that makes your pulse thrum in your ears if you're green. Me? It just sharpened my focus.

I keyed my comms, voice low but steady. "Echo, Cowboy. Give me eyes. What's the latest from your perch?"

For a moment there was a crackling pause, then his voice came back in a calm, clear stream. "Roger, Cowboy. I've been tracking you since you made entry. You're all tucked in near the southwest corner. No eyes on you from where they're standing."

"Good. Talk to me about the tangos."

"They've swept all the villas. Now they're concentrating their manpower on two villas—two and four. Most of the foot mobiles are clustered there. Got a few loitering near the main entrance. Looks like they're setting up for something—maybe defensive, maybe staging for the next phase. Too early to tell."

"Activity in the quarter?"

"Two trucks with mounted PKs, patrolling slow and tight around the streets and perimeter roads. Same pattern—slow enough to spot a straggler, fast enough they're not an easy target. Whatever you do, watch your movement. Those PKs will ruin your day if they light up while you're trying to exfil."

I grunted under my breath. PK machine guns—belt-fed, 7.62x54R, mean weapons that could chew up soft targets like ours in seconds. That was a problem. A big one. Those guns weren't there for show—they were there to make sure no one got out alive. We would need them gone if we were going to extract without a messy chase afterwards.

I clicked back. "Roger. Keep eyes up. Let me know if their pattern starts shifting. We're going to make our move soon."

"Roger that," he came back, but his tone changed a hair. "Scratch that—got movement. One of the trucks just turned off Main onto a street that'll bring it around to your position. ETA: about a minute and a half. You better decide fast, Cowboy—duck or take the damn truck."

Didn't take me more than a heartbeat to make the call. Guys like us lived for this kind of crossroads. The PK was a threat, sure—but it was also a opportunity. Take it, and we would cut their heavy guns in half. Easy choice.

"We're going to take it." I kept it terse and decisive. "Echo, count heads—how many in that rolling coffin?"

"Driver, passenger seat, and... five in the back bed. So seven total."

"Copy that." I turned to the boys, gave them the plan in hushed, crisp bursts. "Truck with a PK's headed this way. We're going to smoke that truck, clean and fast—no wild shots, no noise. Suppressors only. I want them down before they even know what the hell hit them."

I pointed across the street. "Hawkeye, Ninja—cross over, find cover, set up fields of fire. Hawkeye, you're lead. That PK gunner in the back goes down first—can't have that bastard cutting loose. Ninja, drop the passenger up front. I'll handle the driver. Raptor—you start working through the bed, back to front. Tag the guy on tail first, then work your way up. Once our primaries are down, we help clean up the rest. Short, precise bursts. We drop all of them without letting off a wild shot. Got it?"

They nodded—no wasted words.

"Ridley," I said, locking eyes with him. "You're bait. When the truck's right on top of us, you break cover like you're running for your life. Act panicked. Then drop, hands up like you're surrendering. That'll make them slow to check you out. That's our moment."

Ridley nodded without hesitation.

Truth was, I had zero doubt we would pull this off. Everyone was specialized—Hawkeye with the long gun, Raptor a close-quarter monster, Ninja a blade in the dark—but we were all proficient at the fundamentals. Each Delta unit has its sniper—for us, that's Hawkeye—but every single one of us went through sniper school. All Delta are trained to be shooters first. Each operator spends countless hours on the range, putting 5.56 into quarter-sized groups at a hundred yards, from awkward positions, under stress.

So when you have time to set up and take your shot, it's not a question of ability—it's a foregone conclusion. That's what I liked most about this team: there were no weak links.

Hawkeye nodded once, tapped Ninja on the shoulder, and the two darted across the road, moving fast and low, rifles tight to their chests, boots light on the ground. They melted into the shadows on the far side, taking position behind a low stone wall that would give them good angles, HK416s already braced and trained toward where the truck would appear.

Me, Raptor, and Ridley stayed put, rifles up, optics scanning, waiting for that truck to roll into our kill box. Raptor and I fell into a kneeling position, each man raising his rifle, clicking off the safety, and pressing his cheek against the stock.

I looked briefly toward Ridley—injured, but tough enough to do his part. "When you dart into the road... make it believable. Limp a little. Look surprised. Hands up immediately. Sell it. But hit the ground at once. We don't want you getting shot before we take them out."

He nodded. I didn't have any doubts. Guys like Ridley, injured or not, got things done.

The showdown was seconds away. We waited.

It was time to let them meet Delta the hard way.

CHAPTER 27

The headlights cut a path through the dark, bouncing off scrub and sand. The truck was a silhouette first, then a mass of metal and men as it turned the corner about fifty yards up. It crawled forward, slow and deliberate—a wolfpack on wheels—the PK up high in the back, gunners scanning left and right for trouble. They had no idea they were driving into their own funeral.

I crouched low, HK tight to my shoulder, watching as that rust-bucket beast rolled closer, slow and suspicious. The PK gunner in the back bed kept swinging his barrel, eyes peeled, hunting for shadows, itching to let loose at anything that resembled a target. The other gunmen were just as alert, scanning both sides of the street like they knew death was out there. They were right about that.

"Steady," I whispered, my finger resting just off the trigger. "Almost there..."

Twenty yards. Close enough I could see the glint of sweat on the driver's face.

Right on cue, Ridley broke cover—came stumbling out of the trees like some poor bastard on the run. He played it perfectly, legs churning like he didn't know where to go, panic all over his face. The driver's eyes locked on him, and I saw the truck's nose dip as he hit the brakes, tires squealing low against the pavement.

Ridley froze like a deer in the goddamn headlights, hands shooting up. The bed of that truck came alive—the gunmen snapping rifles up, barrels tracking him like hungry dogs.

"Hold," I muttered, already lining up my shot.

Ridley dropped to the ground fast—almost too fast. One of the twitchy gunmen in the back squeezed off a round, bullet whining past Ridley's head so close it probably parted his hair.

"Take it," I barked.

Pfft. That PK gunner's skull just vaporized—head turned into red fog, body slumping over the gun. Hawkeye didn't miss. Never did.

The next instant was pure muscle memory. *Pfft-pfft-pfft*—three suppressed shots so close together they sounded like one. My HK whispered once, and I saw the driver's face disappear in a 5.56 shockwave, his blood painting the inside of the windshield. At the same moment, Ninja dropped the passenger, clean shot through the face. Raptor's man in the back didn't even have time to shout before his throat blew out.

No time to breathe. We kept firing—methodical, silent. The last gunmen in the bed didn't even get their triggers halfway down. Suppressed shots popped off as we mopped them up—two seconds flat from first shot to last breath.

Seven tangos down. Not a sound louder than a whisper and the thump of bodies hitting steel and dirt.

I clicked my push-to-talk. "All tangos down. Nice and clean."

We moved fast—no time to admire our handiwork. The bodies in that truck weren't going to hide themselves.

Raptor was first to the cab. He yanked the driver's corpse out and dumped it into the truck bed with the rest of the dead gunmen. Ninja swung up and into the cab without missing a beat, slid behind the wheel, and eased the truck off the road. He guided it between a clump of trees, killing the headlights.

The truck disappeared into the shadows like it had never been there. No PK. No bodies. No sign of a fight.

Raptor walked over, looking pleased. "Guess what Santa left us in the truck bed?"

"Something that goes boom?" I asked.

"Yup. RPG launcher. Figured it might come in handy if things go pear-shaped."

"It sure will. We're keeping that party favor. Loudest door opener in the arsenal."

Raptor chuckled. "Won't argue with that."

I stepped over to Ridley, who was down on one knee, trying to push himself up. He looked like hell—pale, sweaty, breathing hard. I reached out and gave him a hand, hauling him to his feet.

"Went like clockwork," he said, voice tight, but there was that glint of wry humor in his eyes. The guy was tough, no doubt.

"Yeah," I said, smirking. "Mainly because that distraction of yours was spot on. You played 'scared civvie' like a goddamn Oscar winner. Twitchy-fingers nearly made you a corpse, though."

Ridley let out a breath, half a laugh. "I felt that round, man. It was that close."

I clapped him on the shoulder, but the second I did, I felt how unsteady he was. The blood loss was catching up. That stab wound was starting to drain him dry. No way I was letting him bleed out on me.

"Let me see that cut," I said, already knowing it was worse than he was pretending.

He grimaced but pulled his shirt aside. There was a deep stab wound just above his left hip—messy, dripping, but not arterial. A bad gash, not a killing cut.

"Hawkeye," I called out. "Give him a field patch. Best you can."

Hawkeye nodded, knelt, and opened his small med kit. He pressed a heavy gauze pad directly against the wound to slow the bleeding, then quickly tape-wrapped it tight against Ridley's torso. The pressure would hold it for a while—a field fix, not a hospital—but we weren't going to lose him here.

"Good enough to keep your guts inside," Hawkeye muttered, giving Ridley a pat on the arm.

While Hawkeye patched up Ridley, I kept my back against the truck and let my eyes scan the compound. I turned it over in my mind—we would have to split into two elements. Two-man teams. That meant we would be going in light, underpowered, against a fortified compound with at least ten shooters per villa. There would be no backup, no QRF. The remaining PK-mounted AQ truck was still out there, and when the shit hit the fan, that thing could shred us.

The first time we jumped their truck we had gotten lucky. The element of surprise was ours. That kind of magic was a one-time deal. If we tried it again, we could be the ones surprised—and not in a nice way. We would be sitting ducks if that second truck turned up during exfil.

I pressed my knuckles against my forehead, thinking it through. That PK on the truck we just captured—that was a gift from God, and I wasn't about to waste it. If Ali and Youssef were manning this PK, we would match their firepower. Have a fighting chance at cutting down the other truck before it chewed us up. That meant calling them inside. It meant shifting plans—fast.

I walked over to Raptor. "Change of plans. It makes more sense for Ali and Youssef to come in and take over the PK. That'll keep the other truck from chewing us up when we move on the villas."

Raptor nodded. "I was thinking the same, Cowboy. We sure as hell don't want it breathing down our necks at the worst moment."

"Exactly." I pressed my earpiece. "Ali, change of plans. We need you inside. You and Youssef get to the side gate—Raptor's going to let you in."

"Roger that, Cowboy."

I turned back to Raptor. "Let them in."

Raptor nodded once and peeled off into the dark. I turned to Ridley, who was still propped against the side of the truck, blood-soaked gauze pressed against his ribs, looking like hell but still sharp behind the eyes. And that's what I needed.

I crouched beside him and handed him the tablet Echo had loaded with the villa layouts. "I've got the schematics, but we're not going to have time to run a textbook entry, so I'm leaning on you. You've been inside every one of these villas. I'm going to need your best call on how to crack them open. How do we breach?"

Ridley studied the screen for maybe three seconds before shifting a little, grimacing from the pain, then leaning forward and tapping my tablet. Echo had already piped in the compound schematics—rough layouts of both villas, enough to orient us but not enough for confidence. What I needed was the human intel. Ridley was it.

"Both villas are identical," he said, voice gravelly but steady. "Two floors, rooftop terrace above the second floor. Flat roof, concrete slab, with a parapet all around. Main living quarters are on the first and second floors. Roof's probably unmanned—unless they're expecting trouble."

I nodded. "Interior?"

"Ground floor's got a large foyer right off the main door. That connects to a sitting room and dining area, all up front. Kitchen and a storage room in the rear, with a hallway running straight through. Rear staircase leads up."

I nodded, eyes scanning the plan. "What about second floor?"

"Master bedroom's here." He tapped it. "Faces the rear. Has a balcony. Three smaller bedrooms along the sides. All connected by this hallway. Rear balcony overlooks a tight little courtyard. That's your best insertion point—less exposed, and if anyone's watching, they're focused on the front. But no way to say where they're holding the hostages. Could be upstairs, could be split up."

I nodded, then turned to Hawkeye. "Keep that nano drone warmed up. We launch when we're in position behind the villas."

"Roger that," he replied. "Wings are folded and ready to fly."

Just then, I heard soft footfalls and turned. Raptor came jogging back in with Ali and Youssef flanking him, both geared up and ready for trouble. I motioned them over to the truck and pointed at the mounted PKM.

"Ali, Youssef, you two stay here. Man the gun, keep an eye out for that other truck. When I give the word, you roll out, intercept, and light them up. Echo will send you its exact location before that. If it shows up during our breach, I want you laying down steel before they get eyes on us."

Ali nodded, hand on the feed tray. "We won't miss."

"Copy," Youssef confirmed. "They won't pass."

I turned back to my guys. Time to cut the pie.

"We're splitting up," I said, voice low but firm. "I'm with Ninja—we're taking Villa 2. Raptor, you're with Hawkeye. Villa 4 is yours."

Then I looked to Ridley. "Normally, Hawkeye runs overwatch on our ops. But tonight we need boots inside both targets. That means Calhoun's stepping up."

Ridley gave a nod. "He's solid. Cool under fire. Better shot than I ever was. You'll need to get on his net. He runs channel sixteen sub one."

I dialed it in on my radio and keyed up. "Calhoun, this is Cowboy. You read me?"

"Roger that, Cowboy," came the response, crisp and cool—British accent as smooth as cold steel. "Spotting from the eastern roofline. I'll keep the sky clear for you."

Perfect.

I looked back at Ridley. "Time to kick in some doors, pal. You better sit this one out. Nothing to do with your fight—you've already bled more than enough for it."

He gave a weak grin and pushed himself upright just an inch. "Understood."

No arguments. He knew the score.

I went on, "Depending how this shakes out, we might need someone to lead the hostages to the side gate while we deal with whatever's left. You think Maddix is up to it?"

Ridley didn't hesitate. "Yeah. He got a little cut up, but he's solid. Big guy. You need a mule to carry scared civilians, Maddix is the man for it."

"Good. That's the backup plan. If I give the word, he leads everyone—including your bunch—out the side gate. No delays. No hero shit."

"Understood. You give the word, we move. Go raise some hell."

I didn't even need to say a word. The moment he said it, me and the three operators—Raptor, Ninja, Hawkeye—snapped back in instinct.

"Hooah."

It wasn't for show. It was an old habit.

We were all Rangers before Delta. And so was Ridley. That word wasn't just a battle cry—it was a nod of respect to a brother who had earned it.

I stood up and looked over my team. Each man nodded. No speeches. No handshakes. Just warfighters ready to do the dirty work.

I checked my watch. **2340 hours. Twenty minutes to zero hour.**

Time to move.

CHAPTER 28

We moved like shadows through the trees, a four-man wedge gliding silently toward the villas, boots sinking into the dry dirt, rifles up, heads on a swivel. The air was thick—not just with heat, but with something darker. A low-pressure kind of stillness that came before a storm. Only this one didn't bring rain. Just blood.

The villas loomed ahead in the dark, hulking outlines against the faint star-glow. Two stories each, clean white plaster now turned gray under moonlight, the kind of suburban opulence that was hiding terror behind its tiled roofs and arched windows.

We stopped under a cluster of gnarled trees about fifty yards behind the targets. From there, we had line of sight on both rear balconies. I dropped to a knee and scanned the upper balconies while Hawkeye unpacked the nano drone kit like a surgeon prepping for a transplant.

"Bird's in the air," he whispered as he launched the drone.

The little bird quietly took off, nearly silent, its thermal optics and low-light cams spinning into action. We watched the feed on the tablet. Villa 4 first.

Before we could get a solid peek, Calhoun came in on the radio. His voice was low, but there was ice under it.

"Cowboy, Calhoun here. Got eyes on something foul on Villa 4 roof. They're stringing up two bodies on the terrace of Villa Four. Dead guards. Hung by the neck from the roof rails like some medieval warning. Bastards are staging a show."

My jaw locked tight. I didn't need to see it to picture it. A couple of poor SOBs, probably the first to challenge the intruders, left dangling in the wind like some grotesque warning sign. This wasn't just some last stand—they were setting the stage for a sick, twisted broadcast. I could feel Calhoun's fury radiating through the radio waves.

"They were good lads," Calhoun said. "Local tribal boys, but solid. Brave. Never flinched on an op. And now these AQ shits are putting on a puppet show with their corpses." His voice dropped, low and dangerous. "It's taking everything I've got not to pull the damn trigger and drop the bastards right now."

I could picture him up there, laying prone with his long gun, finger curled on the trigger, crosshairs dancing over skulls. I felt the same black heat boiling in my gut—not the fast kind that makes you reckless, but the kind that sharpens your edges. Cold fury. Focused hate.

I exhaled slowly. "They're setting the stage for the main act. Some macabre little show they want to kick off at midnight. Terror theater."

"Bloody cowards," Calhoun muttered.

I nodded, even though he couldn't see it. "We'll end it before they raise the goddamn curtain. Keep eyes on, Calhoun. Hold back till we go loud."

A pause. Then: "Copy that. I've got eyes on the front of both villas. Just give the word. I'll start stacking bodies."

"Hold position for now. Eyes up."

"Roger that." A clipped reply. I knew that tone. The man was a sniper sitting on a powder keg of righteous wrath, same as the rest of us.

I clicked off comms and turned as Hawkeye slid up beside me, peering down at his drone tablet. His voice, normally the definition of calm under pressure, had a new edge—not loud, not emotional, but taut like piano wire.

"Two guards on the rear balcony of Villa Four," he said. "Main bedroom's got three people. One man—hands tied behind his back. The others—a woman and a kid. Girl, maybe ten."

"Status?"

He didn't answer immediately. Just kept staring at the feed.

"They're... motionless."

A cold weight settled behind my ribs.

"Motionless?"

He looked at me. His eyes were hard, like glass that had seen too many fires. "I mean they're not moving. Could be unconscious. Could be worse. I can't confirm without getting the drone closer, but I can't risk it. Balcony guards will spot it if I push."

That wasn't like him. Hawkeye usually didn't offer opinions or maybes—he gave facts. If he was hedging, it meant the situation was bad.

And if it involved a kid...

I could feel it in his voice—a tremor beneath the ice. He didn't show rage, didn't need to. But it was there now, smoldering like coals behind his words.

I nodded once. "Copy. What about ground floor?"

He switched the feed. "Living room's lit. Two more hostages—male and female. Hands behind backs, hoods over their heads. Kneeling in the corner."

"Probably the couple from outside the gates," I muttered, thinking about how two clueless souls who wanted to have a good time found themselves cast in a horror movie instead.

"Looks like it. Other side of the room—AQ goons putting up a black flag. Big one. Arabic scrawl all across it in white. You know what that means."

Yeah. I knew. I didn't need to read the damn thing to know it was their banner of death. A backdrop for a snuff video. I had seen enough of those flags in burnt-out compounds and laptop hard drives from Afghanistan to Yemen. Propaganda trash. Calling cards for sick bastards in masks with knives and stolen bravado, feeding their sick ideology to an audience of fellow degenerates. All timed for midnight. All theater for some twisted cause.

Ninja Man, crouched behind me, didn't say a word. But the way his knuckles turned white on his suppressed HK416 told me everything.

"We're burning this set to the ground," I muttered.

Hawkeye gave a curt nod. "Copy that."

He flew the drone over to Villa Two. The tiny bird zipped through the shadows and curved around the second villa. He kept it high—couldn't risk a close peek with two guards stationed on the rear balcony, smoking and muttering to each other, not knowing their hours were numbered.

Twenty yards back, the drone's lens peered into the master bedroom.

"Main bedroom—one man, hands tied. Alone."

I frowned. “Only one?”

He zoomed in a bit, but kept his distance. “Yeah. No sign of anyone else.”

“Ridley said family of three—couple and a ten-year-old.”

“Then they’re locked up somewhere inside. Rooms without windows. I don’t have line of sight.”

Damn it.

We didn’t have time to run a full fly-through. No time to map every room. That meant one thing—adapt on the move, improvise, dominate. This op was going to be held together with grit, violence, and partial intel.

“We don’t have time for a full sweep,” I said. “We take what we have and improvise the rest.”

This wasn’t going to be clean. Hell, it wasn’t even going to be surgical. It was going to be brutal. But we would get them out. Or die trying.

I glanced at my watch. **2345 hours. Fifteen minutes to zero hour.**

I looked at my team. Ninja was already up and re-checking his rig. Raptor stood silent, eyes narrowed, jaw tight. Hawkeye packed up the drone gear without saying a word. Every one of us had the same thought behind our eyes.

There were kids in there. Families. Strung-up corpses on rooftops. Hooded civilians kneeling beneath a terrorist flag. We had seen what happened when you waited too long. We had buried the consequences.

Not tonight.

Not this time.

We were going to paint those walls with AQ blood before the bastards could press record.

CHAPTER 29

We didn't speak. Just exchanged that final look—the one where you confirm without words that if this was the last time you were seeing each other breathing, it was a damn honor.

Ninja cracked his neck left, then right. Hawkeye flicked his safety off. Raptor tapped his fist twice to his chest, then pointed at the villa like it had personally insulted his mother. I gave a slow nod, and we split, two-by-two—death in twin pairs, stalking the night.

We moved like shadows toward our designated kill boxes—Ninja and I to Villa Four, the other two ghosts to Villa Two. Each footstep was placed like we were on glass. No shadows broken, no stray noise.

The breach plan was tight and mirrored. One gunman each, both villas, back balconies. Take the shots, climb up, get in, secure the hostages. Once every noncombatant was safe except the two hooded ones downstairs, we would lower them out the back and then go loud on the main floor. AQ wanted to start a show—we were going to cancel it with high-velocity lead.

I took my position and locked onto my target through the IR scope—bearded prick in a black vest holding a battered AK and scanning the darkness. Ninja had the other guy—skinny, cocky, AK slung loose.

"Cowboy ready," I whispered.

"Hawkeye ready," came the calm reply.

"Ninja set."

"Raptor's hot."

I gave the word. "Send them to hell."

Pfft. Pfft. Pfft. Pfft.

Four suppressed shots sliced through the night like whispers from the Reaper. Four bodies crumpled and fell.

"Two down. Balcony's clear," I whispered into comms.

"Copy. Villa 2's clear," Raptor responded.

Go time.

Ninja and I were already in motion. We sprinted low across the dirt, boots quiet, weapons tight. The wall was old stucco with just enough irregularity for a foothold if you knew how to move. I hit it at speed, planted a boot in a crevice, and launched up—fingers catching the stone lip of the balcony's underside.

I swung once for momentum, then used the flex in my arms to get a second boost. My knee hooked over the rail and I rolled over silently. Ninja mirrored the move, a blur of black gear and zero hesitation.

We were on the balcony. Inside, moonlight bled in through the curtains.

We entered fast and clean, weapons sweeping. Bedroom clear. I was already on my knees beside the woman and the kid. Little girl, maybe nine or ten. Both had a smear of blood at the side of their heads—blunt trauma. But they were breathing. I pressed two fingers against the woman's neck, then the girl's. Pulse steady. Relief washed over me—a rare visitor in this line of work.

The hostage—the man tied to the chair—had eyes wide with shock. Mouth taped. Hands lashed behind his back. He was trembling but silent.

I leaned in close, peeled the tape off slow, and whispered, "U.S. Army. You're safe. But stay quiet. Nod if you understand."

He nodded fast, eyes glassy. Guy probably thought the end had come, only to get delivered by two shadows from nowhere.

Ninja kept watch on the door, rifle up and breath calm like a monk at war. I slid my knife from my belt, cut the man's bindings. He rubbed his wrists, breathing deep, eyes watering.

I keyed comms. "Three hostages secure, second floor, Villa Four. Woman and child unconscious but breathing."

"Copy," came Raptor's voice. "Same here. We've got our three—woman and kid were locked in the bathroom. All accounted for."

Good. Phase One, complete. Took us under two minutes, start to finish—from dropping those balcony guards to breaching the villas and securing the hostages. That's the kind of timing we drilled until it bled. Not perfect, but close enough for combat work. Countdown was in the red now. Every second was a crackling fuse.

But the real storm was yet to start.

I keyed my comm. "Maddix, this is Cowboy. You copy?"

He answered before the static even cleared. "Copy, Cowboy. You get to the hostages?"

"Affirmative. Six secure. Meet us at the pine grove, fifteen meters west of the generator shed with the red diesel tank—near the stone wall with the vine creepers. Two minutes."

"Copy. On my way," he replied, cool and ready. I didn't expect less.

I slung my rifle tight, leaned down, and lifted the woman. Still out cold but breathing steady. Ninja had already scooped the girl up in his arms, her limp head tucked against his shoulder like she was sleeping off a fever. The husband looked like he had been dropped into Hell and handed a map he couldn't read, but he was upright and moving. Good enough. We motioned him to follow, and he did—legs shaky but moving. I didn't give him time to feel sorry for himself.

We hustled back to the balcony where Ninja had already rigged a tactical assault ladder—carbon fiber rods inside webbing. Lightweight as hell, strong enough to hold all of us and then some. Hooked fast and firm over the stone railing with its self-locking clips and tensioned loops. No creaks. No clangs. Just a silent black ribbon leading down into the dark.

Ninja went down first, one arm clutching the girl, the other working the rungs like he had done this a thousand times. He had. It wasn't the most graceful carry, but more often than not, battlefield extraction was more brute than ballet.

I waved the husband forward. "Move it. Now. Don't freeze on me."

He looked down and hesitated.

"No time for vertigo, pal. You want your wife and kid alive, get your ass moving."

He got the point and obediently followed—clumsy, fumbling, but fear did wonders for speed. Ninja had already laid the girl on the ground and was waiting below with arms raised just in case the guy slipped.

Then I swung the woman across my shoulder, adjusted her weight, and started my descent. Yeah, we could have used harnesses, ropes, or even a fireman's grip if we had time, but we didn't. Speed was life right now, and shoulder carry was the fastest. Not graceful, but gravity did half the work. Fast descent. Smooth enough landing.

We left the ladder rigged—plan was to come back this way and re-enter the villa. Same way we had left. Same angle. Clean kill lane.

We moved in a crouch to the tree line, weaving through brush and rocks till we reached the spot—pine grove behind the red-tanked generator. Maddix was already there, crouched behind a tree with an MP7 slung across his chest, sidearm drawn low. When he saw us, he slid the pistol back into his leg holster and stood waiting.

Big guy. Damn near Raptor's size—built like someone crossed a battering ram with a Marine recruiting poster. Just a flicker of a thought that crossed my mind. No time to admire the symmetry of warfighters.

But I did clock the tightness in his movement, the slight hitch in his shoulder as he slung the MP7 back. Hurt. Not down, but limping through it.

We clasped hands in a firm shake.

"Maddix."

"Cowboy."

That was it. No room for poetry. You don't waste words when the enemy's got a stopwatch.

Then I saw them—Raptor and Hawkeye walking out from the trees nearby, flanking three more survivors. A husband and wife, both mid-thirties, and a little boy maybe ten. Pale, wide-eyed, breathing hard. But breathing.

That made six rescued now—plus the four Maddix had tucked in the safe room earlier.

Ten civilians. Ten lives. Not bad for a warm up.

I nodded at the group. "You're taking these six, plus the four in the safe room. Move fast and quiet to the clump of cedar trees beside the east side gate—the one near the cracked stone wall. Ridley's waiting there. We'll call you when the exfil's hot."

Maddix didn't blink. Just said, "Copy."

I shifted the woman toward him. "She's coming to, but still woozy. You carry her—her husband's still in shock, barely upright."

He took her like she was a gym towel. Guy was built like a damn rescue crane. Slung her over his shoulder with one hand and turned to move.

I gave him the last bit. "Clock's ticking. Two left to save, ten minutes to deadline."

Maddix gave a final nod and moved out with the hostages, disappearing into the trees like a slow-moving tank with cargo.

I turned to the team.

"This is it. Final push. We've got two left to pull before the clock hits zero. All hits go simultaneous. Maximum confusion, total chaos. Calhoun's on overwatch—ex-Brit Army, Pathfinder Platoon sniper. He'll start dropping targets outside the moment we breach. Ali and Youssef take out the truck with the second PK. Copy?"

Fist bumps all around. Hard eyes. No fear.

I glanced at my watch. **2350 hours. Ten minutes to zero hour.**

Somewhere inside that house, two people were about to die unless we carved our way through hell to stop it.

CHAPTER 30

I keyed my mic as Ninja and I moved in the shadows beneath the villas, sticking close to the outer wall of Villa 4. The tactical ladder we had left hanging from the second-floor balcony was still there, barely visible in the moonlight.

"Echo, Cowboy," I murmured. "Send the grid on that second truck with the PK to Ali. Tell him to position for cutoff—he'll have a shot when that thing charges toward us once we light this place up."

"Copy that," Echo came back, voice crisp in my ear. "Sending now."

Ninja grabbed the first rung and started climbing. I followed, boots finding each carbon-reinforced step. It flexed but didn't give—the ladder was light as hell, but strong enough to carry a goddamn horse if we needed it to. We cleared the rail in seconds and slid over the balcony like ghosts.

We passed through the empty bedroom to the upper landing and crouched low. Ornate wooden balusters lined the curved rail—real antique finish, probably a luxury villa before AQ turned it into a slaughterhouse. Below us, a spiral staircase wound down to the ground floor. I held up a hand. Ninja froze beside me.

Seven tangos.

Seven AQ boys were down there, clustered in their little execution theatre. The guy hostage had been moved. Now he was kneeling dead center in front of the black flag tacked to the wall like some sick theatrical backdrop. Hood still on. Three gunmen stood behind him—AKs up. Center guy wore a chest rig with a big-ass blade in a sheath so visible it might as well have had neon lights.

Ninja leaned in close. "That one with the knife's feeling real tough and macho."

I didn't miss a beat. "Might be the last thing he ever feels."

The hostage couldn't see a damn thing with that hood on, but his body knew. He was trembling so hard it looked like he was seizing. Almost tipped sideways once. One of the gunmen grabbed his collar and yanked him upright like a prop in a puppet show. Didn't want the star to fall over before the curtain rose.

Center of the room, a laptop was set up on a plastic table. Camera lens aimed at the flag—and the poor bastard kneeling in front of it. Some twitchy tech-type was bent over the keyboard, checking angles, adjusting lighting. Probably streaming this crap live to some encrypted server in some godforsaken hole. Another guy stood beside him like some low-rent producer.

Ninja whispered, voice low and tight, "They're setting up for a snuff video."

No argument from me.

In the far corner, the woman was still kneeling. Hooded, bound, trembling worse than the man. I couldn't see her face, but I didn't need to. Her body was jerking in fits, pure terror racking her bones.

By the main door, two more AQ goons lounged against the wall with rifles slung low, watching the scene like it was their version of pay-per-view. Smirking, shifting feet. Savages warming up for the bloodsport. Probably placing bets on how fast the guy would bleed out.

We couldn't see what was directly under us—angle was too tight—but we knew better than to assume it was clear. Might be more scumbags under the landing watching the stairs. But we didn't have time to sweep. The longer we waited, the closer that knife got to the hostage's throat.

I tapped my radio again.

"Ali, Cowboy. You in position for that truck?"

Ali came back calm and steady. "Affirmative. We are set between their location and the villas. They move—we shred them."

"Good. Stay cold. You'll hear the fireworks in about a minute."

Next, I switched channels.

"Calhoun, Cowboy. Eyes on?"

"Affirmative," he replied. "Five tangos in front of Villa Four. Five at Two."

"Alright. Villa 4 first. Do a silent fifteen count, then drop as many as you can. Move sights to Villa 2 after that. You copy?"

"Solid copy. Good hunting. Starting countdown... now."

I looked at Ninja. "Time to ruin their show."

He didn't say a word—just nodded and pulled a flashbang from the rig on his hip, placed it beside him like a priest setting down a Bible before a sermon. One meant to send these bastards to hell, not save them.

Then we both brought our HK416s to shoulder and leaned forward over the railing just enough to get eyes on the living room.

"Cowboy, this is Calhoun," Calhoun's clipped British voice came in smooth through comms.

"Lined up. Green in five... four... three... two... one."

Pop—crack.

The suppressed shot from Calhoun's HK417 echoed like a dry cough across the villa row. That sound was the curtain call for the two sentries posted by the main entrance as Ninja opened up with two suppressed shots.

One round smacked the first guy dead in the face—his head snapped back and he collapsed against the doorframe. The second barely turned before Ninja's round punched through his neck. He twitched once and folded, blood misting the air behind him.

Clean.

Ninja dropped the rifle to his sling and snatched up the M84 flashbang. Pin out with a flick—he made it look like art.

Meanwhile, I wasn't wasting time. Sighted in on the three bastards behind the kneeling hostage.

Two smooth trigger pulls. First round punched through the sternum of the bearded jackass on the left—his body went rigid before tipping backward like a felled tree. Second guy caught the round in the mouth. Down he went in a gurgling heap.

The middle one—the one playing executioner, knife sheath swinging from his belt—must have had a sixth sense. He dove right as I fired. My shot grazed his upper arm, but it wasn't the kind of wound that put a man out of the fight.

I didn't have time for a follow-up shot. Ninja lobbed the flashbang down that very second.

Clink. Clack.

The flashbang hit tile and rolled like a coin before coming to a stop in the center of the room.

We ducked behind the thick wood of the balcony railing, turned our heads, eyes shut tight. We were ready. Our ballistic eyepro cut the worst of the flash. Our comms-integrated ear pro—Peltor ComTac IVs—automatically compressed the blast down to something survivable. Without them? That bang would have sounded like a freight train in our skulls and lit up our vision like the surface of the damn sun.

BOOM.

Light like God cracked open the world. The room below lit up like a magnesium flare. A wall of sound rolled through the villa and hit hard enough to rattle my molars. Plaster cracked. Furniture jumped.

The M84 delivered all 180 decibels of love—loud enough to make your ancestors flinch in their graves. Somewhere downstairs, a grown man screamed like a dying goat.

Most of the AQ scumbags dropped where they stood—blinded, deaf, confused. A few staggered, rifles forgotten, eyes blinking at ghosts that weren't there. One fired a blind, panicked shot into the wall. The camera guy and his tech buddy curled up under the damn table like a couple of interns during an office fire drill.

The two hostages—hooded, scared out of their minds—got a little mercy. The cloth dulled the flash for their eyes. But the sound? That was another story. Their ears would be ringing for days, if not bleeding. But they were alive. And if they managed to stay that way through the next five minutes, they would just need therapy. Not surgery.

And now, it was time to clean up.

CHAPTER 31

We came off that landing like wolves let loose. Boots pounding the spiral staircase, rifles up, barrels slicing air.

I was first down the curve, sweeping the room through my optic. Ninja stayed on my six, smooth as a shadow, finger ready on the trigger.

The living room below was chaos—bodies staggering, dazed, trying to recover their senses in the fog of flashbang hell. That kind of sensory nuke fries your brain for a good minute or two.

Two gunmen who had been outside found their feet and their balls just in time to rush back in through the front door. Bad call. Ninja dropped them both before they cleared the threshold—two suppressed shots that hit like punctuation marks. One crumpled forward into the tiles, the other hit the wall behind him and slid down like a busted scarecrow.

Ninja broke right toward the kneeling woman, moving fast and low. He holstered the sidearm he had drawn mid-sprint and yanked her up with one hand while his rifle covered the door with the other.

I pushed forward toward the black flag and the poor man still kneeling there, his hood shaking like he was stuck in a seizure.

The bastard with the knife—executioner-boy—was behind the kneeling man, squinting through the burn in his retinas, reaching out like a blind man. Flashbanged, half-blind, he still had the instinct to finish the job. Knife in one hand, the other grabbing for his victim's hood like he was trying to drag him back to hell.

Maybe he was committed to the cause. Or more likely, he was just a psychopathic freak who didn't like leaving work half-done.

Didn't matter.

I leveled my rifle and punched a round through his head. Top of the bridge, just above the nose. Skull cracked like a melon and he went down behind the hostage like a dropped puppet, dead before gravity caught up.

No hesitation. No mercy. Not for scum.

"Ninja, stash them!" I barked. "Store room, back wall!"

"Copy."

Ninja moved, pulling the woman along with one arm while covering the open front with the other. I grabbed the hooded man, yanked the sack off his head—young, mid-thirties, soaked in sweat and damn near catatonic—and hauled him upright with one hand, rifle steady in the other. No time to play therapist.

"Move," I told him, and pushed him along toward the store room at the rear of the living room.

We were halfway there when movement flared in the kitchen doorway. I caught it with the edge of my eye. A muzzle rise. Instinct kicked in.

I shoved the hostage forward into the store room, twisted sideways and ducked in behind him. Rounds smacked tile and plaster. Some hit me—three or four impacts along the front plate of my vest. Didn't punch through, but felt like getting slammed in the chest with a sledgehammer.

Angled hits—glanced off, but the jolt knocked the air out of me. I grunted and stumbled sideways, dazed.

Ninja's return fire was immediate—two short bursts that turned the shooter into meat paste against the doorway.

I was still staggering back into the store room, trying to catch my breath, when something moved in the shadows to my left.

Another one. Close.

He came at me from behind a stack of boxes with a blade, fast and low, arms tight like he knew what he was doing. I caught the shimmer of the blade an instant before he struck and pivoted. Jammed the stock of my rifle into his arm, driving the blade wide. He snarled—young, fast, strong—but he wasn't trained.

I crushed his knee sideways with a brutal stomp. Something gave with a sharp crack, and he screamed through clenched teeth as he dropped.

But he wasn't done.

He clawed at my vest with one hand and swung the knife with the other. I caught his wrist, twisted hard—metal clattered to the floor—and we went down in a tangle of limbs and rage.

I let him get a taste of the fight, then pulled my knife from its sheath.

The blade slid home under his ribcage, angled up.

His breath caught. Just once.

Then nothing.

I shoved him off and stood, panting, blood on my gloves, heartbeat trying to punch out through my chest.

The room went still again, except for the wheezing hostage and the fading echo of boots outside. Ninja appeared a second later, rifle up, ready to end any threat still breathing.

"You good, Cowboy?" he asked, voice even.

"Yeah," I muttered, wiping the blade on the dead man's shirt.

It was best to leave the two hostages in the storeroom, out of any direct threat of their being caught in a crossfire. They were still shell-shocked—ears ringing like an artillery bell tower, heads low, breathing hard. That flashbang had scrambled their hearing, but the hoods had spared them from the worst of the blinding light. Their eyesight was back. Terror still etched deep in their faces.

Ninja knelt by the woman, gave her a calm palm-down hand signal—*stay down, stay safe*. I did the same to the man, then pointed to the room floor, tapped twice—*wait here*. Their eyes tracked us, blinking, rattled, but they nodded. Survivors.

We eased the door shut behind us.

Back in the hallway, I swept right, rifle high. Ninja mirrored left.

Then we heard them—two long, violent bursts from a PK machine gun. Deep, guttural, like a buzzsaw chewing through steel. That thing didn't talk—it roared. Belt-fed, 7.62x54mmR Soviet dinosaur, iron sights, ugly as hell but meaner than sin. Hundred-round box on the side. Sounded like it spat at least forty rounds in the two bursts.

I glanced at Ninja.

"That'll be Ali and Youssef lighting up the second truck," I said.

Ninja gave me a sideways grin. "That must feel good—letting AQ chew on their own damn ammo."

Two seconds later, Ali's voice crackled in our comms.

"Second PK position eliminated. All gunmen killed. No survivors."

"Copy," I said. "Good work. Take control of the entrance gate. It's still under AQ guard. Last thing we need is a QRF storming into the Quarter and flanking us from behind."

"Moving now."

I looked over at Ninja. "Hold security at the main entrance. Full coverage, tight arc. Light up anything that doesn't look like us. I'll go check the rooftop."

He nodded. "Roger. Setting up on the front, weapons tight."

My real reason for heading to the rooftop was partly tactical, but it was more for Calhoun.

He had told me what they did to the two guards—hung them from the terrace rail like meat. Said he knew them. Said they were solid. The kind of men who didn't fold under pressure, didn't quit when things got loud.

And the sound of his voice when he said it... that hit different. That tight-jawed, soul-cutting fury you only get when someone kills your brothers dirty.

I knew that weight. I had carried it more times than I cared to count. You work with someone, bleed next to them, and then some scumbag parades their body like a trophy? That sticks with you. Sticks in your gut like a blade.

So I was going to take them down. Let them rest right.

I moved fast and quiet through the house, rifle ready, safety off, scanning each shadow like it owed me money. Up the staircase I went toward the second floor, and hit the next set of stairs that led to the rooftop terrace. On the landing, I paused, back to the wall by the terrace door. Couldn't assume it was clear. We had missed enough tricks in this place already.

That's when Raptor came in on comms.

"Villa Two is clear. Tangos inside and out are down. No further movement."

"Roger that," I said. "Shift over to Villa Four. Secure Ninja's position. He's holding the main breach. Keep the perimeter locked down."

"Copy. Moving."

I scanned the light switch panel just inside the threshold and flipped on the terrace floodlights. White light flooded the rooftop—harsh halogens mounted high on the villa's roof corners. Anyone hiding up there just got flashbanged by reality.

I spun out, fast and low, rifle up in a tight shoulder pocket, muzzle slicing air.

Clear right. Sweep left. Then—

Two gunmen near the front edge of the terrace. One crouched, one standing, both turned away from me. They were posted up watching the villa perimeter, rifles loose, fingers near triggers, trying to make sense of the mayhem going on down there.

They flinched when the lights hit—blinded, too slow to react, still adjusting, barrels wavering.

Two quick suppressed bursts—four rounds, center mass. Both dropped where they stood, rifles clattering across the stone tiles.

I moved up, slicing the angles, clearing the left flank, muzzle tracking every shadow. Roof behind the water tanks—clear. Solar panel racks—clear. Small utility room—clear.

Terrace secured. I walked back to the door and killed the terrace lights.

Didn't want to end up a silhouette with a bullseye stitched across my chest. No telling which rooftop might be hiding a lone AQ asshole with a scope and a grudge.

I crossed the roof, boots scuffing across the concrete, and made my way to the two bodies hanging from the terrace railing. Heads down, boots swaying slightly in the breeze. Ropes tied tight, necks broken clean. AQ had strung them up like trophies— their twisted idea of psychological warfare. Hang enemy fighters out in plain view, let fear do the rest.

Not on my watch. Time to bring them down. Let them rest with dignity.

"Not leaving you like this," I muttered, and pulled out my blade.

I grabbed the first man by his vest, lifted him up to slack the rope, then cut him loose. I eased him down like he was still breathing. Did the same with the second. Laid them both side by side, flat on their backs, hands on their chests. Quiet. Dignified.

Soldiers. They earned that, at the bare minimum.

That's when Calhoun's voice crackled in my ear. His voice was tight, but there was a pulse behind it.

"Cheers for that, Cowboy. Didn't think I'd see them down with a bit of dignity."

I paused, hand still on one man's vest. "I know how it feels. You fought with them?"

"Aye. Both of them. We shared rations and rounds more than once. Wasn't right, the way they went. You did right."

"I've lost brothers, too. You don't leave your own strung up like meat. Just following the code."

"Damn right," Calhoun replied. "You fight for the living, but you honor the dead. That's how we roll."

I looked out toward the edge of the roof. The city was dark again. Tense. Waiting.

"Hold your position, Calhoun. You've got the highest perch in this whole sector. Eyes on that front gate. You see a fly twitch in the dark, I wanna hear about it before its wings finish flapping."

"Understood. Eyes sharp."

I checked my watch. **2358 hours. Two minutes to zero hour.**

The silence felt unnatural now. Like the city was holding its breath. We had pulled the plug on the macabre circus AQ had set up, but this was just the warm-up act. *Midnight Scimitar* was coming—their grand finale of blood and flame. And we were standing right in the middle of the stage.

It was going to be a long night.

CHAPTER 32

The hostages were safe. For now.

But I knew better than to get sentimental. We were still deep in the belly of this beast. The streets outside were a maze of shifting loyalties, blockades, and angry men with old Soviet rifles and fresh grudges. It was a boiling stew of half-baked militias, AQ fighters, and whatever psychos crawled out after midnight looking to settle tribal scores with an AK and a Molotov. We would have to snake through that madness before we even sniffed the safety of the U.S. embassy compound.

And hell—even the embassy wasn't a sure bet anymore. *Midnight Scimitar* had that on their hit list too. If this city tipped fully into chaos and the Yemeni government folded like wet cardboard, no compound, no wall, no flag would protect us. Not for long.

But that was tomorrow's fire. First thing was getting the hell out of that villa before someone dropped mortars on it.

I came down from the terrace, boots slow and quiet on the stairs. The smell of gunpowder still hung thick in the air, laced with the tang of blood and heat.

Just as my boots hit the top-floor landing, Ali came over comms. "Cowboy, we've got control of the main gate. And saved one of the guards AQ had captured. He's hurt but will live."

"Solid copy. Good work."

"But there's movement outside—foot mobiles and three trucks hanging around about two blocks out. They've got eyes on the gate. Looks like they're expecting it to open."

I checked my watch. Zero hundred hours. Midnight. Witching hour.

"Yeah," I muttered. "They're waiting for the horror show to kick off. Must think the big bloodbath's about to roll out from here. Midnight Scimitar's opening act. Stay put, Ali. Eyes on that crew. I want to know the second anything moves."

"Copy that, Cowboy. Holding."

I linked up with the team downstairs. Ninja, Raptor, and Hawkeye. All three looked like they had been through hell and back, but none of them looked ready to quit.

We had a problem. We had 21 souls that needed exfil—me and the three operators, Ali, Youssef, Calhoun, Maddix, Ridley... and twelve terrified civilians, most still dazed. Two SUVs weren't going to cut it.

And with the city tightening like a noose, we didn't have the luxury of second trips.

I laid it out straight. "Alright, gents. We stay longer than ten minutes, we're inviting inbound fire. We've got 21 warm bodies to move and two SUVs sitting outside the side gate. We're short on wheels, and we sure as shit aren't calling for an Uber."

"Don't they do flying carpets around here?" Ninja asked, looking all serious.

"I think you need to book in advance. They don't have an App yet. Any other bright ideas?"

"Alright, then what about those two AQ pickups? The ones we ventilated earlier. Any AQ we bump into might think we're one of their own."

I nodded. "That's what I'm thinking. They're beat to hell, but they've got PKs mounted, and they look like they belong. That might just buy us a few seconds of confusion if we roll past an AQ checkpoint. At least long enough to get clear. If they figure us out mid-transit, we've got firepower up top to punch through."

Raptor added, "We can load civilians into the SUVs and operators into the pickups. Keep firepower forward and rear."

"Good. That's the stack," I said. "Ninja, haul ass and get the second truck. It's parked where Ali and Youssef served hot lead to the last batch of idiots. Bring it back here, fast and tight."

Ninja grinned. "Be back before you guys miss me."

"Doubtful," Hawkeye muttered. "We like the peace and quiet."

As Ninja jogged away, I was about to nod at Raptor and tell him to grab the two rescued civvies from the storeroom. But then I took a look at Raptor and stopped myself.

The man was a six-four, 250-pound war machine, face painted up like a Halloween nightmare, and built like he had been raised on a diet of steel and rocks. The two hostages we pulled out earlier had already been through enough. Having a guy like Raptor walk in on them in the dark might send them straight to cardiac arrest.

So I sighed and patted Raptor's shoulder. "Hold the line here. You and Hawkeye stay sharp. I'll get the civvies."

He gave a quick nod. No argument.

I moved inside, cutting across the foyer. The villa was dark, still smelled like blood and cordite. I keyed my comms as I walked.

First, I pinged Calhoun. "Calhoun, time to move. Pack up, head for the side gate. We're rolling soon."

He came back quick, voice still carrying that stiff British calm. "Acknowledged. I'll be there shortly."

Next, I hit Ridley. "Ridley, you copy?"

"Go ahead."

"Calhoun's on his way. He'll link up with you in two minutes."

"Copy that."

"You move all civilians through the side gate. Assemble them near the two SUVs, the ones parked by the bakery wall."

"Already prepped. Soon as he's with us, we're gone."

"Keep it quiet. No hero shit."

"Roger that."

I reached the storeroom and opened the door slowly. The two inside—both looking like geeky twenty-five-year olds—flinched hard at the creak. They looked like ghosts. Eyes sunken. Nerves fried.

"Easy," I said low, not stepping in too fast. "You're safe. We're getting you out now. Just stick with me."

They nodded like bobbleheads, too shocked to speak. I guided them out gently.

I led them out, keeping them tight between me and the wall. Back in the courtyard, Ninja pulled in just in time—driving the second AQ truck we had jacked earlier. A rundown Toyota Hilux with a

PKM mounted like a mechanical vulture in the bed. Lights off, engine low. Mean as hell.

We loaded up fast. Me, Ninja, Raptor, Hawkeye, and the two rescued civvies. We crept toward the front gate, engines purring low, every man scanning the shadows.

I raised my binos. A hundred meters out from the main gate, we saw them.

Three trucks. Dozens of AQ fighters, clustered like ants on a carcass. AKs slung loose, some holding radios, one with a grenade launcher. Each one of them looked twitchy, ready to let loose at a moment's notice. Two of their trucks were dead ringers for the ones we had captured—same models, same PK mounts. Tension thick enough to carve with a Ka-Bar.

I could see it in their posture—they were ready for violence. They just didn't know which direction it was coming from yet.

Ninja leaned toward me, voice dry. "Boss, you left out a tiny detail earlier."

"Yeah?" I kept scanning.

"Yeah. That part about us having to literally shove through a gathering of pissed-off AQ trucks at the front gate. Kinda important, don't you think?"

I smirked. "Maybe you should brush up on your situational awareness, Ninja. There's only one way in or out of here wide enough for a truck. Where'd you think we were going, the roof?"

He muttered, "Told you we should've booked that flying carpet when we had the chance."

Raptor chuckled from the back. "Flying carpets don't come with PKs and RPGs. These do."

"Right," Ninja shot back. "Because nothing says 'covert exfil' like blowing up half a city block."

"Buckle up," I said. "We're not sneaking out of this one. We're kicking down the damn front door."

Hawkeye added, deadpan, "Can't wait for the Yelp review."

I took one last look at the enemy line. Fingers twitching on triggers. Restless, like jackals sniffing blood.

And us, riding two of their own war wagons, about to punch through like a battering ram with a bad attitude.

No time for finesse now.

They wanted a show?

Fine.

We would give them one. Curtains up.

CHAPTER 33

Raptor and Hawkeye took position in the shadows on either side of the main gate. Each had an RPG slung low, fingers already finding the grips like they had been born holding them. I watched them get into position, backs against the wall, calm as surgeons before a cut.

I raised two fingers to Ali, then dropped them.

He hit the switch inside the guardroom. A low mechanical hum rumbled up from under the earth.

The bollards—fat steel pistons designed to stop a ramming truck dead—started to sink into the ground. Inch by inch. Every second dragged like wet rope.

Outside the gate, the AQ fighters were getting twitchy. Cigarettes flicked away. Rifle butts adjusted. They could hear the machinery too. Could feel the tempo changing. Like animals sensing the coming quake.

They knew something was coming.

They just didn't know it was death.

I glanced up at the moon. Pale, bloated. Midnight had passed. This was zero hour.

As soon as the last bollard sank into its housing, I signaled Ali again.

The heavy steel gates shuddered, then started to part.

Steel hinges groaned. Not fast, not clean—just heavy and deliberate, dragging tension behind them like a predator dragging a corpse.

Out front, I saw heads turning. Necks craning. Figures backing up a step. One of the AQ trucks flashed its headlights twice—some kind of signal, maybe an all-clear.

From their angle, all they saw was two of their own pickups inside, both lined up neatly. Familiar silhouettes. Friendly vehicles.

Good. The bait was set.

Ali and Youssef stepped out of the guardroom, casual as locals heading to the corner store. Ali even gave a sharp chin nod and a quick tap to his chest, the way locals greeted fighters. Youssef did the same. They moved toward the trucks like it was all routine.

Right then, I saw Raptor shift his stance.

He braced against the wall, lifted the RPG tube to his shoulder. Breathed out. Locked in.

Hawkeye mirrored him on the opposite flank, perfectly in sync. Both aimed for the AQ trucks with PKs mounted—our biggest threat if we rolled out into that crowd. Take those out, we punch the enemy's teeth down their throat.

I heard Hawkeye's dry whisper. "Targets locked."

"Send it," I murmured.

FWUMP. FWUMP.

Twin launches. The RPGs flew like screaming banshees, fire trailing their fins. Time slowed. The warheads screamed across the short distance, arcing just slightly.

WHAM.

First warhead detonated mid-engine, flipping the target truck into the air in a ball of flame and twisted metal. Tires launched skyward. The gunner disintegrated—one second there, the next gone like dust in the wind.

BOOM.

The second rocket struck just behind the cab, hitting the ammo cans. The blast carved the truck open like a tin of beans. The PK flew in a smoking arc and came down spinning like a sawblade.

The whole area outside dissolved into hell.

Gunmen scattered, shouting over each other in Arabic. Some dove for cover. Others stood frozen, stunned. A few raised rifles and just started spraying blindly.

Then Ninja went full savage.

He opened up with the PKM mounted in the back of our truck—full auto, belt-fed hate. The muzzle flashed like a strobe, and the sound punched the air like a jackhammer in a war zone.

The rounds tore out like a buzzsaw in hell—*thwack-thwack-thwack*—ripping into the chaos.

A line of fighters tried to scatter left. Ninja raked across them like he was mowing dry grass. One got spun clean off his feet, blood spraying in an arc. Another got stitched from hip to throat—his chest opened up and he collapsed face first, twitching.

The truck that hadn't been hit yet caught a full burst across the grill. The engine coughed once, then seized up in a puff of black smoke and steam. Ninja adjusted and walked the rounds up across the hood—shattering the windshield, vaporizing the gunner who had tried to climb in.

It was carnage—bodies falling, fighters screaming, some throwing their weapons and running.

I stood behind the blast shield in our truck's passenger side, hand on my carbine, teeth clenched.

"Time to leave!" I bellowed.

Everyone moved at once.

Ali and Youssef dove into their trucks. Raptor and Hawkeye leapt into the back bed of ours, RPGs slung, rifles up. I jumped into the passenger seat and slapped the dash.

"Go!"

The tires screeched as we surged forward. Burnt rubber and diesel fumes filled my nose. We plowed out the gate, past the mangled remains of the AQ trucks, the gunmen still reeling. We tore through the smoke-choked courtyard, rubber screaming, fire reflecting off shattered glass.

I looked out the window. One of them tried to aim something—probably an old Type-56. Didn't matter. Hawkeye tagged him before he could blink.

We swung left hard, wheels skipping over the curb, then gunned it down a narrow side street. Headlights off. Engine snarling like wolves off the leash. Our second truck followed tight behind, keeping formation like a loyal dog in a street fight.

We tore around the final corner and hit the back side of the Quarter—our rendezvous point.

There they were. Ridley, Calhoun, Maddix, the rescued civilians, and the rest of the team. Packed tight near the two SUVs, looking like ghosts under the low streetlights. Engines already idling. Doors open. Ready to roll.

The cavalry had arrived.

Time to load up and get the hell out before the city burned down around us.

CHAPTER 34

We soon rolled out from behind the Quarter like a blunt instrument—four vehicles deep, moving tight and deliberate.

I was in the lead truck, riding shotgun, my rifle across my lap, eyes scanning the road ahead. Ali was my wheelman. Ninja stood in the back like a sentinel from hell, his gloved hands gripping the handles of the PKM, face paint cracked with sweat and soot, eyes burning.

Right behind us were the two SUVs. Packed tight with civilians and Ridley's crew. Youssef drove the second vehicle with Ridley riding passenger, eyes on everything. Calhoun took the wheel in the third SUV. His sleeves were rolled up, sweat on his brow, shotgun laid between the seats like a friendly reminder.

Hawkeye brought up the rear in the second PKM-mounted truck. Raptor manned the gun, helmet low over his brow, scanning rooftops with that dead-serious stillness that meant he was already planning who to shoot first if things went loud.

We rolled out from behind the Quarter like we were kicking down the door of hell. The convoy took a right down a narrow alley littered with broken pallets and a half-burned trash bin. We popped out onto one of the main roads leading east.

That's when I got a proper look at Sana'a—and it wasn't pretty. The streets greeted us with fire and trash and the smell of smoke-thick despair.

The city looked like it was starting to rot from the inside out. Smoke drifted across the rooftops in oily tendrils, rising from fires that no one seemed to be putting out. I saw burned tires stacked at intersections like makeshift barricades, their flames licking the night sky.

Some roads were lit by flickering bulbs strung up on half-collapsed power lines. Others were black as a tomb. Electricity flickered from time to time—here a buzzing streetlight, there a neon sign still pulsing over a shuttered shop.

The city was in pre-collapse mode—no rule of law, no chain of command, no real government presence. Just pockets of armed militias holding turf with blood and bravado.

Armed groups roamed in twos and threes—some with rifles slung across their backs, others dragging them lazily like bored executioners. Half were probably stoned out of their minds. The other half were waiting for someone to shoot so they could justify lighting up the block.

Gunmen stood on corners like self-appointed gatekeepers. Teenagers with chrome pistols tucked into basketball shorts. Men in sandals and AKs resting on their shoulders like garden tools. They watched us like wolves—unsure if they should bark, bite, or run.

I scanned every corner, every alley. Ninja swiveled slowly with the PKM, the belt fed, the lid clamped. No idle chatter. He was in the zone.

Then we hit a bottleneck.

A group of six gunmen had set up shop in the middle of the road. Scarves wrapped around their faces, AKs held loose but ready. One of them stepped forward, arms out, like a traffic cop in a bad dream. Another popped a few rounds into the air—more for show than anything, but still enough to make the tension spike.

Ali slowed the truck, not stopping, but rolling in like a slow-moving battering ram.

"Careful," I muttered, my eyes on the lead man. He looked like a wannabe field commander—no plate carrier, just a *shemagh*, ammo vest, and a half-wild look in his eye. Probably hadn't slept in days. Probably hadn't showered for longer.

Behind me, I heard the soft metal creak of Ninja shifting position. He didn't say a word—just swung the PKM forward, zeroing in on the center man like a hawk locking on prey.

The effect was instant. You could feel the energy shift.

The lead gunman froze. His swagger evaporated. I saw it—the flicker of second thoughts behind his eyes.

One guy at the edge took a step back. Another lowered his rifle just slightly. They didn't know what to do—run, shoot, pray?

That big black PKM might as well have been the Grim Reaper's scythe.

The leader turned to his buddies, said something fast. The guy who had fired in the air lowered his rifle. Each guy backed up a few steps. Ninja didn't move, didn't blink. Just held that PKM center-line, the barrel aimed square at their nervous hearts.

Ali kept the truck rolling. Not fast—just steady. Enough to make it clear we weren't stopping, and if they didn't want to become organ donors, they would better move.

We rolled right through, forcing them to step aside. One slapped the back of the truck weakly as we passed. Ninja didn't flinch. Just tracked them with the muzzle until they were behind us.

Ali gave a low chuckle. "Bunch of tough guys till the PKM winks at them. Should've handed them a white flag and a diaper."

I let out a grunt. "City's unraveling, man. That right there was a checkpoint yesterday. Now it's just six dumbasses trying to feel important."

I glanced around again as we pushed on—rolling into the belly of the beast, steel and sweat and just enough ammo to make it count.

Fires burned to our left—maybe a gas station, maybe just someone's shop that caught a Molotov. Smoke curled skyward. You couldn't tell what was destroyed by airstrikes and what was just part of daily life now. This place had been through civil war, tribal war, and now AQ wanted a piece of it.

This city... it was coming apart at the seams. The Yemeni government was losing its grip one block at a time. Too many warlords, too many agendas, too many AKs in untrained hands.

I glanced in the side mirror. Still tight formation. Hawkeye's headlights bobbed behind us like steady ghosts.

The embassy might hold for now. High walls. Marines. Armored gates. Enough firepower to make a rebel cell think twice.

But after what we saw at the Quarter? The dozens of AQ fighters, the hardware, the coordination?

That wasn't some ragtag militia with pickup trucks and a prayer. That was a trained, armed, and funded op with intent.

The embassy wouldn't hold forever. It was only a matter of time before the whole city buckled, and the walls came down. I wasn't sure how long the stars and stripes would still be flying over that embassy compound.

I gritted my teeth. One problem at a time.

We cleared the chaos and took a hard left around a blown-out pharmacy. Tires squealed. We aligned again.

And then we saw it—the final stretch.

About a mile of broken asphalt, potholes, and twisted street signs. At the far end, tucked behind concrete blast walls and a ring of Hesco barriers, loomed the U.S. Embassy compound—dull beige, ugly as hell, but right then the safest square footage in the whole damn country.

The American flag still flew at the top. Bent slightly in the wind. But still there.

I keyed the mic on my tac vest. "Last leg. Stay tight, eyes peeled. If anything moves, we light it up."

Raptor came on comms. "Copy that. Let's put this baby to bed."

CHAPTER 35

As we got on that final stretch, that's when it hit me. I needed to call this in. Immediately.

Marines at that gate weren't going to see a friendly convoy—they were going to see two AQ-style gun trucks barreling toward a U.S. compound with pintle-mounted PK machine guns and a column of unmarked vehicles.

Twitchy fingers. Hair triggers. Too damn much could go sideways.

I flipped to comms. Called Caroline.

"Cowboy to Caroline. Come in."

Caroline's voice came back clear and direct. "Go ahead, Cowboy."

I had already updated her when we left the Quarter—hostages safe, minimal injuries, mission success—but this was a different kind of heads-up.

"We're thirty seconds out. It's a four-vehicle convoy. Two technicals with mounted PKs—that's us. SUVs in the middle, full of civilians and agency personnel. We're going to look like a hostile convoy. You better warn the Marines at the Embassy gates not to light us up."

"Consider it done," she replied. "I'm near the gates. Marines have your description and they're standing by to verify. I'll update them about the trucks."

I let out a breath. Not relief—just one less thing that might kill us. But then the other part of her message hit me.

"What do you mean you're near the gates? Are you at the Embassy?"

"Affirmative. We've already pulled out of the safe house. My team and Atwood are at the embassy. We're consolidating. Minimizing targets. One stronghold, not five."

Made sense.

I nodded, even though she couldn't see me. "Good call. Better to have one Alamo than a dozen Benghazis."

Truth was, I had already been thinking the same. After what we saw at the Quarter—well-armed AQ cells converging with speed and discipline—they weren't just probing anymore. They were moving pieces on a board. Planning something ugly. And we were the prize on the table.

If AQ had lookouts in the neighborhoods—and I would bet my rifle they did—then any convoy with Western faces or armored SUVs would light up their comms like a Christmas tree. Too many locations to defend, and not enough shooters to defend them. We couldn't afford to play zone defense. Best option was to consolidate all friendlies, all firepower, behind the thickest walls we had left.

Bringing everyone under one roof was the right call. Even if that roof was about to take a pounding.

"Copy all," I told her. "See you in sixty."

I killed the call and looked out the windshield. Ali kept us steady. His hands were tight on the wheel, eyes flicking from mirror to mirror. Behind us, the two SUVs with Ridley and the civvies hugged our six, and Hawkeye's truck kept the rear end locked down like a tail gunner in a bomber run.

The American flag came into view first. Then the walls. No frills. Tall, blast-resistant concrete. Squatting behind two layers of T-wall barricades and sandbagged firing positions. The front gate was a steel monster, painted tan, with anti-ram barriers laid out like iron fangs.

The truck's tires crunched gravel. We slowed as the gate guards raised a hand.

Two Marines stepped out from behind the sandbags, rifles ready. Kevlar, Oakleys, desert boots. One had an M249 SAW light machine gun across his chest. The other had that unmistakable *who-the-hell-are-you* stance, his M4 raised just enough to keep you honest.

They looked us over hard, but only for a second. I leaned out the passenger window.

"Captain Blaze. We've got rescued hostages, friendlies, and wounded. Clearance from Caroline Maddox."

The lead Marine gave a quick nod. "Roger that. You're cleared. Hold one."

He stepped back and waved his partner to the gate control.

The gate clanked and hissed as hydraulics brought it to life. The thick steel slabs groaned open like a vault door cracking in slow motion. Behind us, the rest of the convoy kept tight. The two SUVs, the second truck, all rolled past the barriers and into American soil—or as close as you could get to it in Yemen.

We pulled into the overground parking area—barebones but fortified. Spotlights overhead, camera domes watching from corners. Not exactly

Baghdad Green Zone, but it beat the hell out of the furnace we had just come from. The lot had space for maybe a dozen vehicles, but right then it felt like a damn airfield.

We rolled to a stop—four vehicles cooling down like beasts that had just sprinted through hell. Engines ticking, metal hissing from heat. The stink of spent gunpowder and diesel still hung in the air.

I hopped out, boots hitting the concrete with a thud that echoed off the walls. Dust, blood, and sweat clung to me like a second skin. But the first breath of non-smoke-filled air hit my lungs like a shot of bourbon.

I took a look back—convoy intact. Nobody missing. Nobody dead.

That counted for a lot.

Caroline was already coming out the side doors, moving fast. Tactical pants, sleeves rolled, Glock on her hip and hair pulled back so tight it looked like she was about to brief the Joint Chiefs. Eyes sharp, steps deliberate.

There was a flicker in her eyes when she saw me—just a pause, a microsecond of relief or something like it. She stopped a few feet away.

"You're late," she said in mock seriousness.

I gave her a dry look. "Traffic was murder."

A small smile tugged at the corner of her mouth. She looked like she hadn't slept in days—but then again, neither had I.

"How many wounded?" she asked, stepping closer.

"Civilians are mostly shaken," I replied, pulling off my gloves. "Couple of cuts, one with a bullet graze—nothing critical. But Ridley and Maddix got cut up worse during CQB. You'll want your medics on them first."

She gave a quick nod, already scanning the convoy. "Triage is prepped inside. Second floor's clear for intake. The medic team's just coming out now."

And right on cue, four guys came sprinting out of the side doors—pushing carts loaded with trauma packs, I.V. kits, and stretchers. They moved like they had been rehearsing this for months.

Ridley was helped down first, though he tried his best to get out himself. Maddix was limping, favoring his left leg.

While the medics swarmed, I spotted Calhoun by the third SUV. He was standing tall but worn, sweat drying on his collar, eyes scanning the perimeter out of pure habit.

I held up a hand and walked over to them.

"Hell of a job," I told them, voice low and solid. "You boys held the line. Couldn't have asked for more."

Calhoun gave me a tight nod.

Ridley winced as a medic examined him but managed a grin. "Was good having Delta on our six for a change. Don't usually get that kind of backup."

"You earned it," I said. "You boys did real work out there."

I gave Ridley a firm shoulder tap and stepped back, watching as the medics guided them toward the inner corridor.

Then I turned and made my way back to Caroline.

She was watching the medics work, arms crossed but relaxed now that the chaos was under a roof and behind a gate.

"All three of them—they're solid. Did exactly what needed to be done, no hesitation," I told her.

"I've seen them operate," she said, voice quieter now. "They're damn good. Still... I can only imagine what it's like watching you and your team run the play. Controlled chaos?"

"Something like that." I shrugged. "We were lucky tonight. If we'd been five minutes later, those bastards would've lit the place up. They weren't there for a snatch and grab. They came loaded for a massacre."

She gave a short nod, her jaw tightening. "Zero civilian casualties. That's a damn good result."

"For now. But the embassy's not going to be a safe haven for long. AQ haven't thrown all their cards yet. This was just the opening volley."

"I know." Her voice dropped to a near whisper. "That's why we need to talk. You, me, and Atwood. Briefing room's ready."

She looked me over for a second. "You need a breather before we go in?"

"I'm good. Just tell me there's coffee in that briefing room."

"It's bad coffee," she replied, already turning toward the hallway. "But it'll kick you in the teeth if that's what you're after."

"Perfect. My system's too used to bad coffee. Wouldn't want to give it a shock with good brew in the middle of a warzone. Just want my boys to grab a bite as well."

Caroline pointed down the hallway past the access door. "Your guys can grab a bite in the embassy mess—first right after the checkpoint. Burgers, coffee, whatever's left. Not gourmet—but better than MREs."

"Everything's better than MREs," I muttered. "Thanks."

"I'll have something for you in the briefing room too," she said over her shoulder before disappearing inside.

I turned back and walked toward the trucks where my guys were peeling themselves out of the steel and dust, emerging one by one, shaking off the adrenaline dump like dogs drying off after a storm.

Hawkeye had parked himself on the tailgate, cleaning blood off his boots with a rag that used to be a T-shirt. Ninja was rolling out his shoulders like he had just gone twelve rounds with a bear. Raptor crouched nearby, shaking sand out of his helmet and cursing softly.

"Alright, war dogs," I said, stepping up. "Embassy mess is down the hall, first left. Burgers, caffeine, and maybe a soft chair if you ask nice. You've got fifteen. Then we go hot again."

Ninja looked at me like I just told him Santa was real. "Hot food *and* chairs? What's the catch?"

"No catch," I replied. "Just don't fall asleep chewing."

He still looked hopeful. "Any word on milkshakes?"

"Yeah," I said. "They're fresh out of sprinkles and fairy dust too."

Hawkeye chuckled. "Long as the coffee doesn't taste like axle grease, I'll consider it a win."

"I wouldn't get your hopes too high. All I can say is it'll be strong stuff. You want flavor, join the French Foreign Legion."

Raptor grunted. "If it ain't MRE chili mac, I'm in."

"Don't break the furniture," I said, nodding toward the embassy doors. "We're still guests here."

"Remember you're saying that to the human bulldozer," Ninja quipped, looking at Raptor.

They headed off toward the mess, loose and limping, the kind of tired that lives deep in your bones but hasn't won yet.

I took a breath, squared my shoulders, and walked back toward the inner corridor.

CHAPTER 36

The embassy hallways were quiet, white, and humming with recycled air. Clean, professional, too sterile for what we had just been through. Like stepping into a different country.

The briefing room was two turns and one security checkpoint away. The Marine on duty scanned my badge and waved me through without a word.

Inside, the room was compact and clean—glass wall for visual intel, big screen with static feeds from the outer perimeter, a whiteboard covered in scrawl, and a long table dead center with folders, maps, and a couple of half-drunk water bottles.

Caroline was already inside, tapping something into a tablet.

Atwood stood at the far end, sleeves rolled, suit jacket slung over the chair, looking like he had been awake since last week.

On the chair waiting for me—blessed sight—was a plate with a burger wrapped in foil, a paper napkin folded like someone gave a damn, and a mug of coffee putting out more steam than a busted radiator. The smell alone was enough to get my synapses firing again.

I dropped into the chair like my bones had signed a surrender treaty.

Atwood gave me a nod from across the table. "You pulled off a miracle at the Quarter."

I shook my head as I unwrapped the burger. "Nah. Just did the job. My boys—those guys are the miracle. But it's going to be a long night."

I peeled back the burger's foil, steam rising off the patty like it had been waiting for me. Took a long pull from the coffee. It tasted like it was brewed with radiator water, but the caffeine cut through the fog behind my eyes like a scalpel. Exactly what I needed. Then I bit into the burger. Greasy, hot, loaded with cheese. I leaned back, chewing slow.

Caroline and Atwood were both watching me, politely giving me a moment of peace. No talking. Just the rustle of foil and the hum of AC. I could tell they were itching to get into it, but they had manners. That earned respect in my book.

I swallowed, wiped my mouth with the napkin, and gave a small grin. "Alright, let's talk business."

"Safe house completely cleared?" I asked.

Caroline nodded. "All personnel accounted for. Everyone's here now."

"And the happy family? Al-Mansour and his two rays of sunshine?"

She chuckled. "Separated. Hassan was making too much noise, trying to blame everything on his father. We stuck him in a quieter room before someone smothered him with a pillow."

I smirked. "Well, Al-Mansour's intel saved the Quarter. If we hadn't gotten there when we did, that place would've turned into an execution livestream buffet."

Atwood nodded grimly. "Agreed."

"But," I said, my tone shifting, "those civilians shouldn't have been there. Families? Kids? What the hell were we thinking putting ten-year-olds in a powder keg like that?"

Atwood looked like he swallowed a thumbtack. "They were scheduled to leave first thing tomorrow."

I let that hang in the air, then moved on. No sense kicking a man who already knew he screwed up.

"What's the situation at the airport?"

"We passed the alert to Yemeni forces," Atwood said. "They've reinforced checkpoints, upped patrols around the terminal, and we're told the area is under control."

I looked at him flat. "You believe that?"

He sighed. "Doesn't matter if I do. It's all we've got."

I nodded once. That was the reality. No backup coming. No cavalry.

"What about the embassy? Evac plans in motion?"

Atwood shook his head. "Not tonight. The ambassador has been assured by the Yemeni government that things are contained. Says the rebels haven't moved past the eastern perimeter all day."

Caroline crossed her arms. "He's still worried about optics. Wants to project strength to D.C."

I studied their faces. Neither of them bought the company line.

"Has he been outside lately?"

"No," Caroline said. "Not since about nine this morning."

"Maybe someone should put him in a truck, take him on a scenic tour. Let him see the checkpoints, the gun trucks, the twitchy militias playing street cop. No one's out there anymore unless they're ready to shoot their way home.

They didn't argue. I leaned forward.

"This city's on borrowed time. Hours, maybe less. Militias everywhere. No law, no control. Hell, I wouldn't step outside for a burger without a suppressed carbine and body armor. The way it looks right now, Sana'a falls before dawn. And if it does, we're boxed in here."

Caroline gave me a nod, jaw tight. "That's why we wanted to talk to you first. There's someone we think you should meet. Deputy Chief of Mission—her name's Dana Prescott. She's sharp. Feet on the ground, not here for politics. She knows the ground's shifting and she's not afraid to say it. If anyone can knock some sense into Ambassador Leland, it's her."

"Then maybe she's our Hail Mary."

Atwood raised a hand like a coach calling a timeout. "Alright. I'll track down Prescott. She's somewhere in the building. Give me two minutes."

He was already on the move, phone pressed to his ear.

As he stepped aside to make the call, I leaned back in my chair and scrubbed a hand down my face. Felt like sandpaper on concrete. That burger was sitting heavy in my gut—in a good way—and for one dumb minute I let my body think I was done for the night.

Then it hit me like a mortar—Staff Sergeant Logan Davis. The Marines.

"Goddamn it," I said, sitting up straight.

I had forgotten the fourth target under Midnight Scimitar. The Marine unit at the forward ops site, south of the city. I had told Logan I would be there if it went sideways. If they got pinned, I would hit their flank.

I turned to Caroline. "You got any traffic from the Marines at the forward site?"

She looked up from her notes. "No. Nothing. Last check-in was an hour ago. Why?"

"They were on the damn target list," I said. "I talked to the Sergeant and the Marines were dug in, but they won't hold if AQ brings serious weight. You know what they like to do with Marines who run out of ammo."

She nodded grimly. "I'll reach out to the watch floor. See if anything popped in SIGINT."

I gave a short nod. "What about the Marine reinforcements? Still inbound?"

"Yeah. My update says they touch down at 0230."

Before I could dig further, my comms lit up. An unexpected call from a man who shared my last name.

CHAPTER 37

My comms crackled—tight, clear, with that clipped embassy comms discipline.

"This is Echo Station for Cowboy. Be advised, you've got an incoming priority call—origin Camp Lemonnier. Caller requesting direct link. Do you want it patched secure?

"Copy, Echo Station. Patch me in secure," I said, tapping the side of my headset. Then to Caroline, I nodded. "Need to take this."

But she was already pushing back from her chair. "Atwood wants me with him—Dana Prescott's just two doors down." She flashed a quick hand signal. "Back in two."

I watched them step out.

"Cowboy, you're live on channel. Go ahead."

I adjusted the comms and leaned forward. "This is Captain Blaze."

The line crackled—then the exact same four words came back at me: "This is Captain Blaze."

Not feedback. Not an echo. Just a damn mirror. My brow twitched.

"Who is this?"

"Gotcha, didn't I, Rockstar?"

I didn't even fight the grin. There was only one man alive who called me that name.

Ryan Blaze. My older brother.

He started it when we were kids in Colorado—back when I thought Axl Rose walked on water and I strutted around the barn with a bandana tied over my mop of long hair, Guns N' Roses blasting from Dad's pickup. I was eleven and ridiculous. Ryan was thirteen, already stronger than most grown men, and he would just shake his head and say, "There goes Rockstar again, practicing his Grammy speech."

"Jesus, Ryan," I said, leaning back in the chair with a grin. "For a second I thought I was talking to a ghost."

"C'mon, little brother. After all that Delta training, you still spook that easy?"

"I just thought they didn't let lunatics prank-call embassies on secure lines."

"Only during office hours," he laughed. "What's your excuse, rookie? Still hitting the wrong button on the headset?"

"I was busy saving your diplomats. What were you doing— still polishing your boots in the FOB?"

"Negative. I was prepping my squad to clean up whatever crap you stirred up. You know—real Marine work."

"I'm shaking in my boots. Remind me again, which one of us passed selection on the first try?"

"Oh please. I benched three plates when you were still playing air guitar in the barn."

"I was eleven, you oversized yak. And Mom still says I'm better-looking."

"Yeah, well, Mom's got a soft spot for strays."

He laughed. That low, rough, familiar sound that hadn't crossed the airwaves in a year. I cracked a grin. Couldn't help it. Felt like home again, if only for a heartbeat.

But just like that, the air shifted. We both felt it. The war had a way of finding its way back in.

Ryan's voice dropped. "So how bad is it over there, Ax?"

I glanced at the door, still shut, and dropped my tone.

"It's hanging by a thread. City's ready to go full collapse. We've been rushing around all day, barely stopping a massacre at midnight. AQ's moving like they got a damn playbook. I'm trying to knock sense into the ambassador—get him to greenlight the evac before it's too late."

"Yeah. I know how these suits work. They'll debate it to death and call it policy while the building burns. Always lands on guys like us to clean it up last-minute."

"No argument here."

"I had to damn near throttle a couple officers just to make sure our C-17 goes wheels up in time. We'll be up in ten. Touch down in Sana'a at 0230, come hell or high water."

"Good," I said. "I'd been wondering when you'd hit the ground. We'll need backup once this place starts unraveling. It's gonna be loud when it happens. Nobody here's ready."

"Copy that. How's my Staff Sergeant Logan doing? You talked to him?"

"About an hour ago. And man, was I in for a surprise when he mentioned you. I like him. Solid guy. Didn't flinch when I told him AQ might come knocking. How bad's it out there?"

"Bad. His boys are catching hell from an assault force, maybe sixty heads or more. He's holding the line, but he knows no cavalry's coming till I get there."

"Shit," I muttered, then added, "I told him—once I wrapped up my current op, I'd push to his flank if it got too hot. That was my plan before you called in. I was just about to saddle up."

"Then do it. If you take off some heat, Logan's boys'll hold. They've got spine, but I don't want another Fallujah happening on my watch."

I could hear real tension in Ryan's voice as he said that.

Fallujah. A firefight that turned into a meat grinder. We had lost too many good Marines in that city. I pictured the grit-caked faces of exhausted Marines, pinned down behind sandbags and half-collapsed walls, calling in reports nobody would answer for hours. No one with a uniform and a soul ever forgot it.

I adjusted my grip on the radio handset. "Don't worry, Ryan. I'll give them hell. Logan'll get some breathing room. Just keep that bird hot and wheels on the tarmac."

"Good. You hold the fort, Rockstar. I'm bringing the muscle."

We stayed silent a beat longer than needed.

Then I said, "See you on the ground, brother."

"Count on it. Stay sharp, Axel."

"You too, Ryan."

The line went dead, but the fire in my chest was just warming up. Ryan was coming, and he would be bringing thunder. But for now, it was my move.

Time to raise hell.

CHAPTER 38

I brought up the sat-map on my tablet, fingers sweeping over the terrain outside Sana'a, tracing a line from our safehouse to the dustbowl Logan's squad was holed up in. Then I keyed my comms and punched in Logan's frequency.

"Logan, this is Cowboy. You copy?"

There was a pause, then the line buzzed alive with gunfire in the background. Sounded like a warzone—and that's exactly what it was.

"Copy, Cowboy. We're still vertical. But we're catching it hard. About hundred AQ fighters pushing," he replied, trying to sound steady.

"How bad?"

"Under heavy fire. Lost our drone uplink, we're blind past 200 meters. They're trying to cut off our north wall. We're holding the line. For now."

The 'for now' did some heavy lifting in that sentence.

I looked back at the map. His forward ops site was a dust-choked corner outside the city—no easy approach, few good fallback points. I zoomed in on an adjacent ridge.

"You think you can hold off for another couple of hours until Ryan and his crew can get boots on the deck."

There was a pause. Not the scared kind—just the math kind. Logan ran the numbers in his head.

"If you're asking if we'll still be here—I'd bet on it. Might be ugly, but we're not handing over our flag. AQ wants this ground—they're gonna have to bleed for it."

Spoken like a Marine. I could hear the grit in his voice like he had chewed it with breakfast.

I checked our position, did some back-of-the-napkin timing.

"Copy that. I'm en route. Thirty minutes, tops. I've got a four-man element, all door-kickers. Not a full-blown QRF, but we make noise and break things. Might be enough to knock AQ back on their heels."

Truth was, a proper Quick Reaction Force would have rolled in with MRAPs, air cover, and more firepower than a Fourth of July parade. We were four guys, light on armor, heavier on attitude. Not ideal. But in a knife fight, sometimes the meanest guy wins.

"That's all the edge I need, Cowboy. You bring hell—we'll hold the gates."

"Copy that. I'll have my tech, Echo, reach out on a secure channel. He'll feed you regular ISR. You'll get real-time eyes on AQ movement. Helps you track them and shift your defenses."

"Much appreciated. I'll send him my priority target grids. You land a couple hits in the right direction, we can stem the tide."

"Will do. Hang in."

I flipped to Echo's channel.

"Echo, this is Cowboy. You online?"

"Standing by, Cowboy."

"I'm sending you Staff Sergeant Logan's coordinates now. Feed him ISR coverage on a loop—drone eyes, thermal, whatever you got. Logan's team's getting hammered. Without your recon, they'll get rolled."

"Got it. I'll run high-altitude feed and thermal overlay. Any specific targets?"

"He'll feed you that. Get him what he needs."

"Roger that. Eyes in the sky, always."

I cut the line and toggled Raptor's channel.

"Raptor, this is Cowboy. Saddle up. We roll in ten. Pack heavy—we're going in to smack AQ off our Marines."

"Copy, Cowboy. What's the loadout?"

"M240Bs, SAWs, M4s with M203s. We're also bringing the RPGs we stole off the last batch of AQ. This isn't a surgical strike—we're throwing the kitchen sink. Dump everything we got. Our boys'll get steamrolled if we don't."

This was the heaviest metal we had left in-country. M240Bs—belt-fed medium machine guns that hit hard past a thousand meters and could make whole AQ trenches second-guess their career paths. Add a couple M249 SAW light machine guns for suppression, and M203 grenade launchers to drop hate on enemy cover. Enough firepower to rip a hole straight through the assault line and create some serious chaos.

Raptor replied: "Loud and messy. Just how I like it."

"Good. Load fast."

I ended the call and looked back down at the map when the door opened.

Caroline walked in, Atwood at her six, and between them, a woman I didn't recognize. Tall, confident stride. She walked like she owned every inch of air between her and the desk. Sharp suit. Sharper eyes. She looked like someone who hadn't had a hair out of place since 1997.

Atwood started to speak. "Captain Blaze, this is—"

But she cut him off with the kind of authority you didn't argue with.

"Dana Prescott," she said, stepping forward and extending a firm hand. "Deputy Chief of Mission. CIA's briefed me. That was a hell of a job getting our people out of the Quarter."

"Just doing our part, ma'am."

She nodded once. "I'd like your assessment. How bad is it out there?"

I liked her already. No fluff. No warm-up act. Just right to the point. I laid it out straight—no sugarcoating.

"It's bad, ma'am. City's overrun. Militias own the streets—mostly AQ and Houthi, but there are a few smaller crews sniffing around too. I've been through five districts and didn't see so much as a checkpoint manned by government forces. If the Yemenis still hold anything, it's small pockets. Maybe the airport, if we're lucky."

She didn't flinch. Just processed it like someone used to bad news.

"But those pockets," I continued, "are shrinking. AQ's tightening the knot, one block at a time. They're not rushing. They're strangling."

She folded her arms, waiting for the bottom line.

"If we don't roll out tonight, under cover of darkness, we'll be pinned in this place come sunrise. And when that happens—evac's off the table. This place will be a kill zone."

She took that in like someone used to bad scenarios. Cold analysis. No dramatics.

Just then, my tablet pinged. I glanced down. It was Echo—ISR uplink from the drone. Thermal overlays, motion tracking, and coordinates on Logan's squad. Red blotches clustered like bacteria around his compound. I tapped into the feed. AQ was stacking bodies on the north and west perimeters, like they were building their own human barricade.

Dana must have seen my jaw twitch, because she asked, "More bad news?"

"Yeah," I muttered, eyes still on the screen. "Marines holding the forward ops site are catching hell. AQ's throwing everything they've got at them. Feels coordinated—waves of contact. They're not going to stop till every last one of our guys is down. And if the FOS falls—" I looked her dead in the eye, "this place is next. Every Houthi and AQ cell with a radio will zero in on the embassy. They'll converge here like flies on blood."

Caroline looked away, biting her lip. Atwood shifted uncomfortably. Dana just nodded once, slow and deliberate.

I closed the tablet. "That's the lay of the land, ma'am. And that's all I've got time to tell you. I need to move. We're going to hit the AQ position from the rear—buy those boys a little breathing room."

She didn't waste time. "How bad is it out there for them?"

"Rough estimate?" I swiped to Echo's tactical overlay. "About a hundred fighters. Heavily armed. Coordinated assault."

"And how many men do you have?" she asked.

I looked up from the screen. "Four. Me and my three operators."

She stared a moment, then said it like a statement, not a question. “Four operators. Ten Marines. Against a hundred heavily armed fighters.”

“Yep.”

“That winnable?”

“Nope.” I cracked half a grin. “Not if it’s a stand-up shootout. But we’re not playing by the rules. We’ve got the element of surprise, and we’re not going through the front door. We hit their rear—raise some hell, throw them into chaos. That’s our edge.”

She gave me a tight smile. “You’re planning to be the chaos.”

“That’s the idea.”

She nodded, satisfied. “Well, if anyone can pull it off, it’s you, Captain. I’ll go twist the ambassador’s arm until something cracks. We’ll get the evac moving.”

“Appreciate that,” I said. “What’s the evac protocol timing once the decision’s made?”

“Standard full drawdown takes two to three hours,” she replied. “But with a gun to the head—like there seems to be right now—we can crash it in under an hour.”

I nodded, doing the mental math. That meant they would go into full emergency drawdown—classified material burned or shredded, hard drives yanked and destroyed, comms shut down, embassy communications blacked out. Every trace of American presence erased. Half the embassy would turn into a bonfire before the first evac van rolled out. It wasn’t as simple as loading a bus.

“I’ll be back in an hour,” I said, “and hopefully, the wheels are in motion by then.”

"Will we have safe passage to the airport?"

"If we don't, we'll bulldoze our way through. When Marine reinforcements land at 0230, the airport should hold up for a few more hours—there's only so much 30 incoming Marines can do, it's not like they can permanently fend off an entire army of AQ and Houthi fighters combined."

"Understood," she said, extending her hand again. "Good luck, Captain."

I shook it—firm, quick. The way pros do when time's short and the stakes are high.

I turned to Atwood. "I'll be on comms the whole way."

He gave a nod. Caroline didn't say anything at first, but I caught her eyes for a second—there was something there.

She stepped close—just enough for the others not to hear. Her voice was low and even. "You come back in one piece, Cowboy."

I gave her a nod. Just enough to say I heard her.

Then I walked out, boots echoing down the corridor, headed to meet my team in a room beside the embassy's service entrance.

CHAPTER 39

I cut through a side corridor, past a busted AC vent humming like it was dying slowly. Found the guys in a squat room near the service entrance—cement floor, flickering fluorescent light, smelled like a mix of oil, gun grease, and hot metal. Felt like home.

My team was there—Ninja, Raptor, Hawkeye. All three geared up and looking like they were heading to war, which, technically, they were. Rifles slung tight, sidearms holstered, plate carriers snug, NVGs clipped and ready, gloves half-on. All business.

What I didn't expect was to see Ali, Youssef, and Calhoun in the same damn room.

Ali was leaning against the wall near a stacked crate of bottled water, arms crossed. Youssef stood by the window, checking the side mirror angle on one of the Land Cruisers outside like he was fine-tuning a getaway. Calhoun sat on a metal chair, one leg over the other, the picture of patience with an undercurrent of cold, coiled rage.

I stopped in the doorway. "You three take a wrong turn on the way to the embassy café?"

Ali didn't smile. "We heard where you're going."

"Yeah, about that," I said, folding my arms. "This isn't exactly a CIA-sanctioned run. No green light, no backup. More like...a personal favor to some Marines who are getting chewed up as we speak, and no one else is coming to help. You don't need to be in on this."

Calhoun raised a brow. "So what, you're literally going cowboy? Just you and your team charging AQ lines?"

"I'm doing it on my own call," I said, nodding at my guys. "Even for them, this was optional."

Raptor looked at me like I had just told him gravity was a lie. "Seriously?"

Ninja leaned back against the wall and cocked an eyebrow. "Boss, no offense, but save the feel-good speech for the suits. You really think we're gonna let you run off solo with a machine gun and play Rambo on AQ? Come on, man."

Hawkeye, dry as ever, muttered, "He's got that look again. You know—the 'just give me one belt-fed and a Red Bull' look."

I couldn't help smiling. Bastards had my six whether I asked or not. "Didn't think so. Just had to say it out loud."

Youssef stepped forward, hand on his chest like he was testifying. "Look, I know I'm just the driver. Not Delta. Just a humble soldier boy. But you show me one American who can drive in Sana'a faster than me, I'll eat my boots. You want to get there fast, and maybe get back alive? Then I'm coming."

Ali gave a sideways nod. "And I can't let the great Delta Force stumble off into the night and get lost. I'm the only one who can read half the road signs you'll pass. Someone has to make sure the commandos don't get lost and end up in Houthi central."

Then Calhoun stepped up—quiet, steady, British calm behind those stormy eyes. "My boys were butchered by AQ, mate. Strung up like warnings on a roadside pole. You think I'm gonna sit this one out?"

I looked around the room. Jawlines set. Every pair of eyes already miles ahead, in the fight. There was no convincing left to do. They had made their calls.

"Alright," I said. "Mount up."

We pushed through the side door to the service lot. Two Toyota Land Cruiser 78s idled quietly under the sodium lights, exhaust puffing slow clouds into the cool night air. They looked like any dusty NGO rig you could see parked near a Red Cross camp— dust-caked, scratched, anonymous.

But under the skin, they were beasts. Steel-plated bodies. Bullet-resistant glass. Run-flat tires. Reinforced underbellies to handle mines. Comms gear packed in the console, extra fuel cells strapped to the rear. They weren't pretty, weren't fast—but they were stubborn as hell. They could chew through a kill zone and come out the other side coughing smoke.

We weren't rolling out for recon. We were going to punch through hell and drag the Marines out by the teeth if we had to.

I gathered the crew beside the first vehicle, under the flickering exterior light. Everyone stood still, waiting.

"Ten Marines are holding a forward base about two clicks outside the city edge," I told them. "No air support, no QRF—just guts. AQ's throwing everything they got at them. Full frontal assault. If they go down, this embassy's next. We're going to roll in from the rear and hit them hard. Fast, brutal, no mercy. Break their spine. Take out their crew-served heavy weapons, scatter their lines, cause enough chaos for the Marines to get some breathing room. Then we exfil before they realize what the hell happened."

Nods all around. No questions.

Ali climbed behind the wheel of the lead Cruiser. I took shotgun. Hawkeye and Calhoun slid into the back seats, locking rifles between their knees.

Youssef stepped into the driver's seat of the second vehicle, flexed his gloved hands, and gave a low whistle like he was about to race the Dakar Rally. Raptor rode passenger. Ninja took rear.

Two beat-up trucks, seven men, and enough firepower to start a local war.

Doors slammed shut, and the cabins filled with the low clack of mags locking in, safeties getting checked, and headsets syncing up.

Night was on our side. And we were about to make it rain fire.

We rolled out of the embassy like wolves off the leash—two armored Land Cruisers moving fast and mean through the night, blacked out and pissed off. No matter what the streets threw at us, we didn't stop for anything. Not for the skinny kid waving an AK at a fake checkpoint, not for the pile of junk tires some genius thought could serve as a roadblock. Youssef didn't even tap the brakes. That V8 growled and chewed right through.

We were heading into the northwest outskirts of Sana'a. Dust-bowl terrain littered with half-finished buildings, concrete skeletons from projects long abandoned. I sat shotgun in the lead truck, tablet in hand. Echo had fed in the layout of the forward ops site—Logan's little Alamo.

A grainy, sat-fed top-down of the forward ops site (FOS) popped up. Dusty terrain, busted concrete, some jagged terrain rising on the north side—textbook no man's land. The operating site sat in the middle of it like a sore tooth. Rough rectangle—about 100 meters long, 80 meters across. Surrounded by sandbags, Hescos, and old-school concertina wire. A cage with ten Marines in the middle, and AQ hammering at the bars. It could handle probing attacks—but not sustained hell.

North side was the problem. It faced rising terrain—a low, craggy ridge about 150 meters out, running slightly northwest to southeast. Broken stone walls and scattered scrub brush. Echo's latest data showed AQ were embedding two machine gun nests and at least two RPGs up there—perfect overwatch. Once they got about their business, they would rain hell on the Marines.

The west side of the site was flatter—gravel access road, a few busted sheds, and scattered shell-shocked buildings. AQ had infiltrated that zone too, using doorways and windows for cover. Assault teams were leapfrogging forward, five- to six-man fireteams with AKs, trying to push the perimeter. They had one technical in the mix—flatbed with a mounted machine gun and two gunners.

South and east flanks were cold—no movement, no pressure. That's where we were headed.

"Ridge is the anchor," I said over the net. "We snap it, AQ loses their overwatch. Hawkeye, Raptor, Ali—you flank west side. Take the high point. Ninja, Calhoun, and I are coming in from the east. Youssef holds the trucks. If we call for medevac, you come like hell. No delays."

"Copy all," Youssef said. "Engines stay hot. I'll keep the coffee warm."

We pulled off the road and cut west across rough terrain, suspension grinding like teeth. Both SUVs ran night vision assist, screens glowing green as we pushed through dry brush and rubble-strewn flats. No headlights. Just shadows moving with intent.

The night air buzzed with distant gunfire. Muffled cracks, rising and falling. But no heavy stuff yet—no PKM chatter, no RPGs punching the sky.

We crested a low rise, and the echoes of sharp, angry gunfire became louder. Rifle rounds cracking the air. That was no probing contact. This was a full-on gunfight.

I leaned forward, watching the ridge through the windshield. That low spine of terrain to the north of the FOS was starting to come alive. I keyed the comms.

"Logan, this is Cowboy. We're one klick out. Coming in dark from the north. Got Echo feeding us real-time—looks like your ridge is getting busy."

Static hissed, then Logan's voice came back, loud and raw.

"Copy, Cowboy! We've got movement all along the north edge! Got visual on at least two machine gun crews digging in on the ridge. RPG teams too—saw two runners with launchers heading that way five mikes ago. They're prepping to lay it on thick!"

"Yeah, we see it," I replied. "Drone feed shows the crews are just now getting set up. No belt loaded yet. No rounds fired."

"Not yet. But once they're in the fight, they'll pin us down hard. I got a sniper trying to get an angle.

He's trying to get clear shots, but if those gunners dig in first—"

He didn't finish. A burst of automatic fire ripped across his channel—raw, close-range.

Logan came back, breathless. "—if he can't get them in time, those guns are gonna pin us hard. And once they're locked in, AQ's assault teams'll walk right up our western flank."

"Negative," I said. "That's not happening. We're coming up the ridge from behind. We'll take those gun teams out of the equation."

There was a pause. Then Logan's voice came back. "Copy that. You clear that ridge, we'll hold the west long enough for reinforcements to punch through."

"Roger that. Sit tight. It's about to get western up there."

We would clear that ridge or die trying. We weren't about to let good men die on a lonely ridge while the world looked the other way. Those Marines weren't alone—not anymore.

CHAPTER 40

I cut the comms, then tapped the screen of my tablet. The drone feed confirmed what Logan said—two machine gun crews setting up on the crest, each with three men, and two more RPG gunners hovering nearby. One team was digging in just behind a slab of rock with a sandbag brace. The other was lower down, closer to the center, setting up on a patch of broken masonry.

We circled around the far side of the ridge and pulled behind a rusted-out construction shack maybe two hundred meters from the ridge's backside. The air was dry, still. I popped the door and stepped out into the black, night vision on. The world turned to green ghosts and jagged silhouettes.

We split into two teams. Hawkeye, Raptor, and Ali moved out wide to the west, low and fast, angling toward the ridge's far end. Their job was to sweep along the crest and cover the flank.

I took Ninja and Calhoun. We headed east, hugging broken terrain, moving under cover of low walls and half-built cinderblock shells. No chatter. Just controlled breathing and the soft click of gear.

The ridge was steep, chewed-up terrain—scrub brush, loose rock, broken concrete slabs left behind by someone who never finished whatever the hell they were building out there.

As we edged nearer, I could hear shouting in Arabic, heavy boots scrambling over stone. AQ was rushing to finish setup. One machine gun nest was dug in near the center, with another roughly 40 meters to the west. One RPG team rotated between a stone wall and an old generator shack. The second was perched near a crumbling archway at the far western edge—right in Hawkeye's projected path.

We crept up along the east slope, hugging the low terrain, flanking the center nest. Heard them before we saw them—muted Arabic chatter, radio static, the rattle of a belt being fed into the PK machine gun. Maybe eighty yards out. That was our nest.

Calhoun was already up in overwatch, belly down on a slab of reinforced concrete, sniper rifle braced, eye on scope. His voice crackled in my ear, calm and dry as ever.

"Cowboy, eyes on the nest. Three-man crew at the crest—machine gun's on a bipod pointed down toward the compound. One's feeding the belt, one's bracing the legs, and the last idiot's trying to line up the tripod like he's never seen war before. Twenty meters to your ten o'clock, up two levels of rock."

"Copy," I whispered. "I want that gun gone, not just the crew. No one's scrambling back up here to use it later. We're going close."

"Copy. RPG team's just behind them. Two with tubes, third one with reloads. Moving slowly."

"Call it when you're set."

"Lining one up now. Give me thirty seconds."

We started moving—me and Ninja crawling under a low wall and moving left in bounds. Dust kicked up under our boots. I switched to suppressed fire. The Glock rode quiet on my chest, but I had the HK416 in hands, short barrel, tight sling. Ninja mirrored me—low, quiet, locked in.

I saw movement behind a half-built retaining wall. A sentry, probably a runner. He turned his head too slow.

Pffft. Ninja's suppressed round caught him under the ear. He folded like wet laundry.

We came across two more AQ fighters moving toward the gun—probably backup for the crew. They never saw us coming. Ninja put one down with a tight pair to the chest. I took the other through the throat with the Glock. We dragged them into the brush and kept going.

Calhoun's voice came back, just as I spotted an RPG-toting guy shouldering his launcher. "Locked on RPG man."

A single suppressed crack echoed across the slope, barely louder than a soda can popping. The man dropped, launcher and all, and rolled lifeless down the incline.

"Good hit," I muttered.

We were thirty yards from the crest, the gun team still hunched over their PKM. They had no clue death was sneaking up on them.

The ridge lit up a moment later—AK fire cracking overhead. Someone finally noticed their buddies were getting dropped. Bullets snapped past us, hitting rock and dirt, spitting up dust like angry hornets. A burst of AK fire whizzed past my left side—too damn close. Ninja ducked and dropped to prone, returning fire in short bursts.

I dove behind a broken slab and fired from cover, tapping one in the leg and another in the gut. They dropped hard. One tried to crawl, but Ninja stitched him.

Gunfire raged from the compound below—Logan's Marines were still giving as good as they got. But I knew if we didn't shut that PKM down immediately, we would be neck-deep in Marine body bags.

We pushed forward, leapfrogging from cover to cover. I dumped a mag, slapped in a fresh one, and crawled the last fifteen yards up to a low wall just shy of the machine gun nest.

I moved in. Ten yards from the nest. Grenade in hand. Eyes on the gun team—sandbagged pit with a PKM machine gun ripping fire down toward the FOS. I judged the arc. Clear line.

"On target," I whispered. "Popping frag."

I yanked the pin, side-armed it over the ridge lip, and dove behind a boulder. Less than two seconds in the air, then it vanished behind the sandbags.

Half a second later—*WHUMP*. The ground shook. The ridge lit up orange, dirt and body parts spraying in a sick halo. Screams and shrapnel flew. The PKM stopped singing.

I rose, eyes scanning through the haze—PKM was twisted junk now, two of the crew dead. One was crawling, barely conscious. Ninja stepped up and finished him, one suppressed shot to the head.

"First nest's out," I spoke into comms. "Gun destroyed."

Before I could catch my breath, another staccato burst lit the dark—tracers snapping across the slope and down toward the compound. Second machine gun nest had opened up and was hammering the Marines. Orange streaks clawed through the sky.

I keyed up. "Raptor, sitrep. That second gun's lighting up the compound!"

No reply. Nothing but static.

Then—*BOOM*. A dull, sharp explosion echoed from the far side of the ridge. A flash lit up the rocks like lightning. The gun went quiet.

Raptor's voice crackled in.

"Second nest's toast, Cowboy. RPG solved the problem."

"Copy that. Nice timing."

Now it was cleanup. Calhoun and Hawkeye opened up with their suppressed M110s, picking off AQ fighters trying to fall back toward the western slope. I saw one go down mid-sprint, arms flailing. Another dropped before he could raise his rifle.

Another burst—Raptor's SAW light machine gun chewed through a shadow trying to run downslope.

Me and Ninja pushed through the smoke and dust, clearing out the last stragglers on the north ridge. Short bursts, fast movement, surgical.

By the time we hit the far end of the ridge, the firing had thinned out. Bodies lay where they had dropped. The AQ assault on the north side was broken. The ridge was ours.

"Ridge is clear," I said. "Repeat, ridge is ours."

Below us, Logan's boys were still lighting up AQ positions, but the volume of incoming fire had dropped. The assault was unraveling.

Bodies lay scattered in the dust, weapons still warm in dead hands. Smoke drifted low across the rocks like a bad omen, but my guys were alive and still putting in work—one suppressed shot at a time. Calhoun and Hawkeye were chewing up the stragglers trying to regroup on the west side of the FOS.

That firing from the ridge had turned the tide, made AQ think twice. Now their fighters were breaking, some peeling back, others hesitating behind those busted cinderblock shacks like maybe their assault wasn't such a great idea after all.

I keyed the mic. "Cowboy to Logan. North ridge is clear. Both gun teams eliminated. No more RPGs. No more threats up here."

There was a short pause—gunfire still popping in the background—then Logan came on, and this time his voice wasn't as tight.

"Copy that, Cowboy. We're dug in tight. West side's still hot but we've got it locked now. You boys just saved our asses. Thanks."

I shook my head even though he couldn't see it. "Save it for the bar, brother. You'd do the same in a heartbeat."

"Damn right I would."

I scanned the dark again—nothing moving but smoke and silhouettes limping west. I checked my watch. 0100 hours. Reinforcements weren't landing for another hour and a half. A lot could still go sideways in ninety minutes in a place like this.

I keyed up one more time.

"We're heading back to the embassy. This city's about to fall off the edge. High likelihood we start evac tonight. If that happens, I don't want you and your boys stranded out here. You copy?"

"Yeah, I copy." Logan's tone shifted—he understood what I wasn't saying.

"If we give the word, be ready for a full exfil. Controlled demo. Take down your comms, ammo, weapons—hell, even the coffee maker if you have to. Leave AQ nothing but scorched rock and splinters."

"Roger that," he replied, all business now. "We'll prep the EDP. You take care of things back at base."

"Roger that," I replied, relieved that Logan was all keyed up on an Emergency Destruction Plan.

I signaled to the team— index finger twirled, then jabbed south. Time to peel off, regroup, and roll out. We were halfway down the north ridge, boots crunching over loose shale and shell casings, before my comms crackled again.

Echo's voice came through, sharper than usual.

"Cowboy, copy?"

"Copy, Echo. Go on," I said, wiping sweat and dust off my NVGs.

"Hassan Al-Mansour just took the U.S. ambassador hostage inside the embassy."

Goddammit. Just when I thought the night couldn't get darker, it did.

CHAPTER 41

I froze mid-step. "Echo, say again. Hassan did *what*?"

"He's got a live frag grenade. Repeat—*live frag*—in a secured meeting room with the ambassador, Atwood, and a DS agent. Thumb's on the spoon, pin's out. Says if anyone shoots him or tries to rush in, he lets go and we're scraping suits off the walls."

I stared into the night, mouth dry as chalk. "Echo, how the hell does a detainee in U.S. custody inside a secured facility get his hands on a goddamn grenade? Last I checked, our boys weren't walking around embassy halls with frag pouches on their hips."

"I've got no clue how he got it, Cowboy. Zero. Might be internal compromise. I'm pulling every second of security cam footage from the last hour—tracking who slipped it to him, how they did it, and if there's more out there."

"Make it top priority," I said. "I want eyes on whoever handled that thing before it got to Hassan. If there's one grenade in play, there could be more."

"Roger that," Echo said. "Already spinning up the facial recog subroutine. I'll run badge scans too, check who accessed restricted zones. I'll find the son of a bitch."

Then his voice leveled out. "Patching you through to Caroline now."

There was a click. Then her voice came on—tight, low, controlled, but I could hear the stress under it like a wire about to snap.

"Cowboy."

"Caroline, talk to me. What the hell happened?"

"We got played. Bad. Walked right into it."

"Yeah? No shit. What happened?"

"Hassan asked to speak with someone from CIA—said he had real intel, something that would help us stop the attacks. We were stretched thin. FOS barely holding. Dana was all over the ambassador to initiate evacuation, and Atwood and I were doing what we could to stop this city from falling apart. And we knew Hassan was tied into AQ's planning loop. He timed it perfectly."

"Keep going."

"So Atwood went to see him in the secured interview room—thought we'd take the shot. Hassan told him he'd only talk if he got full immunity for himself, his father, and his brother. Said he wanted out—new identities, U.S. resettlement, the works. Not a black site in Poland, but a backyard in Pittsburgh."

"Sounds familiar."

"Right. Atwood told him we already had a deal with his old man. Hassan didn't care. He didn't want a vague CIA promise and black site limbo. He wanted a passport and a cul-de-sac. Atwood told him that would depend on the quality of intel."

"Let me guess. Hassan wanted it from the horse's mouth."

"Exactly. Said he'd only give up intel if the ambassador gave him his word personally."

I bit back a curse. "And the ambassador thought he'd play hero and walk out with golden intel."

"Pretty much. Dana didn't like it, but the ambassador saw a way to avoid evacuation if Hassan's intel was real. Thought this would 'turn the tide'. He overrode her."

"So what happened?"

"They went in. Atwood, the ambassador, and a Diplomatic Security agent. Hassan was seated at the table. Calm. Cooperative. Two minutes in, he reaches under the table, pulls out a grenade—God knows where he stashed it—pulls the pin, keeps his thumb on the spoon. No one had a clean shot. Now they're locked in there. He's demanding a vehicle at the service entrance in exchange for the hostages."

"Jesus Christ."

"We're buying time, but... we don't know how long we've got."

My mouth was dry. "And nobody knows how he got the frag?"

"Negative. Echo's running surveillance. DS did a sweep, but either they missed it, or someone passed it to him. Most likely a mole."

I knew this could go sideways at any second.

"Copy all," I said, jaw clenched. Then I clicked back to our tac net.

"All call signs, race back to the Cruisers. Now. Embassy's hot."

No one asked why.

We all just ran.

Boots pounded hard on dirt and stone, gear rattling, breath fogging in the cold night air. The adrenaline hadn't left our blood yet—not after the ridge fight—and now it kicked even harder.

As we sprinted downhill, I keyed the tac mic.

"Listen up," I barked, wind in my throat. "Hassan's gone full rogue. Took the ambassador, Atwood, and a DS agent hostage inside the embassy."

"What?" Raptor burst out. "How?"

"Live frag grenade. Thumb's on the spoon. Pin's out. He pulled it from under the damn table during a meeting."

"You're kidding." Ninja almost yelled.

"Negative. Ambassador, Atwood, and a DS guy. Hassan says he'll blow everyone up if we don't give him a car and let him walk."

"What the hell? Where did he get a frag?"

"I don't know how he got the damn thing. Echo says they're checking security footage and supply inventory now. Either DS missed it on the sweep or someone handed it to him."

Hawkeye spoke up, voice sharp: "Tell me we get to breach and shoot that little shit in the mouth."

"Negative," I said. "He's holding that spoon. You shoot, it's frag soup in there."

We reached the Land Cruisers, piled in hard and fast. Ali gunned the ignition, wheels kicking gravel as we tore off down the ridge road, suspension groaning under the weight of operators and gear.

The city burned in front of us, orange glow rising behind the dark skyline.

"Strap in," I said over the engine roar. "We're heading back into the fire."

No one argued. We were past that point.

And this time, we weren't just rescuing CIA assets or dodging machine gun fire. We were about to walk into an embassy hostage standoff with a live grenade and the fate of U.S. command in Yemen hanging in the balance.

We flew through Sana'a like the devil had a drone on us. Ali was driving like he stole the thing—second gear screeching, shocks bottoming out every time we clipped a crater in the street. Night air whipped through the busted vent, thick with dust and smoke and a city that knew it was dying.

My brain was three clicks ahead, running through breach scenarios and worst-case outcomes. Grenade goes off—boom—ambassador, Atwood, DS agent, all gone. Yemen collapses into chaos by morning. Hell of a Tuesday.

That's when Caroline came back on the net.

"Cowboy, it's Caroline."

"I'm here. Go on."

She hesitated a second. That told me more than words.

"Khalid wants to talk to you."

Her voice had that brittle edge again—tension cracking through the calm.

I blinked. "Come again?"

"He's volunteered to speak with Hassan. Said he might be able to calm him down."

"And he wants *me* first?"

"Correct. He specifically asked for you. Said he'll only try if he can speak with you beforehand."

"What's the angle?"

"I don't know. Maybe guilt. Maybe ego. Maybe he just thinks you're the only one who won't lie to him. Look, I don't pretend to understand it, but you and him... there was something there in that safehouse. Some kind of... man-to-man connection. I don't get it, but I'll grab any damn straw I can reach right now."

"Is this his play for leverage?"

"I don't think so. Honestly? We're out of cards, and he knows it. If there's a shot, we have to take it."

I nodded to myself. Not because I liked it. But because I knew it was probably the only card left.

"Patch him through."

I leaned back against the seat as the Cruiser tore around a corner, engine growling.

I had walked through a prison in Houthi territory, survived fake checkpoint ambushes, crushed an AQ assault on a Marine outpost—and now I was about to play hostage negotiator through a jihadi father trying to save his son with a live frag in his hand.

Yeah. The surprises just kept coming.

CHAPTER 42

"Captain," the voice came through the headset—calm, deep, measured.

Khalid Al-Mansour.

"Yeah," I replied. "I'm here."

I let the sentence hang with an unspoken question. He never knew my name, as in his presence, Caroline had always addressed me by my rank.

There was a pause, then Al-Mansour asked, "You remember our conversation about my son Hassan? About how close to the edge of the abyss he was, looking into the dark?"

I stared out the windshield at the chaos bleeding past—Sana'a in full breakdown, shadows rolling across alleys, smoke climbing from somewhere north. And I thought about the kid, barely twenty, with a grenade in his hand and a suicide speech in his throat.

"I remember," I said, low and grim. "Looks like tonight he stepped over. There is no edge anymore. Only the fall."

"I know," Al-Mansour replied. "And I understand there's no coming back from what he's set in motion. No forgiveness. No redemption."

Al-Mansour didn't even try to come up with an excuse. He was just a man laying down the truth.

The man wasn't blind. He saw Hassan for what he was—a brainwashed zealot drunk on blood, vengeance, and holy war. He knew Hassan wasn't holding that grenade as leverage. He was holding it like a final prayer. A martyr-in-waiting. And Hassan wasn't going to waste the chance to take out a high-value target like a U.S. ambassador.

That's why Al-Mansour had said it straight—no forgiveness, no redemption. Not for Hassan. Not after this.

I waited for him to go on. The rumble of the engine and the crunch of gravel under our tires were the only sounds. I had come to understand that Al-Mansour never wasted words. Every word was a chess piece. When he spoke, it was calculated. Intentional. Every phrase a stepping stone to something bigger.

"I'm going to walk into the room," he finally said. "I'll try to talk him down."

I pictured the layout: a secure room in the lower levels of the embassy, dim light, stale air. Hassan holding a grenade with a death grip, the ambassador and two good men within the kill radius. A single twitch from Hassan, and we would be scraping flesh off the walls.

"You sure he'll listen?" I asked.

"No," he said plainly. "But I am the only one who might reach him."

His voice stayed calm, but something in it had changed—a weight behind the words. Not fear. Not even hope. Purpose.

"You need to understand, Captain," he continued. "This is... extremely volatile. One wrong word, one wrong move... Anything can happen."

He didn't need to spell it out. The frag grenade. One twitch, one slip of a thumb, and it all goes up.

"I know," I said. "You walk in, you're betting your life on hope."

"Yes."

I didn't say anything. I was listening. And I was trying not to think about how many ways this could end badly.

Then he shifted gears. Quietly, carefully.

"There is something else," he said. "You believe—perhaps grudgingly—that my younger son, Ibrahim, is not like Hassan. That he is... caught up in all this."

I blinked once. He's not talking tactics anymore. He's talking legacy. Blood. I stared out the window at the streaks of smoke curling into the night sky.

"Yeah," I said. "I do. Not sure if he's completely blameless, but he does come across as a kid in a cage built by other people's choices."

"Exactly," Al-Mansour replied. His voice was almost soft now. "He's young. Too young to carry the weight of what I have done. What his brother is doing now."

He paused again. That silence carried real pain this time. The kind that lives in the marrow.

"I ask you now for a promise." Al-Mansour's voice softened just a notch. "If I save your people—your ambassador—can you assure me that Ibrahim will not suffer for the sins of his brother and father?"

There it was. The real ask.

"What do you mean exactly?"

"I mean that whatever happens to me—or to Hassan—my son Ibrahim deserves a future. A chance to start over, away from this war? A chance to live free of our shadows?"

His voice didn't tremble, but something cracked in it. Just a little. Like glass flexing under pressure.

I understood what he was doing. This man wasn't negotiating for himself. He was putting his life on the line… for one shot at saving what little good he had left.

This wasn't about leverage. This wasn't even about stopping a son. It was about freeing another. A dying man's last card to save what was left of his family.

He understood he had barely minutes to make any kind of impact on the hostage situation. No time for paperwork and ironclad guarantees. He wouldn't take Caroline or anyone else's word for it. But somehow, due to some indefinable connection we seem to have created, he was willing to trust my word.

I ran a hand across my face, swallowed hard. Then I spoke.

"Khalid, I know you understand we don't have time to get you papers or lawyers or guarantees. But I can give you my word. If you save those three hostages, I'll work every angle I can to make sure Ibrahim gets a shot at a new life. No blood guilt. No retribution."

There was a pause. Then Al-Mansour exhaled—and I heard something shift in him. Resolve. Not hope.

"That is all I needed to hear," he said.

Another pause, but this time it was heavier. Not hesitation. A man checking the weight of what he had chosen.

"I respect you, Captain. As a warrior. And a man of honor. If I have your word, then I will save the hostages," he said, voice hardening. "No matter what."

I felt it like a knife under the ribs. He meant it. Every word.

He was going to walk into that room, face his son, and do whatever it took. Try to talk him down. If that didn't work, take the blast. Maybe both. But he would get those people out.

He had done terrible things once, sure. But tonight, he was about to do something goddamn righteous.

"Then may God go with you," I said.

"Thank you," he replied, voice low. "May God protect you, Captain."

The old man meant it.

And before the call dropped, I spoke again. Not sure why. Maybe it felt right.

"It's Axel," I said. "My name."

There was a pause.

"*Shukran*, Axel," he said quietly. "I am honored. Good luck."

"Good luck, Khalid."

The line went quiet as Khalid got off the call. I waited for Caroline to get back on.

CHAPTER 43

I stared out the windshield like it was a blank screen and I was trying to project a goddamn miracle onto it. But no amount of squinting would change what was about to happen inside that embassy meeting room.

Three hostages. One grenade. One fanatic with the pin already pulled and the spoon clenched in his sweaty grip. And one father who had decided this was the only hand he had left to play.

From the way Khalid spoke, the tone in his voice—it was clear. Hassan wasn't bluffing. He was waiting, biding his moment, like a true believer who knew the finale had to be cinematic. And Khalid, desperate to carve a clean future for Ibrahim out of the blood and smoke, was ready to make himself the buffer between life and death.

I had no doubt what was coming.

I ran the scenario over in my head a dozen different ways in those first few seconds, heart thudding like I was the one about to walk into the blast radius. I had seen the secure meeting rooms. All three of them. Secure? Sure. Vault? Not quite.

The room Hassan had taken over was one of the two corner secure suites—reinforced concrete walls on two sides, and ballistic-rated one-way glass on the other two. That glass was thick, layered, resistant to most small arms. But it wasn't frag-proof. You cook off a grenade in there, the pressure wave's got somewhere to go—and it's through those windows. Outward. Away from the source.

That gave the hostages a shot. Not a great one. But better than if they were inside a steel coffin.

When those glass panels gave under the overpressure, some of the blast force would vent outward. Not all of it, but enough to give the poor bastards inside a fighting chance. Blast always searched for the weakest link. If that link was tempered glass, it would shatter out into a hallway. Much better than bouncing off steel walls and turning the inside into a frag blender.

And a body—Hassan's or Khalid's, thrown between the blast and the hostages—could change the math. If Atwood and the DS agent had the reflexes to grab the ambassador and hit the ground, maybe get behind a table... they might survive the blast radius, maybe even the frag spray. Nothing stops fragmentation dead, but every layer slows it down. Wood. Flesh. Steel. Position mattered.

Didn't change the fact that if Hassan let go of that spoon, it was going to be chaos.

The second Khalid got off the call, my brain kicked into overdrive. I could almost see that room in my mind like a 3D model—long table in the center, steel-framed with a thick wooden slab, bolted into the floor. Chairs on both sides. Atwood and the DS agent would have been seated near the door, flanking the ambassador. Hassan had them in a tight kill zone. Probably had the grenade low, under the table, hand clamped tight on the spoon.

Khalid wasn't going in there for a conversation. That ship had sailed. He was going in to throw himself on his son's suicide switch. That was the only plan left standing.

My comms crackled. Caroline's voice cut through, cool and direct, but I heard the edge under the calm. "What do you think? Should we send Khalid in?"

"He's the only card we've got," I said. "Hassan's going to pop that grenade no matter what. He's already crossed the threshold. He's in that dark place now, full of rage, delusion, martyrdom. That frag's going off. The only thing we can try to control is who lives through it. And Khalid will do whatever he can to keep those people alive."

"You think he can talk Hassan down?"

I shook my head even though she couldn't see me. "Not a damn chance in hell. Only scenario I see ending with hostages still breathing is if Khalid gets that frag out of Hassan's hand. And even then, with the pin already pulled and that spoon barely hanging on..." I let out a breath. "Boom's almost inevitable. Khalid's going in there to jump on that grenade if he has to."

There was a pause.

"Send him in," I said. "But first—get everyone the hell away from that meeting room. Clear the halls. Those glass walls will pop outward and take down bystanders if they're too close."

"Copy that," she said. "We've cleared most of the floor already. You think he's really planning to shield them?"

"Yeah. He's not doing this for glory. Or guilt. He's doing it because he knows the only future his son Ibrahim has depends on those three men walking out of there alive."

I didn't say what I was really thinking—that Khalid Al-Mansour had walked the long road of atonement and he had hit the final mile marker.

Redemption wasn't in the cards. But legacy? That was still on the table. And legacy meant keeping those three people alive.

I could hear her take that in.

"You still have Atwood and the DS guy on comms?" I asked.

"Yes. Earpieces in."

"Then patch this through to them—verbatim. Khalid is coming into the room. No sudden moves. But the second he's within arm's reach of Hassan, they hit the deck hard. Take the ambassador with them, and get behind whatever solid furniture is in there. Table legs, desk, even the far corner of the room if they can get there. That's where the concrete walls meet—blast will vent out through the glass. If they hesitate, they're toast. But if they move fast, and Khalid uses his body to block the worst of it, those three might walk out alive."

I paused, jaw tight.

"Tell them to move *fast*. The second they see Khalid lunge, they go down. Don't wait for the boom. There won't be time. The hostages will take some injuries. No way around that in a confined space. But a body between them and the blast... that changes things."

She was quiet again for a beat. Then: "Understood. I'm on it."

And with that, the line went dead and I stared forward again, every muscle taut like I was already in the room. Watching it play out in my mind.

Khalid stepping in. Eyes locked on his son. The quiet calm before the storm. And then—

Hell.

Hell with a chance of survival.

And sometimes, that was the best you got.

CHAPTER 44

We were still five minutes out. I sat up front, window cracked, air slicing across my jaw like a razor, eyes locked on the red-glow map on the tablet in my lap. The embassy perimeter shimmered just beyond the next cluster of streets.

I hit the mic. “All stations, this is Cowboy. Stand by for update on a possible detonation scenario inside the secure room at the embassy. Al-Mansour’s heading in unarmed to try to stop it. This is his play—he's going in to save the hostages.”

The team stayed quiet for a beat.

Then Raptor broke the silence. “Man’s walkin’ into his own funeral. Some fanatics you just can’t talk down. Their faith’s wired to detonate.”

Ninja was next. “Brainwashing ain't just belief. It’s architecture. Hardwired. Sometimes the only way to stop ‘em is to shut the circuit down at the source.”

Hawkeye came on over comms, voice flat as iron. “You live by the sword, sometimes the only redemption left is dying by it clean. That man’s doing what most men can’t.”

I nodded to myself. No dramatics. Just cold facts from guys who had danced with death long enough to know what it costs.

I gave it a few seconds to settle. Let the weight of it hang. Then something hit me sideways.

“Wait a second,” I muttered, mostly to myself, gears grinding behind my eyes. “He asked for a vehicle.”

Raptor turned. "What?"

"Hassan," I said. "Demanded an escape vehicle at the service entrance in exchange for releasing the hostages."

"Yeah, and?" Hawkeye prompted.

"And Khalid's convinced the frag's going off no matter what. So why bother with the bullshit cover story about a getaway car?" I let the words hang as the realization snapped into place. "Unless that vehicle's not meant for escape at all."

Ninja leaned forward. "You think he's planning to blow himself up at the side entrance?"

"Yeah. And you know what that means. This isn't a suicide play. It's a breach plan. If he opens the service entrance with a blast, AQ's got boots waiting outside to come storming in."

I felt a chill crawl up my back.

If AQ fighters were waiting just outside that service entrance, and Hassan opened the door with a grenade blast? It would be open season on every diplomat and Marine inside.

My comms crackled at that moment.

Echo's voice came in sharp. "Cowboy, we've got something. Guy who recoded the access card to the armory? Yemeni local, embassy IT contractor. Name's Qasim Al-Zubaydi. Been on embassy maintenance support for two years."

"You saying he pulled an M67 from the armory?"

"Yep. Used admin-level override to bypass logs. Slipped past the tracking system."

"Where the hell is he now?" I asked, already feeling the walls closing in.

"Still inside. Didn't badge out. I've got all cams running facial ID."

I chewed on that. "Why the hell is he still inside the embassy? He knows he'll get ID'd from footage—why not vanish?"

"Been asking myself the same thing," Echo replied. "Hold on..."

A few seconds passed. Then Echo came back sharp.

"Got him. Utility room near the southeast quadrant. Ten meters from the service entrance. He's sitting at a workstation, eyes glued to a laptop."

"What's he watching?"

"Live feed from the cam outside the secure suite. He's watching Hassan's hallway. He's watching it go down."

My gut went cold.

We weren't dealing with a hostage taker. We were in the middle of a breach op disguised as a suicide stunt.

"He's part of the second wave," I spoke urgently. "If Hassan fails to blow the door open, he's the fail-safe. He opens it manually."

"Looks that way," Echo confirmed. "Guy's waiting on a trigger."

I weighed my options. Even with a mole inside, breaching that service entrance wasn't going to be a walk in the park for AQ. They might have greased the skids with an inside man, but this wasn't some back-alley checkpoint they were walking into—it was a hardened U.S. embassy.

I had seen the layout. Hell, I had been through it myself during a pre-op brief inside the embassy's southeast security post. That entrance was a goddamn fortress in miniature.

First, you had the outer vehicle gate—big beast made of reinforced steel, blast-rated, thick enough to stop a vehicle laden with explosives cold. That gate didn't swing open just because someone whispered the magic word. Access was electronic and monitored from inside—usually by security guys staring at a wall of monitors. No one was just strolling through it.

Right past that was the buffer zone—a kill box if there ever was one. Maybe fifteen, twenty feet deep, boxed in tight by twelve-foot concrete walls. The kind of place where you get stuck and regret your life choices. You drive in, outer gate closes behind you, and then you wait while the inner gate decides if you are friend or foe. If you are carrying any bad intent in that space, you are dead meat before the second gate even thinks about moving.

Then there was the inner barrier. Another tight choke point. That's the one that got you inside the actual embassy grounds. Locked tight unless someone buzzed you through. On good days, staffed by a DS agent or local guard. On bad days... well, this was one of the bad ones. If the mole's job was to crack open that outer gate at the exact second the inner blast went off—then, all bets were off.

So even with a mole inside, AQ had their work cut out for them. But they weren't just winging it. Those guys had set one hell of an elaborate plan in motion. They had mapped this out, probably down to every camera blind spot and pressure sensor. Hassan wasn't just a distraction—he was a fuse. The blast was never about escaping. It was about breaching. Throw enough chaos in the system, and people stop watching the gates. Or worse—someone opens them from the inside.

This wasn't some half-assed martyrdom op with one guy and a backpack. This was an orchestrated breach with layers. AQ had gone surgical. If I sat back and hoped the layers of concrete and steel would hold, we would be mopping up diplomats and Marines with body bags by dawn.

"Echo," I snapped, eyes scanning the dark ahead of our vehicle, "patch me through to Ridley or Maddix. Now."

"Copy that. Give me five seconds."

I knew both Maddix and Ridley were banged up. But injured or not, those two were pros. They had been chewing on embassy security since I was still cutting my teeth in Ranger bat. They knew the floorplans, the routes, the angles of fire. If anyone could organize a quick reaction team for a hard stop at that side gate, it was them. They could read a situation and react like Delta operators in civvies.

End of the line was coming fast. And I needed killers, not excuses.

"Cowboy, this is Ridley. What've we got?"

Voice rough but steady. No wasted breath. No bullshit.

"Listen carefully. Forget the secure room and the live frag situation. There's about to be a breach at the service entrance. I need you to take whoever the hell you trust—Maddix, DS agents, Marines, janitors with mop handles—I don't care—and get to that entrance now. You copy?"

He didn't hesitate.

"Solid copy. I'm moving. Maddix is with me. We're taking anyone with a badge and a gun. We'll hold that breach point."

"Make sure that door stays shut, Ridley," I said. "You open it, we lose the embassy."

"You got it, Cowboy. We'll hold the damn line."

The comms went dead.

Ali swung the Cruiser around the final bend, the embassy walls now looming ahead like a goddamn war monument rising from the heart of Sana'a.

CHAPTER 45

"Skip the front," I told Ali. "We're going to the service entrance."

Ali nodded, face tight, eyes locked on the narrow back road that snaked toward the embassy's service entrance. We weren't headed for the main gate. The real war was about to kick in from the southeast corner.

That's where the breach was going to hit. The rest was just theater.

I sat up front, rifle across my chest, boots braced against the floorboards. The Land Cruiser's suspension was chewing gravel and potholes like it owed us favors. Raptor was already un-slinging the SAW light machine gun off the rear seat mount. Ninja Man was checking his mags, eyes like stone.

Then Echo's voice cracked in through the comms—low and fast.

"Cowboy, grenade just went off inside the secure room. Full detonation. Not sure about survivors inside."

I flinched like someone punched me in the ribs.

"Copy," I said.

"Other bad news is the mole moved right after the boom. Picked up a weapon—AK-103 stashed under the table in the utility room. He opened the inner gate manually, shot both guards in the cabin. Now he's inside the gatehouse, sitting behind the control console."

That sonofabitch was fast.

I pictured it—door swinging open, two DS guards taken completely off guard, muzzle flashes, blood, bodies slumped. And then that bastard sliding into the chair behind the console like he owned the damn place.

"He's going to open the outer gate," I growled. "That's the play. We're almost there. Keep eyes on. Feed me everything you've got, real time."

"Roger that," Echo snapped.

That's when the line beeped again—priority channel. Caroline.

Her voice was low, almost hollow—like she had just watched a ghost walk off the battlefield. "Cowboy. He did it."

I didn't need to ask who she meant.

"What happened?" I asked, eyes scanning the tree line as we took a tight curve toward the southeast compound.

She exhaled. "Khalid went in. Did what he could. Talked to him, threatened him, begged him. But nothing got through—he had that look. You know the one."

Yeah, I did. I had seen it in villages from the Korengal to Haditha. Eyes like dark glass—no soul behind them, just purpose soaked in blood and belief.

She continued. "Khalid rushed him. Tackled him to the ground. They went down hard, into the corner. And then..." Her voice faltered for half a beat. "The grenade went off."

The guy had meant it. Every damn word.

"The hostages?" I asked.

"They're alive. They hit the floor just in time, pulling the ambassador down. Table and Khalid shielded them. Everyone's concussed, ears ringing, and Atwood's got shrapnel in his thigh. One guy's throwing up from the shock, and the ambassador's temporarily deaf. But they're breathing."

I let out a breath I hadn't realized I had been holding. The hostages were alive. Banged up, shaken, but breathing. That was something.

"That's good."

"He knew he was going in there to die," Caroline added quietly.

I didn't answer. Just waited.

"He asked me for a bulletproof vest before he went in. Wore it under his loose shirt. I remember thinking it was pointless. A vest wasn't going to save him from a grenade. I figured maybe it was just... psychological. Something to make him feel braver."

Her voice, usually steel and spine, came close to breaking. "But now I get it. He wore it so it'd take a little more of the blast. Just enough."

I nodded, jaw tight. "You're right. He knew what he was doing. Gave his life so the other son could live."

A second of silence passed. But I couldn't let her stay there—not when a breach was about to happen.

"Caroline," I said, my tone sharpening. "We'll deal with all that later. Right now, listen up, we've got a breach incoming at the service entrance. Strap in."

Just as I said it, our SUV crested the rise like a war horse hitting the high ground. The whole southeast quadrant snapped into view. My binos were already up. The rest of the guys didn't say a word—they were too busy locking in.

The outer gate was wide open.

The steel bollards were down.

What the hell?

Then we saw two pickup trucks burning rubber straight toward the gate, kicking up a rooster tail of dust like they were on a suicide run. Each bed was packed with armed men, rifles up and ready to roll.

Raptor leaned forward, hand already on the door latch. "That's it, Cowboy. Breach in progress."

"Eyes on," I snapped. "Weapons ready. Glass anyone with an AK."

But then the game twisted.

The outer bollards hissed back to life. Hydraulic power surged. The thick steel pillars began going up slow but steady, like the earth itself was pissed off.

The lead pickup never saw it coming. It slammed full speed into the rising bollards.

The crunch was biblical.

The front axle crumpled like tinfoil. Bollards punched clean through the truck's undercarriage, steel spearing the engine block and flipping its nose up like a rearing horse. It hung there like a gutted animal, front tires spinning mid-air. Men inside scrambled like rats in a drowning cage. One flopped halfway out the shattered side glass. Another tried climbing out the bed, rifle dangling.

And the gate—it was sliding shut. The massive blast-rated slab groaned as it started to roll inward.

"Son of a bitch," I muttered. "Somebody's fighting back."

I keyed up. "Caroline, hang on a minute. Switching over."

Flipped to Ridley's channel.

"Ridley, this is Cowboy. You in the guard post?"

His voice came on, sharp. "Yes. Took out the mole. I'm inside. Closing the gate now."

"Good work," I started, but then my binos caught movement—rooftop across the street, high side. Skinny bastard in man-jammies shouldering an RPG-7. My gut went cold.

"Ridley! RPG on the roof, twelve o'clock high—GET DOWN, NOW!"

Too late.

A flash—white-hot and savage—lit up the night like a slap from hell.

Even as I shouted, the rocket-propelled grenade streaked toward the entrance, trailing fire like a comet from hell—and detonated inside the buffer zone just inside the outer gate. The blast tore through the buffer, sending smoke and fire rolling into the compound like a demon's breath.

I tried to raise Ridley again. "Ridley, come in. You good?"

Silence. Goddamn silence.

No static. No breathing. Just silence.

"Shit."

Hawkeye was already halfway out the window, M110 rifle dialed in, finger on the trigger.

"Ali, stop here. Angle the truck—give Hawkeye a lane."

Ali didn't even blink. Swerved the vehicle into position with the kind of precision only years in combat will buy you, giving Hawkeye the clearest lane to the rooftop.

Hawkeye fired a second later. One clean crack.

RPG guy jerked back like someone yanked his soul through his spine. But by then, he had already shouldered another round. As he collapsed, his hand jerked as he squeezed the second shot. The grenade shot off wildly, not straight, but high. It flew straight up like a bottle rocket on meth and vanished into the inky sky.

Then came the swarm.

Gunmen poured through the gate. Black fatigues, AKs, chest rigs, the whole jihadi fashion parade. At least fifteen, maybe twenty of them, flooding in. Some were already firing back at defenders inside. More trucks screeched to a halt behind them. Boots hit gravel with more men rushing in. War cries filled the air. And then came the chatter of automatic gunfire from the embassy interior—our defenders firing back.

I toggled back to Caroline.

"Caroline, breach has happened. They're inside the buffer zone. Get every interior checkpoint locked. Pull every shooter you can spare to that corridor. We're coming in through the service entrance. Hit them from the back. Don't worry about the front—Marines have it locked. But we've got to contain this breach now or it's game over."

She responded immediately. "Understood. We're falling back to interior defense lines. Give them hell."

"Oh, we will."

It was time to join the battle. "Ali, push forward."

He floored it.

I glanced at the boys. "This is going to be close quarters, no room for finesse. We cut down everyone still outside the gate at the trucks, then bolt through the gap and cause some goddamn mayhem inside. Goal's simple: chaos, confusion, body count. Make them wish they stayed in the cave they crawled out of."

"Copy that," came the growled chorus.

Steel on steel followed—Raptor racking his M240B belt-fed like he meant to kill a city block. Hawkeye, Ninja and I thumbed safeties off our M249s, belts ready to chew. The cabin filled with the clack and thump of men getting mean.

Three dozen had already breached, slugging it out with a skeleton crew at the inner door. We were about to even the odds—and not gently. This was the part of the dance we knew best.

We roared forward toward the breach.

CHAPTER 46

Ali swung the wheel hard, kicked the tail out, and brought the SUV to a skidding halt—nose-to-nose with Youssef's rig in a tight V-formation that gave us perfect defilade. Real textbook combat parking. Gave us two metal walls of cover and one fatal funnel of fire.

The moment the tires stopped rolling, doors flew open like spring-loaded traps and armed operators came spilling out.

"Stack on line! Go hot!" I snapped.

We took cover behind the angled SUVs, rifles up, eyes locked on the threat downrange.

Five enemy pickups were parked just outside the bollards—lined up nice and neat like they were waiting for a lunch order. Gunmen milled around, rifles slung lazy.

They weren't charging the gate. Not yet. These were the second wave—the vultures. Hanging back, waiting for their three dozen brothers inside the buffer zone to overrun the inner checkpoint before they swooped in for the kill. Probably thought they had it in the bag.

They surely didn't expect hell to pull up behind them.

"Let it rip!" I barked.

Raptor dropped prone behind the front bumper, bracing his M240B medium machine gun against the concrete lip like he was staking a claim on it. "Happy birthday, assholes."

He squeezed. The belt-fed beast bucked in his hands, spewing fire and vengeance. 7.62 NATO rounds slammed into the nearest pickup, punching through doors, torsos, spines, and bone. Windshields vaporized. Whole chunks of the first truck's door peeled off like paper. The driver didn't even scream—just slumped, spinal cord turned to soup. Two guys crumpled in the bed of the truck like marionettes with their strings cut.

I went full auto with my M249 SAW—light machine gun, belt-fed, hungry as hell. My rounds stitched the second pickup like I was signing my name in lead. Hawkeye and Ninja laid down parallel lines of fire beside me, the three of us forming a moving curtain of bullets that turned everything in front of us to pulp and scrap.

Raptor's gun thundered. Ours chattered. It was a goddamn orchestra of death—steel strings, lead percussion. Brass poured out like it was on a conveyor belt.

We weren't firing to suppress. We were firing to erase.

Calhoun took a knee near the rear fender, working his HK416 with sharp, three-round bursts—each one finding a new target, dropping them like sacks of wet concrete. No wasted motion. No wasted ammo. Just pure surgical hate.

Behind us, Ali and Youssef stayed low inside the driver seats, pistols drawn, scanning the flanks. I turned and tapped the side of Ali's door. "Heads down. Don't engage unless you have to. Be ready to roll in case this goes sideways."

"Copy that," Ali said, tightening his grip on the wheel. Eyes forward. No panic.

The ambush hit the AQ force like a hurricane. One truck went up in flames when a lucky burst hit a jerrycan in the bed. Two others were riddled so bad they looked like they had been through a meat grinder. Men screamed, fell, staggered—only to catch another burst mid-limp. A couple tried to retreat, but there was nowhere to go.

We hit them hard. Fast. No mercy.

Raptor saw one make a break for it. "Nope," he muttered, walking his fire across the gravel and stitching the guy's legs out from under him. The man pitched forward, skidded face-first, and didn't move again.

Another tried to raise a PKM in the back of a Hilux. Hawkeye stitched three into his chest before the weapon even cleared the tailgate. The gunner folded over the barrel like wet cardboard.

Sixty seconds. That's all it took. All enemy personnel outside the gate were either dead or dying, and their vehicles looked like Swiss cheese at a scrapyard.

"Clear!" I yelled. "Rifles and pistols. We go in fast, tight, and mean."

We ditched the heavier guns—too long, too loud for tight maneuvering. I swapped to my HK416, checked mag, slapped it home. My sidearm sat snug on my thigh, backup plan ready.

I looked back. "Ali, Youssef—get outta here. Move to the main gate, off to the side. Stay close, engines running. We'll call you in when the zone's clear."

Youssef nodded, already shifting into reverse. "Understood, Cowboy."

They peeled off, swinging wide and disappearing into the side street leading toward the main entrance. Couldn't just leave those trucks out there—too much firepower onboard. And we would need them later. This night was far from over.

I keyed comms. "Caroline, get the inner door boys to hold fire. We're moving into the buffer zone. No friendly fire."

"Copy that," she shot back. Voice tight but steady. "You're clear to advance."

I gave my team the nod. "Let's clean house."

We moved fast, low, tight stack. Six shadows gliding toward the smoke and flame, hearts pounding, muzzles pointed forward, eyes locked on the kill zone.

Time to dial up the violence.

CHAPTER 47

We spilled into the buffer zone like wolves off the leash. The air was thick—burnt metal, cordite, blood. The gunfire hadn't stopped since we came through the gate, but it changed pitch when we entered—panic. The kind of panic that comes when the hunters become the hunted.

My team fanned out instantly, rifles tight to shoulders.

"Stack up!" I barked. Raptor and Calhoun peeled right, covering flanks. Ninja shadowed me, silent as a grave. Hawkeye moved like a wraith in his wake. Orders were sharp and simple: *Make this hell theirs.*

Bursts rattled from AKs up on the embankment. We weaved behind busted concrete blocks. I took one man in the gut—mid-sprint, gun raised, too slow. Two taps center mass. He spun like a rag doll and hit the pavement hard. I stepped over him, scanning fast—this was a slaughter box, and we had just lit the fuse.

Ten yards in, three fighters popped out behind a wrecked Toyota. I dropped to a knee and squeezed three controlled shots from my rifle. Three down. One twitched, then stilled. I kept moving.

Left side, Ninja's gun cracked—short, brutal bursts. A fighter lunged out of a stairwell—Ninja side-stepped, pistol already in hand, and dropped him with a round through the jaw. Blood misted against the wall like spray paint.

I kicked in a side door to a crumbled admin shed and cleared right. Nothing—just two more gunmen running in the open behind the guard shack. I raised my rifle, put them both down with chest shots, then vaulted the debris pile and pushed forward.

Suddenly—gunshots, frantic and scattered.

Someone ahead of me was firing wild, barely holding the weapon up.

I ducked behind a chunk of concrete and used my optics.

Christ. Ridley.

Blood running down his face, chest heaving, crouched against the shattered wall of the guard cabin. Firing in short, jerky bursts. He was out of it, but still fighting. Three AQ fighters were closing on him—steady, deliberate, rifles raised.

I surged forward.

"Ridley!" I roared.

They looked up. Too late.

I slammed into the closest one with my full weight—sent him flying back, rifle knocked aside. The second spun on me—my rifle was up, but too close. I let go and jammed my Glock into his ribs. Two quick shots. He dropped in a wet pile of meat. Third man was raising his AK. Two shots to the head. The man crumpled like a puppet with cut strings.

I dropped to my knees beside Ridley. "Jesus, you're alive."

He blinked. "Didn't think I was."

"Me neither," I said, checking his pulse. Still strong—wounded, bleeding bad, but alive.

"Sit tight," I muttered, dragging him into a darkened corner behind a slab of broken wall. "You're not dying here, you hear me?"

"Copy," he croaked, half a grin breaking through the blood.

Behind me, the others were tearing through the courtyard.

Hawkeye double-tapped two fighters trying to scale the inner gate. Then he surged forward, switching to a Glock—quiet, deadly. He cleared another stairwell of two men.

Calhoun fought like a demon—HK416 dry, switched to Glock, clearing a path through the smoke. One guy grabbed him from the side—Calhoun dropped his mag and shoved the pistol under his chin—POP. Deadweight fell backward like a sack of meat.

Ninja moved with surgical precision. Two fighters tried to box him in—one went for his legs, the other flanked. He shot the first in the kneecap, then spun and drove his knife straight through the second's clavicle, twisting once for good measure.

Raptor took a round to the arm and kept moving, wrapping it up in duct tape mid-run, blood soaking his sleeve. He shot two fighters through the same hole in the wall and then slammed a massive shoulder into a third one who was trying to line up. The man went flying, back of the head hitting a wall, breaking his neck, killing him instantly.

A guy like Raptor slams into you, you don't get up.

I stepped out from Ridley's position, reloaded my Glock, and moved up to a final cluster of fighters near the gate—six of them, pinned but still resisting.

"Come on, you bastards," I growled.

I charged.

They weren't ready.

The first two raised their rifles—too slow. I double-tapped both.

One tried to flee. I kicked his leg out and dropped my knee on his throat. He gurgled once and went still.

Another leapt at me with a knife. I caught his wrist mid-swing, slammed his face into the wall, then stabbed him twice in the gut. He buckled.

The last two fired from the hip. I dove behind a cinder block and flanked left. One round clipped my thigh—burned like fire—but I pushed through and shot them both as they tried to reload.

Suddenly, it all went silent.

We stood in the middle of the buffer zone, surrounded by the stench of blood, oil, and gunpowder. Thirty-something bodies, dead or dying, lay across the concrete and blood-soaked gravel, twisted into shapes they weren't meant to hold.

My vest was bloodied, most of it not mine. My Glock was dry, my HK was hanging by the sling, and my blade was tacky with blood. I wiped it on a dead man's sleeve.

"Clear," I said into comms. "All stations, buffer zone is clear."

I limped back toward Ridley, who was still conscious but barely, breathing heavy, face pale but fighting to stay with us.

I crouched beside him, checking the makeshift pressure bandage Calhoun had slapped over his side. Blood soaked through it fast. His eyes were glassy, unfocused.

"You stay with me, brother," I said. "You didn't crawl out of a goddamn RPG blast just to die in my arms."

He didn't answer, just nodded, trying to bring on a smile that wouldn't come through.

The others regrouped around me. Breathing heavy. Bleeding, scratched, bruised—but standing.

We had held the line.

With knives, pistols, and sheer fucking rage.

CHAPTER 48

I keyed my comms. "Maddix, this is Cowboy. Buffer zone's clear. Repeat, buffer zone is clear. Ridley's alive, but he's hit bad—needs a stretcher team. Now."

There was a short pause. Then: "Copy, Cowboy. Coming out."

A moment later, the inner gate creaked open, slow and cautious. Maddix stepped through first, flanked by three DS agents. They looked like they had been through hell—smudged faces, torn sleeves, but weapons ready and eyes alert.

Maddix stopped a few feet from us, surveyed the battlefield like he was trying to count the bodies. "Jesus," he muttered, a half-grin on his face. "You boys play rough."

I grinned back. "Better rough than dead."

He scanned the corpses scattered across the concrete. "Thirty-plus bodies in a hundred feet. Remind me never to pick a bar fight with you."

But then his eyes landed on Ridley and the grin vanished.

"Shit," he cried out, and rushed over, dropping to a knee next to him. "We thought he was gone."

"Me too," I said. "Found him shooting like hell, bleeding out by the cabin wall."

Two embassy medics jogged in right on cue, kits out, calm and efficient. They didn't waste words. Got to work fast, checking vitals, patching lines, and loading Ridley onto a stretcher.

"Get him inside," I told them. "He's still got fight in him."

They nodded and hustled him through the gate.

I turned to my guys. "We're holding here. Take up perimeter at the outer gate. We're not done yet."

They moved like clockwork, setting up behind concrete dividers and burned-out vehicles. I was about to call Caroline, get the damn gate closed and bollards back up, when I heard the hydraulic hum.

Bollards rising. Outer gate swinging shut.

She was already jogging down the steps from the embassy's main building, suit jacket off, hair tied up, blood on her cheek that wasn't hers. She had that look in her eyes—controlled fury and no time for bullshit.

She stopped in front of me, scanning the zone. "You OK?"

"Still vertical."

"I was at the inner gate with Maddix. Saw the whole damn show," she said. "You and your boys just wiped out a company-sized element in five minutes."

"We get performance bonuses for that?"

She snorted. "You want a medal, or you want the gates shut?"

"I prefer the gates shut. Looks like you've already got that covered."

She smirked. "As soon as I saw you clear the last one, I called the main control center. Told them to override the guard cabin and shut everything. Figured you'd want the gate sealed ASAP."

"Good instincts."

"Professional paranoia," she said.

"Well, whatever it is, it works just fine. What's the sitrep on Atwood and the boss?"

"Atwood looks like a car crash but he's stable. The ambassador's half-deaf, which is probably doing him a favor."

I blinked. "How come?"

She smiled grimly. "Dana Prescott's been chewing his ass off nonstop. He's lucky he can't hear it for now. She didn't wait for his signoff—ordered the evac the moment the grenade went off."

"She had authority?"

"She's number two. When the ambassador's incapacitated, she becomes acting chief of mission."

I nodded. "Smart call. Hassan laid that trap slick as hell. It was a lead-in to something bigger. We shut it down, but this isn't over. AQ and the Houthis won't back off. They've had a taste now—and they'll come back with bigger teeth. We can cut down squads, but not whole armies."

"I know."

"Which means," I said, glancing at my team, "we can't sit here waiting to get overrun. Prescott's evac order still stand?"

"Yep. She's mobilizing now."

"Good. We need to get out of this place soon. Before all access routes are cut off."

Caroline didn't argue.

We stood there a moment in silence, both of us watching the outer gate finally shutting and final bollard lock into place. Smoke drifted low across the tarmac from the wrecked enemy trucks. I scanned the road outside—dark, empty, but it wouldn't stay that way long. That silence felt like the kind that comes before an explosion—or a storm.

I didn't need to say it, but I did anyway. "That quiet out there won't last."

She nodded, her jaw tight. "How long before they come back?"

"No idea. But it's time." I turned to her. "We need to pull the Marines out. Now."

She looked at me. "How long will that take?"

"Not long. I already gave their Sergeant a heads-up to prep for evac. They'll be out within minutes of the call."

"Then make the call. I'll update Dana."

She turned and jogged inside, heading straight for Dana Prescott's war room. I patched up Logan on comms.

"Logan, this is Cowboy. How you boys holding up?"

"We're good enough. Three of mine are banged up—took frag and one caught a round in the thigh. But we clamped 'em down, stopped the bleeding. They're breathing."

"Good. Listen up—embassy's been breached. AQ got a team inside, but we shut it down. Situation's fluid. You copy?"

He didn't hesitate. "Solid copy. You want us in?"

"Affirm," I said. "Initiate full emergency destruction protocol. Burn the ops site. Then grab your crew and roll out for the embassy. Loaded for war."

"On it. Five mikes. We're coming in stacked and pissed off."

I cracked the faintest grin, despite the seriousness of the situation. That was the right attitude. No questions. No stalling. Just action.

Logan was coming in with heat. We were going to need it.

"Roger that. Expect contact en route. When you hit the compound perimeter, call me. Don't let anyone else open the damn gate."

"Roger that. Moving out soon. ETA thirty mikes."

The second I got off, Caroline's call came on comms. I wasn't expecting good news. Turned out, I was right.

"Got a new problem," she said. "Crowd's started forming outside the front gates. Dozens so far. Chanting *'Death to America'*."

Of course they were.

I exhaled slowly, eyes back on the horizon. "Here we go. I'll see you inside in a couple of minutes."

I turned to the boys, still keeping eyes out around the burned-out trucks and spent shell casings.

"Time to head inside, gentlemen. Gates are sealed, Marines are posted. We're not holding ground out here anymore. And the party's just getting started out front."

The two Marines guarding the inner gate stepped aside as we moved in, rifles tight to their chests, expressions locked down.

As we walked through the service gate back into the compound, I briefed the team.

"Front gate's heating up. Local fan club's outside the front gate yelling 'Death to America'. Loud enough to shake windows."

Calhoun was the first to speak: "Guess we're trending again."

Ninja grunted. “Man, they need some new material.”

Hawkeye nodded. “Yeah, I miss the classics—‘Yankee Go Home,’ or ‘Big Satan.’ At least those had some variety.”

The chuckles faded as we stepped deeper into the compound. The weight of what was coming settled back over our shoulders like body armor soaked in blood.

The battle wasn’t over. It was just changing shape. And now, we had a full-blown siege brewing at our front door.

Time to dig in.

CHAPTER 49

The air outside the front gates had turned thick—thick with heat, hate, and the kind of crowd energy that makes your trigger finger twitch. The noise started low. A hum. A ripple. Then it swelled—

"*Allahu Akbar!*"

"*Death to America!*"

The chants were rising like waves—guttural echoes bouncing off sandstone walls and steel gates. Over and over. Throats raw. Voices manic.

They didn't chant in unison—there was no rhythm. Just chaos. Anger thrown like bricks at the night sky.

I stood at the embassy's front gate with a fireteam of Marines, M4s at the low ready, every set of eyes laser-focused through NVGs. The gate's armored barrier was shut, reinforced with steel and concrete, but it might as well have been made of glass the way the crowd was growing—about a couple of hundred now, maybe more. Some stood on the hoods of old sedans and pickups, waving flags and black banners, others screaming into the hot night air like they were revving up for a religious riot.

Flashbulb pops went off here and there—cell phone cameras, documenting their own rage. Young men held their phones high with one hand and waved rusty AKs with the other.

Then came the first shot.

A crack—rifle fire—aimed at the sky, not at us. A celebration shot.

Another followed. Then three more. The kind of warning fire that said: *We're warming up.*

Crowd didn't flinch. If anything, it got louder. Bolder. The line between demonstration and mob was starting to blur.

I turned my head, jaw tight. "We're one Molotov away from hell breaking loose."

Next to me, Ninja stood arms folded across his rifle. "This ain't a protest, Cowboy. This is a prelude."

He was right. We weren't looking at civilians anymore. We were looking at a fuse, and someone was about to light the match.

I scanned the outer perimeter, expecting to see the Yemeni police in their usual slapdash cordon—blue uniforms, AKs slung carelessly over their backs. They were supposed to act as the first buffer between us and this mess.

But they were fading. Some had just drifted away like fog. Others stood there pretending to care, faces blank, shifting weight like they were waiting to join the other side when it kicked off.

"Cowards," Raptor growled, shaking his head.

"No," I muttered. "Opportunists. Cowards don't stick around long enough to see who wins."

Cowards or collaborators? Didn't matter. They weren't going to help.

I turned as Dana Prescott approached. Her blouse was sweat-soaked, sleeves rolled, phone clenched in one hand, half a folder of classified cables in the other. Hair in a knot, dark eyes sharp. She had been in the ops center pulling evac levers since Caroline got the ball rolling.

She stopped beside me, took in the crowd, the chants, the smoke curling from trash piles, and the nervous tension rippling through the Marines at the gate.

"This situation is turning to shit by the minute," she said, straight to the point, no wasted breath. "Everything you told me, and everything I've seen you do in the last two hours? Spot on. I trust your instincts. What's your call?"

I looked past her—toward the rising voices, the growing crowd, the distant pops of celebratory gunfire that always turned real a few minutes later.

"Evac protocol was the right call," I told her. "But we're almost out of time."

She looked me square in the face. "Why?"

I pointed out through the gate. "After what happened out at the buffer, AQ and Houthis aren't going to stop. Local cops have already started disappearing. That out there isn't a crowd anymore. That's camouflage. AQ fighters are slipping in with them, waiting for a signal. And they won't come with a few AKs this time. They'll bring RPGs, maybe mortars. When that happens, we won't be able to hold ground. Once they breach the wall, it's a slaughterhouse."

Dana nodded. No flinch, no disbelief. Just a look that said: *I was afraid you'd say that.*

Her voice was calm but urgent. "I coordinated with CENTCOM. A C-17's wheels-down at Sana'a Airfield at oh-two-thirty. That's our evac bird."

I stiffened slightly but kept my face neutral. I knew that flight. That was the same flight Ryan was rolling in on with thirty Marines. Of course, I didn't mention that to Dana. Too personal.

“That’s the same flight bringing in the reinforcements,” I said instead. “Good. Adds some weight to our exfil. Lowers the odds of the airfield falling before we get there.”

I checked my watch. 0140 hours.

“That gives us fifty minutes till wheels down,” I said. “We need to be mobile in thirty. Hard deadline. Think that’s enough time to finish evac protocol and round up everyone?”

Dana looked at her watch, then back at the embassy building behind us. “Normally? No chance. But this isn’t normal. I’ll get it done.”

She turned, already dialing someone before she finished turning, voice firm and clipped as she barked out orders.

I turned to the team. “Roof,” I said. “Now.”

The five of us moved fast—me, Ninja, Raptor, Calhoun, and Hawkeye. We hit the north stairwell and climbed two flights. My boots echoed off concrete steps slick with sand tracked in by chaos.

The rooftop gave us eyes on the city. Sana’a wasn’t asleep—it was simmering. Roads choked with vehicles and foot traffic. Random fires burned in alleyways and trash heaps.

And that chanting—it hadn’t stopped. It had multiplied. Angry, rhythmic. Like war drums.

I dropped to a knee near the northeast parapet and pulled down my NVGs. The green haze filled my world. I scanned for movement, edges, rifle barrels sticking out of third-story windows. Too much motion. Too much noise. Too many bodies. All of it a soup of threats I couldn’t shoot at yet.

“Echo, this is Cowboy,” I said into comms. “Talk to me.”

Echo's voice buzzed in my ear, calm and clinical. "Got eyes on your whole perimeter. Overhead drone feed looks hot. Crowds building fast outside the north and west walls. Front gate's surrounded—estimate over two hundred now. Scattered armed elements within. Not overt. Yet."

"Any movement?"

"Plenty. But check this—I've got two technicals. Old Hilux flatbeds. Both with PKM's on pintle mounts. Both sitting about two blocks west of the embassy. Lights off. Looks like they're waiting on a green light."

It all fit the pattern—fighters hidden among the mob, and now trucks with machine guns mounted at the back. The attack was coming, no doubt about it.

Raptor whistled low. "Looks like a fuckin' parade float from hell."

"We got thirty minutes, maybe less," I said. "When this goes, it's going to go full force."

Calhoun leaned in. "The civvies are the problem. They're walking cover."

Ninja nodded beside him. "Yeah, we can't light up a crowd to get one guy with a rifle. AQ's counting on that."

"Just hope we don't start the evac convoy into a goddamn hornet's nest," Hawkeye muttered, adjusting his scope as he settled into overwatch.

I scanned the crowd again. Somewhere out there were people ready to die for the cause. And within the same crowd were people who didn't give a damn about ideology—just looking for blood or loot.

I keyed my mic. "Echo, maintain live eyes. I want updates every time someone scratches their ass in this sector."

"Roger that, Cowboy. Full thermal and IR up. You'll have real-time feeds."

I looked again at the sea of chaos forming outside the walls. The crowd was morphing from a volatile mob into a human smokescreen. Bodies stacked shoulder to shoulder, fists in the air. A thick knot of shouting, posturing civilians backed by hard eyes in the shadows. The kind of crowd where you couldn't tell if the guy screaming for America to burn was just pissed about inflation or waiting for the signal to fire an RPG.

Problem was, some of them weren't pretending. The enemy was inside the crowd. Embedded. Using meat shields and martyr-bait tactics. AQ knew we couldn't shoot our way through that without cable news footage turning it into a war crime by morning.

I scanned the outer perimeter again from the rooftop. Two technical with mounted machine guns two blocks out. Just sitting there, like sharks circling a wounded swimmer. Waiting for blood in the water.

I turned to the team. "Here's the thing. That crowd isn't going away. It's getting thicker. If we roll out the front gate now, we'll be driving through a goddamn bloodbath. Doesn't matter if we take every shot clean—one bullet rips through a civilian and the whole world's going to say we mowed down protestors."

Raptor grunted. "And AQ'll just light a few up themselves and pin it on us anyway."

"Right," I said. "They want a massacre. Even if it means stacking their own dead. That's their win condition."

Hawkeye leaned against the wall, arms crossed. "So what's the move?"

I looked out past the mob, then down at the concrete buffer zone below. "We give them a magic trick."

"Lemme guess," Hawkeye said. "You make forty people vanish without pulling a trigger."

"Close. We sell them chaos at the front gate. Use diversion."

"Talk to us," Calhoun said.

"We make it look like the front gate's about to fall. Controlled chaos. Enough to pull all eyes forward—mob, AQ, rooftops, technicals. Every trigger finger pointed at the main gate."

"You mean feign a breach?" Raptor asked.

"Exactly. We sell them the idea that the outer gate's compromised. Something flashy but controlled. We rig a det charge on the wall or a gate support—make it look like someone's trying to blow in from outside. Might even toss in a few flashbangs, burst fire from our side like we're falling back under pressure."

Hawkeye nodded slowly. "Draw their fighters forward, make them think they've got momentum."

"Right," I said. "AQ won't ignore an opening like that. They'll shift shooters to breach and exploit. Crowd surges forward. While that's happening, we move. Convoy rolls from the service entrance. All assets loaded, no headlights, NVG driving. Quiet and fast."

Ninja looked at me, eyes shining. "Sounds like a plan. You want me to prep a breach charge? Low-yield, directional?"

"Do it," I said. "We set the tempo. Noise buys us time."

Calhoun glanced at his watch. "You think twenty six minutes are enough?"

"Have to be," I said. "We don't have a second window."

The time was 0144 hours. Twenty six minutes to exfil. Tick tock.

CHAPTER 50

Time was bleeding fast.

We didn't have the luxury of second chances or slow decisions. If this plan was going to work, it all had to go like clockwork. So, the moment the idea locked in my head, I started moving.

I turned to Hawkeye and Calhoun, both of them standing on the rooftop beside me, scanning the burning horizon with cold, tired eyes. "Alright boys—grab your glasses and head to sniper overwatch. I want eyes and rifles locked on anything facing the service entrance. Especially rooftops and alley corners."

Hawkeye gave a curt nod. "Rules of engagement?"

"Same as always," I said. "Anyone shouldering an RPG or holding optics and looking the wrong damn way gets dropped. I don't want anyone lighting up our convoy from the flank. Hit them five minutes before we roll."

"Roger that," they replied and took positions.

Next up—eyes in the sky.

I tapped my throat mic. "Echo, this is Cowboy. I need a full grid of threats—gunmen, technicals, anything with wheels or teeth. Start the clock. You've got ten mikes."

"Copy that, Cowboy," Echo replied over comms, already keyed in and cool as hell. "I'm now tracking three, not two, technicals two blocks away behind the crowd lines. Give me ten, I'll paint you a full battlefield."

"Also," I added, "I need a hold site, two blocks out. Off the main drag. Big enough for a couple of trucks to tuck in quietly without drawing heat."

"Stand by... OK, I got you something. An abandoned textile mill on 13th and Al-Wahda. Pitched roof, burned-out top floor, but plenty of shadow and cover on the ground level. You can tuck an Abrams in there and no one would blink."

"Good work. Send me the grid."

Next call—Logan. He answered quickly, voice winded and hot with dust.

"We're moving. Forward site's been demolished—burned every drive and hardpoint, then punched thermite through the floorboards. No evidence left to find."

"How far out?"

"Ten mikes. We're coming in one MRAP and an up-armored truck."

That was going to come in handy. MRAP—Mine-Resistant Ambush Protected. An armored beast on wheels. Looked like the ugly lovechild of a Humvee and a tank. Those things didn't roll into neighborhoods—they announced themselves like judgment day.

"Sending you coordinates to a hold site two blocks out," I said. "Get there and stay cold until I call you. I don't want anyone having eyes on you till we're clear."

"Copy that. We'll be ready."

I cut the line and headed downstairs.

The air inside the embassy was tense, tight—like the walls themselves knew the clock was ticking. Dana Prescott had the place working like a well-oiled machine. Half the lights were dead, but the underground garage glowed with red lamps and low beams. The three black Suburbans were already loaded with State Department and CIA support staff, some still bruised or bandaged from the earlier chaos. Dana stood near the last vehicle, barking last-minute instructions to her RSO.

"Nice work," I told her.

"Not my first nightmare," she said. "These people are ready. The Suburbans roll with the convoy. Two Land Cruisers and two tac SUV are set aside for your team and the Marines."

"How many Marines in all?"

"Seven."

I gave her a thumbs up and checked the time. 0155 hours. My comms buzzed a second later.

"Logan here. We're at the mill. No contact. Holding position."

"Copy, standby."

At exactly 0159, Ninja checked in. "Charges are set."

I stepped into the overwatch room with the detonator clipped to my vest. The breaching charges were in place near the front wall. Ninja had rigged them low and wide—meant to punch out sound and dust, but not enough power to actually compromise the wall's integrity.

More of a theatrical boom. Something loud enough to make the crowd dive and AQ overreact.

By 0203 hours, everything was in place—or damn close to it.

Now came the orchestration. The last-minute check before you light the match and burn the whole playhouse down. Everything had to go down with the precision of a breacher's stack—no hesitation, no confusion, no screw-ups. The only thing standing between us and a massacre was timing, deception, and a whole lot of controlled violence.

I did my final comms sweep, making sure every piece of this twisted puzzle was where it needed to be. But inside, I was already walking the timeline.

We had exactly two minutes before all hell broke loose.

The plan started from the top, where Hawkeye and Calhoun were already belly-down on the roof, rifles fixed, wind calls done.

At 0205, they would take the first bite out of AQ's overwatch— two snipers on the rooftops facing the service entrance, who thought they were invisible, but who were locked in Hawkeye's and Calhoun's crosshairs. They would then take out two more guys hauling RPGs, posted like vultures a block over. Those four were priority threats—they could rip our convoy to shreds before we made it twenty feet.

The second they dropped, Hawkeye and Calhoun would haul ass off the roof and head for the garage. No hero moments, no lingering. Fast in, fast out.

Meanwhile, the Marines at the front gate were already read in. Their job was to put on the best "Oh shit" act of the century. When the breach charge went off near the outer wall—just noise, no breach—they would flinch like fresh recruits and act like panicked squirrels to fall back inside, yelling like the gate was coming down. AQ would think they had finally cracked the perimeter. The mob would surge, thinking they were part of something historic.

Panic. That was the point. Let the mob think they were winning.

That was where Ninja and Raptor came in.

They were crouched near the wall already—hands full of flashbangs, nerves wound tight. As soon as the Marines bailed, they would let loose with the bangers. Four, maybe five—enough to scatter the crowd and fry any AQ trigger fingers lining up shots through the smoke. A few folks would hit the deck, a few would run, and everyone would be blinded, deafened, and disoriented for long enough that they wouldn't see what really mattered.

That would give us a small window—two, three, maybe four minutes tops—when all eyes would be on the front, chaos in full bloom. The enemy would call it a win. But in reality, it was just theater.

The real move came at 0209.

That's when Logan and his boys would punch in with their MRAP—armored beasts that looked like pissed-off bank vaults on wheels. They would roar in from the south, right into the alley where three AQ technicals were idling behind the crowd. Machine guns mounted, ready to follow us and cut us off even if we sneaked out the back.

Logan's crew would open up with .50s and 240s, tear those AQ trucks apart before they ever got a round off. I knew Logan enough by then to know that he would be surgical. He would make sure every round found a target worth killing.

At the same time as the Marines rolled out at 0209, the embassy's service entrance gate would roll open.

That was our exfil point. Simple, quiet, brutal. Seven vehicles waiting below—the embassy's three armored Suburbans packed with civvies, two Land

Cruisers for the Marines, one tactical SUV for me and my crew, and one spare for good measure.

Once the gate cracked, we would pour out like a convoy of ghosts—fading fast, moving hard, following the MRAP like shadows. We would punch through whatever was left of AQ's outer cordon and push for the airport—fast, violent, no radio chatter unless absolutely necessary.

Echo would feed us directions from the drone overhead, eyes in the sky locked on every alley, checkpoint, and choke point between us and the airport.

There wouldn't be time for second tries. We either got out in that window, or we didn't get out at all. It was time to put the plan in motion and pray the enemy kept looking where we told them to.

Everything had to move like clockwork. One wrong tick, and we would all be ghosts for real.

CHAPTER 51

Everything clicked like a well-rehearsed play. Not a single beat missed.

At exactly 0205 hours, the first notes of this violent little symphony rang out—Hawkeye and Calhoun dropped four men from the rooftops with cold precision. Two AQ snipers and two RPG freaks who had been zeroing in on the service entrance. All gone before they knew what hit them.

A second later, the breaching charge went off near the front wall of the embassy—a god-awful bang that echoed down half of Sana'a like Satan slamming a car door. Marines at the front gate pulled off their Oscar-worthy panic routine—yelling, cursing, feigning confusion like they were under attack. They fell back just like we planned. Textbook.

Then Ninja and Raptor did their dance—four flashbangs lobbed into the chaos just outside the outer gate. Thunder, light, confusion. Sounded like the Fourth of July in a barrel. People screamed and scattered. It bought us a few minutes of open window.

That's all we needed.

The MRAP came tearing in like a goddamn juggernaut. Logan was behind the wheel, and that truck's .50 cal machine gun turret chewed through everything that moved. It wasn't a firefight—it was a buzzsaw cutting through cardboard. Three AQ machine-gun toting technicals that thought they were blocking the rear line got shredded. One tried to run. The .50 spat fire and turned it into a rolling coffin.

"Targets neutralized," Logan reported. "Area suppressed. Standing by."

The gate to the service entrance began creaking open.

I keyed my mic. "All units, exfil is live. Convoy move. Now."

Time to get the hell out of Dodge.

We punched out of the service gate at 0210 hours, convoy in motion—three armored Suburbans full of embassy staff, two Land Cruisers, the SUV with Dana, Caroline, and my team in the middle, and Logan's MRAP leading the charge like an angry rhinoceros with a license to kill. I stayed behind the MRAP, close enough to hide in its shadow but far enough to maneuver if it took a hit. Rule of thumb: don't bunch up. Not in a warzone.

The streets were chaos, but the convoy didn't break stride. Locals cleared the roads fast when they saw us barreling through. Few trigger-happy fighters popped off potshots from balconies or alleyways, mostly just to prove they still had a pair. The MRAP didn't even flinch. Anyone who didn't get the message got a healthy dose of 7.62 wake-up call.

At 0220, my radio squawked. Not Echo this time. This voice I knew by heart.

"This is Wrangler, 2nd Platoon, Fox Company. We're on the ground at airport perimeter. Request status of convoy."

Wrangler was Ryan's call sign. Hearing his voice on the air always hit a little different. Me and my brother—we both knew how to keep it professional when the net was hot. No jokes, no stories, no bullshit. That came later, once the guns were quiet and the mics were cold.

"Copy, Wrangler. Cowboy here. Evac convoy en route. Hold current position until arrival."

"Roger that. What's the status of our boys at the FOS?"

"Evacuated. They're leading the column in the MRAP."

"Your team did good." A genuine note of respect in his voice.

That was rare, and I felt it. Then he added, voice back to business:

"Be advised, there's rebel activity at the airport. We're coordinating with government authorities to make sure the airfield and the control tower don't fall."

"Copy that," I replied as I stared ahead, eyes scanning the buildings on both sides of the road.

If AQ took the tower, we would be grounded. No eyes, no airspace, no evac. We would have to fight tooth and nail to reclaim it, and with our convoy loaded full of civilians, that would be a goddamn bloodbath.

At 0225, Echo's voice cut in, sharp and urgent.

"Cowboy, heavy contact near the control tower. AQ fighters pushed hard, but Marines are holding. Looks like they are putting up one hell of a wall."

That was good. Still dicey, but good. The window was still open.

We rolled within a mile of the airport, still no major contact. Logan's MRAP chewed through another flimsy roadblock—some idiot with a burning trash drum and a dream. The convoy kept moving, adrenaline humming, nerves taut.

But at 0226, the whole vibe shifted.

Echo again—this time colder:

"Cowboy, you've got five technicals parked outside the airport gates—machine guns mounted, crews active. Two at the terminal gates, three spread out in a V formation across the street. That's not all—RPGs on rooftops. Multiple shooters, at least two angles."

I looked at the lead MRAP and then at the soft skins following us—Suburbans, Land Cruisers, SUV. They weren't built to slug it out with belt-fed death and top-down rocket fire. Hell, even the MRAP could only take so much.

I keyed back in: "Real friendly neighborhood. These guys really don't want us leaving their country."

Echo came back dry as sandpaper: "Yeah, they're throwing a farewell party. Real classy bunch."

But I wasn't laughing. I stared ahead, jaw locked.

Logan's MRAP could eat a 14.5mm round and keep rolling. The rest of the convoy were armor-lite, barely built to stop pistol rounds let alone belt-fed or rocket fire. More like tin cans when it came to machine gun fire. One burst and we would have blood on the windows. One lucky RPG and the whole convoy could stall out, boxed in and burning.

Machine guns down low. RPGs up high. No cover. No retreat.

It was a kill zone.

I ordered the convoy to halt. Hard brake, low beams, all vehicles staggered tight along the curb. My voice was clipped on comms, but inside, I was weighing the odds—and they weren't good. We were less than a klick from the airport, and the road ahead was a goddamn funnel into the meat grinder.

Only play I had was a recon-by-fire—send Logan's MRAP ahead to make noise and draw fire while the rest of us moved fast and mean. I would dismount with my team and hit the flank, try to peel off some of the pressure. Meanwhile, our rooftop snipers—Hawkeye and Calhoun—would glass the high ground and try to punch out the RPG gunners before they lit us up.

But this wasn't a clean plan. No flank. No prep. No second wave. Time was bleeding out. If AQ sent reinforcements, we would be boxed in fast. And the moment one of those RPGs found a windshield, we would be dragging bodies.

But time was the enemy. We didn't have the luxury to finesse it.

Then the radio buzzed again.

"Cowboy, this is Wrangler. I got the update. Technicals and RPGs at the gates. You're in a kill box. I know."

He continued, crisp and calm—Marine professional through and through.

"Control tower's secured. We're pushing a fire team toward the gate now. Hold your position for two mikes—head on a swivel."

I keyed back a quick copy, eyes still locked downrange through my NVGs. Those technicals hadn't moved an inch. The longer they sat, the more my stomach knotted. Like they wanted us to roll in.

Exactly two minutes later, Ryan came back on.

"Cowboy, advance with two vehicles. MRAP leads, armored SUV trails. Get their eyes on the MRAP. Once they commit, we'll light them up from behind. And I've got two snipers on the tower—RPGs won't be a problem."

I heaved a sigh of relief.

"Roger that. Let's make some noise."

We rolled out.

Logan's MRAP thundered forward, chewing pavement. I followed close behind in an armored Suburban—suspension groaning under the weight, engine humming low. Every man inside was locked in and ready. No one spoke. Just the soft click of safeties going off and gear being adjusted. Combat mode.

The airport gates came into view. Five technicals parked across the road like they owned the place. Sandbags, barrels, gunmen standing beside them with launchers and AKs. No uniforms. No mercy.

The .50 cal on Logan's MRAP was first to speak—roared to life and chewed the middle technical into hot splinters and fire. The gunner flew backward, all limbs and red mist.

That woke the others up.

The remaining four trucks opened up, machine guns barking like rabid dogs. The MRAP took the brunt—rounds pinging and sparking off its armor, but it kept coming like a bull in a minefield.

Seconds later, the real hammer dropped—Marine fire teams inside the airport perimeter lit them up from behind. M249s and M4s stitched death into their backs. Controlled bursts, fast and surgical. The enemy didn't even have time to pivot. Two technicals erupted into flames. One tried to reverse and took a 40mm grenade through the windshield.

Blitzkrieg.

My team dismounted fast—Ninja and Raptor flanking wide, me and Hawkeye laying down directed fire. Targets dropped beside the burning trucks—AQ gunmen caught in the open or trying to run. We hunted them down like wolves.

On the radio, Ryan's voice again. "Both RPGs down. Snipers got them."

I glanced up at the control tower—two sharp silhouettes with long guns pointed downward, calm and steady.

Damn good work.

Within a minute, it was done. Bodies down, trucks burning, the gates ahead swinging open like the gates of Valhalla.

CHAPTER 52

The convoy rolled in fast, sliding through the perimeter and on to the tarmac of the airport like a ghost train—dust-caked, battered, but whole. We parked just short of the gray bulk of a waiting C-17 Globemaster III.

The bird was a beast—built to carry tanks, Humvees, or well over a 100 evacuees with gear. It sat on the tarmac like a guardian angel with jet engines, ramp down and ready to swallow us whole.

Marines began offloading civilians from the vehicles, escorting them toward the ramp. The embassy personnel started filing out of the vehicles—some moving slow, stunned, half-carried by Marines. Others clutched backpacks and kids, eyes wide, feet dragging. They had been through hell, but they were finally about to escape.

Logan's Marines stepped out of the MRAP, scorched and soaked in sweat. Blood on their uniforms, dust in their teeth. But alive.

I stepped out of my SUV, rifle still warm, legs aching, shoulders sore, jaw clenched. The dust of battle still clung to my face, and the taste of cordite was thick in the back of my throat.

Out on the ramp, I spotted Caroline walking with Ibrahim toward the C-17. Her stride was steady, protective, like she was holding the boy's entire world together by sheer will. When her eyes met mine across the tarmac, something passed between us—relief, exhaustion, maybe more than either of us had time to name.

I walked over. Ibrahim looked at me—face pale, jaw trembling, eyes caught in that storm of grief, fear, and a thousand things he didn't have the words for.

I spoke to him. "Your father saved everyone in that room. He knew he wasn't coming out of there."

Ibrahim blinked hard. I pressed on.

"He asked me to tell you something. Said he wanted you to build a life far away from all this—far from hate, far from war. That was his last wish."

Ibrahim swallowed hard and nodded, the tears finally slipping free. I put a hand on his shoulder and squeezed gently.

"You're going to be fine. Now get on that plane."

He turned and followed the Marines up the ramp, shoulders hunched, but walking.

I turned to Caroline. The wind tugged her hair loose from its tie, the lines of fatigue etched around her eyes. But she stood tall, tough, alive.

"We made it," she said, voice rough. "There was a moment... I didn't think we would. But somehow, you pulled off the impossible."

I let out a breath that felt like it came from miles deep. "Story of my life lately. Can't say it's all that fun every time."

Her smile was tired, but her eyes didn't waver. "I hope I run into you again, Axel. Somewhere normal. Somewhere quiet."

"Someplace that doesn't smell like diesel, blood, and bad choices," I replied. "Yeah. I'd like that."

She stepped forward and held out her hand. I took it. The handshake lingered—fingers tightening just slightly, a second too long. No words. None needed.

Then she let go, turned, and walked into the belly of the bird.

And I stood there for a second longer than I should have—watching her go, dust swirling in the wake of something that felt like it almost meant something.

Then I saw Ryan coming out of the control tower gate, helmet under his arm, sleeves rolled, grinning like he hadn't just pulled our asses out of a death trap.

He nodded toward Caroline disappearing up the ramp. "Jesus, Ax. City's on fire, bullets flying, and you're out here sweet-talking the pretty ones."

I shook my head. "Strictly op-related, you old dog. Your twisted brain's always working overtime."

Ryan chuckled. "Someone's gotta keep score while you write love letters in the sand."

We walked up, and I cracked a grin of my own.

"About time you showed up."

"Figured I'd let you soft types get your cardio in first," Ryan shot back. "Didn't wanna hog the credit."

"Oh yeah? We softened them up for you."

"And we cleaned up your mess. Looked like you girls had it mostly handled."

We clapped shoulders, both of us grinning like fools. Blaze brothers—still standing. Still giving each other shit.

Now all we had to do was load up and fly the hell out of Yemen before the devil caught his breath.

I looked back at my crew looking at the two of us with curious expressions. I called them over. Time for a proper intro.

The guys shook hands with Ryan, no frills. Raptor gave a rare grin as he said, "So you're the *older* Blaze we keep hearing about."

Ryan smirked. "The original model. Just with more mileage. But hell of a team you've got. Appreciate you boys pulling my Marines out of the fire. That was some tier-one cowboy shit."

Ninja cracked back, "You more than returned the favor just now. Our asses were about to get fried."

Ryan just smirked and moved on to check in with Logan and the rest of his Marines, leaving us standing in the swirl of exhaust and fading adrenaline. The plane loomed behind us, final destination across the border from that hellhole.

Raptor yawned wide, stretching like a mountain lion. "I swear to God, next op better involve a beach, cocktails, and zero AKs."

Hawkeye nodded, wiping sweat from his brow. "Man, I could use a damn vacation. Somewhere with cocktails and no RPGs. Just no more black ops for at least a month."

Ninja grinned. "How about we do a hostage rescue at a five-star hotel? I'll pack a tux."

I chuckled, the sound dry and gravel-throated. "You divas done whining?"

Truth was, they weren't wrong. We had earned the right to complain—dragged ourselves through the fire and got our people out in one piece. The convoy made it. No civilian deaths. All my boys still breathing, still standing. Not bad for a team of ghosts who weren't even supposed to be there.

It wasn't just about us, either. What we pulled off that night didn't just save the embassy crew. We hit AQ hard. At the same time, took enough of a bite out of the Houthis to stall their advance. Our op stalled their push just long enough for the Yemeni government to regroup, hold Sana'a for another week.

In that brief window, other embassies packed up and got the hell out. Eventually, the red line broke—city fell, and the government packed its things and moved the show to Aden. Same country, new warzone. Another damn chapter in the book of endless fire.

But for now? We were rolling out with everyone intact. Mission complete. Hell of a feeling.

Then Ryan's voice cut across the tarmac.

"C'mon, Rockstar," he called, grinning from the top of the ramp. "Let's get you home."

I gave him a tired grin as I slung my rifle, and gave one last look toward the city lights in the distance—flickering, uneven, smoke curling into the night. Sana'a was bleeding out, but not dead yet. She had lived another night. So had we.

The mission was done. Time to fly. Time to vanish into the dark again.

We climbed aboard, one by one. Marines. Operators. Survivors.

Behind us, Yemen burned.

Ahead? Who the hell knew.

– THE END –

BOOKS IN THE AXEL BLAZE SERIES

BLAZE RETURNS (Book One)

US Marshal Carter has gone missing in Little Butte, Nevada. The Dawsons own the town. A Mexican cartel is moving in. A gang war is coming to town. Blaze returns for one last assignment to find Carter before all hell breaks loose.

LETHAL FORCE (Book Two)

When Blaze takes out a Mexican cartel's operations in Nevada, the cartel sends hitmen after him and everyone he cares about. Bad move. What the cartel doesn't realize is, it has messed with a Lethal Force.

HARD TARGET (Book Three)

When Blaze stops at an isolated gas station, he Prevents an execution about to go down. Blaze's intervention gets a pack of mercenaries after him.

MEAN STREETS (Book Four)

Midnight in New York City. A car stops at an intersection. A girl in the back gives Blaze a distress signal. The chase that begins in Manhattan takes Blaze on a treacherous chase through the city that never sleeps.

UNCHAINED FURY (Book Five)

There is a contract out on Blaze and his old team. Floated by the Cady brothers—ruthless arms dealers who will stop at nothing to get revenge. In this no holds barred game, there's nothing to hold back Blaze's fury.

NO ESCAPE (Book Six)

Chaos erupts in Bison Creek, Wyoming. Two slain officers. Blood-soaked ex-Marine Logan on the scene. A sinister link between a cult and a pharma company. One man will move heaven and earth to get the truth—Blaze.

FEAR CITY (Book Seven)

Blaze heads to Boston after a shadowy group of investors—rich, powerful, and ready to bulldoze anything in their way. Blaze is up against these ruthless players who would sooner bury the truth than face it. They play dirty. But so does Blaze.

DEAD CALM (Book Eight)

The book goes into Blaze's past as a US Army Ranger. Blaze promises to rescue a dying friend's kids from the Taliban. The hunt takes him from Afghanistan to a trafficking network run by the Bulgarian mafia.

NO MERCY (Book Nine)

CIA agents in the Middle East are turning up dead. Blaze must save trapped agents and stop a rogue analyst from blowing their covers. With the Italian mafia and terror outfits in the picture, Blaze has only one rule: No Mercy.

WARPATH (Book Ten)

Blaze and his Delta team head to Mexico to dismantle a powerful drug cartel. But when the cartel brings the fight to US soil and targets Americans, Blaze makes it personal and goes on the warpath.

CROSSFIRE (Book Eleven)

Americans are caught in the inferno As Yemen goes up in flames. Blaze and his team are sent to extract an Al-Qaeda informant, who is the key to saving lives. Facing betrayals and deadly odds, Blaze won't just hold the line—he'll obliterate the enemy.

NEMESIS (Book Twelve – Nov '25)

They killed his brother. They buried the truth. They thought it was over. But Axel Blaze, is coming for them. No rules. No mercy. Just a promise written in blood. The hunt is on. And it won't end until they do. The nemesis is coming.

Printed in Dunstable, United Kingdom

67559708R00190